CODY QUAN
ACT II: MOSAIC DESIGN STUDIOS

RiceDaddy7 Books

FIRST EDITION, DECEMBER 2013

For information about interviews, book signing events, or special discount on bulk purchases, please contact **louisleungauthor@live.com** or visit **http://www.louisleungauthor.com**

Cover designed and illustrated by: Louis Leung

Anchor ISBN: 978-0-991-38091-6

Printed in the United States of America

To Mom and Dad
for their unconditional love.

CHAPTER 13: FOUR YEARS LATER

The weatherman had a cheerful expression about him. Out of all the summers in his thirty-year career, he had never felt more stress-free. His usual routine had now been memorized and rehearsed. Every morning the old codger would give his wife of forty-six years a kiss. Then he would look into the mirror and repeat what he had been saying for the past five months. Then, it was time for work.

"And that's it for sports," one of the anchormen would say. "Those poor Astros. Since their World Series debut, they really haven't caught a break, have they?"

The anchorwoman followed up with a laugh, contributing with "Well, neither can this weather. Geez, has it been five straight months now?"

"Well, let's find out!" the sports anchorman would respond.

Then, acknowledging his cue, the old weatherman dispersed similar news from the day before. Which was the same as the one before that. And the previous one before that.

"Well, guys," the weatherman began reciting, "it's yet another hot and dry day in Houston. Again. Five-day forecast shows not a sign of upcoming precipitation. Back to you!"

He then smiled for the camera. Easiest job in the world, he thought.

Several University of Houston staff members were watching the live broadcast in one of the campus' lounge rooms.

"Shit, more of this goddamn heat," muttered Kirk Santiago, looking at a fellow employee who shook her head in disbelief.

"My underwear gets so sticky," he continued and burped. "It's like melted cheese on my ass!"

Now in his late fifties, Kirk had seemingly worked at the university forever. Over time, he had become extremely fat, exceptionally lacking in hygiene and developed a habit of speaking in crude statements. In short, Kirk didn't care. He broke rules because he was connected with the university higher-ups who protected him. All that brownnosing, however, had made him a natural enemy to the regular employees. It also didn't help that he was assigned the role of supervisor in conjunction with his regular title as I.T. head of security—those combined positions gave him ample opportunity to violate employee and student privacy.

"Ah, well," he concluded with the last bite of his triple meat and bacon cheeseburger. "Guess I don't have to check the weather in the next five fucking days. Same old shit."

Leftover grease from his burger drizzled down his double chin. Rather than using the napkins available to him, Kirk chose to wipe the drippings off with his tie instead. Looking at his phone's clock, he realized he had to return to his office. He pushed himself past a few students as he huffed and puffed his overweight body across campus.

"Hey, you fat jerk!" a female student yelled, "watch where you're going!"

"Squeeze them tittles, honey!" he barked back.

Sweat oozed out of his pores by the time he had reached his desk. Once his perspiration met the leather surface of his chair, he felt comforted by his sanctuary. Like a prison warden, Kirk viewed his collection of webcam feeds from his monitor. Most of the cameras were on the workers he was supervising; he liked to imagine them as pets in their cages. There was one in particular, a gift from fellow supervisor and drinking buddy Rachel Hutchens, that he enjoyed psychologically torturing than most.

"Hey, Cody!" shouted the hellish supervisor, "stop writing emails to non-university personnel. I can see what you're typing behind that goddamn big head of yours!"

Kirk chuckled as Cody scrambled to follow orders. The fat man pulled out some Ruffles; they were on sale at the local Walmart.

"That dumbass," Kirk muttered at the screen. "Never

did understand why Rachel had so much trouble with you."

Cody resumed the usual charade of working on his assignment. Both he and Kirk knew it wasn't a real project. The rotund taskmaster saw fit that Cody was given as much work as possible. Once Friday came, the submitted project would be received by Kirk via USB drive where he would immediately delete the project without checking. Cody discovered this when he decided to test him one week. Rather than putting any real HTML code down, he made a pink and yellow web page with the words "Kirk Couldn't See His Own Dick" repeating in an endless loop. The lack of any reaction confirmed Cody's suspicions.

What an ironic life...I get paid for being miserable, he realized. They wouldn't fire him nor would they allow him opportunity to work on anything significant. He was buried deep in the farthest cubicle in an underground office. The notion of rebelling did not escape Cody, though he couldn't conjure up a point to doing so. He tried to put a positive spin on his spurious work, but pretending to work was work itself. Worse, Kirk rarely left his desk. There were rumors he had inserted hidden cameras throughout the female restrooms around campus. It would certainly explain why Kirk was constantly preoccupied, but so did numerous other things like StarCraft. Cody only knew that whatever his supervisor really did, it wasn't actually work.

It wasn't unusual around three o' clock in the afternoon or so that Cody heard snoring coming from the fat man's office. It reminded him how much his job was a joke; it reminded him how everyone's job in his department was a joke. The government wasted millions of tax dollars on people like Kirk. And it wasn't that Kirk was any good at his I.T. position either—whenever computers broke or received a Trojan virus, he would frantically search Google for the answer. A little baby could do that, Cody thought to himself.

Regardless, there was an advantage with Kirk's daily naps: It meant ample time for Cody to blog. He found therapy in writing, having amassed close to several hundred journal entries over the past four years. Here, he was writing another one:

"June 25, 2009. Wednesday.

Another day, another dollar. What's the point? It just disappears into my mortgage anyway. A thirty-year mortgage. What kind of investment is that? I'm thirty now. Can't believe that shit. Thought I'd have two kids and a nagging wife by now. Where the hell is my minivan? If I traveled back in time and met my fifteen-year-old self I'd tell him lies. I'm too ashamed of revealing that I make money I barely keep, working for Jabba the Hutt."

Cody continued typing for a few paragraphs more. The snoring grew louder inside of Kirk's office. This made it safe for him to turn on his computer's Instant Messenger. Like the Eye of Sauron, once he made himself available online, everyone started messaging him.

"Bubbleman!" typed RainYSkIEs589.

"Chubs," Cody typed back. He was known online as Quanster7.

"Check out my new artwork!"

The person behind RainYSkIEs589 was Rain Yoon, a talented punky hipster far younger than Cody. Rarely did a conversation begin without a request to check out her new artwork. Or to comment on her long rants in the blogosphere. Or to listen to her sing a new song that she wrote. There was no doubt about Rain's diverse talent, but she couldn't commit to anything without wanting to get into another. Chalk it up to youth, thought Cody.

"It's...um...very avant-garde," he commented.

It was an accurate statement to describe her latest masterpiece. The painting consisted of a metal-skinned mermaid diving into a collage of diamond-encrusted seaweed—all of which was taking place at the bottom of a snow globe being observed by a giant girl.

"LOL! Thanks, dude! Wait...what's 'avant-garde?'" she asked.

"It means it breaks the mold. It blazes trails. Maybe it'll start a movement for metallic mermaids," typed Quanster7.

"How do you pronounce that? Is that like 'garden' without the 'e'?"

"Yeah. Or 'guard.'"

The snoring abruptly stopped from Kirk's office followed by a loud thud. He must've fallen off his chair again, thought Cody.

"And what do you think of the coloring. Do you think it's too dark?"

"Hey Rain, gotta go. Fat man's waking up."

"Wait wait wait, dude! Before you go, can you read my journal entry? My brother's being a moron again."

"Look, just show it to Yuki or something," frantically typed Cody. "I have to log off!"

Kirk swept off the pile of potato chips that had fallen on him after his fall. While he was trying to pick himself back up, he collapsed back down again, giving surrender to his weight. He was successful on the fifth try, finally feeling around the desk for his glasses. Upon finding and putting them on, he was reminded of how good it was to see the world in 20/20 vision again. This was especially true as he inspected the webcam images from his monitor. All the workers were hard at work, a sign that they were probably cowering from fear of him. Even Cody was buried in concentration, programming away on Notepad, though Kirk had no idea Cody was actually typing gibberish since the hefty supervisor couldn't read HTML.

"Hey, Cody! Take a damn break, man!" he shouted. "Don't you gotta pee?"

Cody pretended like he didn't hear him. He enjoyed making the obese supervisor muster his way towards Cody's desk.

"Hey," Kirk repeated, "break time, buddy. I'll let you go a little early today. Think I'll head on over to the nudie bar."

"Didn't you tell me you were gay?" questioned Cody.

Kirk stared at him in silence. Cody forgot to address him as 'sir.'

"Sorry, I mean, didn't you tell me you were gay...sir?"

"No, heh heh. I told you...I'm tri-sexual," corrected Kirk. "I'll TRY ANYTHING! HAHAHAHAHA!"

Cody didn't particularly find his lowbrow humor funny.

"What? Not even a chuckle? Eh...I thought it was funny. Yeah, seriously, you're off now. I'm heading to Richmond Avenue. Going to pound my wood. And by pounding my wood I mean I'm going to stick my dick in some vagina! You know what I mean?! You know what I mean?!" laughed Kirk.

He slapped Cody hard on the back. Cody stared ahead without laughing.

"Go. Shoo. You're free! Do whatever it is you Asians do. Play mah-jong with the Joy Luck Club. Hai-yahh! Gongggg!"

Kirk laughed out loud on his way out, though he had a difficult time squeezing his giant frame past the door. Finally, thought Cody, the fat man was walking out of the building. He attempted to turn on his Instant Messenger again, but the computer became buggy. This was no surprise because it was assembled by Kirk and anything by him never functioned properly. Cody had no choice but to sit and sigh, repeatedly wishing their department had a real I.T. professional. After five more minutes of restarting and failing, Cody decided to heed his raunchy supervisor's advice and walked out for some fresh air.

Seeking shelter under a tree, he wondered what he could be doing with his free afternoon. It was far too hot to do anything. He eventually decided it was best to avoid breaking out into a sweat. After all, he had a date later on in the evening. That wasn't very exciting news, however; Cody was on a streak of bad dates. Seventeen by his count.

Perhaps, he believed, tonight would be different.

Wynn Chou would not stop talking.

The date had already become a disaster. She seemed to be an angry woman by nature, occasionally slamming the palm of her hands onto the restaurant table. Regardless of what topic they were talking about, Wynn would find a way to negatively spin it with her circular logic. It would not have surprised Cody if she suddenly got up and punched him in the face; fortunately, that didn't happen. Not literally, anyway.

The sushi dinner ended with a nod and a handshake along with a familiar helping of the "I only date white guys" speech. Cody estimated he could've saved three thousand dollars by now if these girls would've just told him that before agreeing to dinner. The only thing higher than the temperature during the summer of 2008 was yellow fever. Or perhaps it was white fever. Cody had never quite figured out which way it went.

Bitterness was the default attitude for those who felt neglected by the modern progression of interracial dating. For them, it was a foe rather than a friend—a further dissipation of an already narrowed selection. Or was it really that simple? wondered Cody. Was dating for Asians in America an exclusive club with a sign reading "Asian Women Only"? It appeared that way. For Asian men of his generation, it seemed like a far steeper climb. He was only limited to his perceptions, of course. Then again, if it weren't generally true, why were so many young Asian men attending his cousin Duke's dating seminars?

"Hey, wait," Cody stopped Wynn as she headed for her car.

"Whatdoyou mean heywait youdon'ttellmeheywait becauseifthisisaboutwhyyouthink—"

"I just...want...to wish you a good night," he explained.

"......oh okay. Bye!" Wynn replied.

Though she was merely a few feet from him, the chasm might as well have been miles apart. He stood and watched Wynn turn her back towards him, walking away with an air of entitlement to her step. For a brief moment he saw the specter of Daphne Lee in her place. Shaking off that brief moment of dispirited nostalgia, Cody returned to the sushi restaurant, this time to its bar.

"Struck out again, eh, Romeo?" asked the bartender.

He poured Cody a cold Sapporo and gently slid it toward him.

"This is pathetic. I should have more self-respect than this," Cody muttered.

The Asian bartender nodded in agreement. "She gave you the 'I only date white guys' speech, didn't she?"

"Yep," responded Cody. He downed the bottle of beer, bottoms up. "The thing I don't understand is, why is it never a black guy or a Hispanic guy? If Asian-American women don't like us, okay, but what's the deal with this exclusivity towards white guys? And we're not just talking about good- looking white guys either. If Usher and George from Seinfeld both flirted with an Asian girl, Jason Alexander would win. This shit's way beyond me."

"Want my opinion?" chimed in the bartender.

"Sure," replied Cody.

"You believe in the illusion."

Cody raised an insulted eyebrow. "Come on, man. Look at all these tables behind me."

The surreal pattern of most of the couples in the sushi restaurant was of the white male/Asian female pairing.

"And they believe in that same illusion too," continued the bartender.

"You know, you're just like my cousin Duke. He blames the media."

"No. No no. I'm not blaming the media. The media's too dumb to start trends. I'm suggesting that you should undo the illusion about fitting into whatever society is telling you to fit."

"Pardon?"

"Look—if I told you that beer suddenly cost forty dollars, would you just pay me that absurd amount?"

"I thought it was free—ahh, I see what you're getting at," said Cody. "But what if it said forty dollars on the menu?"

"Does the law say that only white men can choose whoever they can date and no one else can?"

"Well, I'm clearly trying," countered Cody. "It's not like I'm not trying."

"Then try harder," answered the bartender. "Look, real talk...we're both Asian. Our parents were immigrants. They drilled assimilation into our heads. When we take 'no' for an answer, that's our parents talking. That shit may work in China or Vietnam, but no motherfucking way do we survive with that mentality here in Texas. The only person that can stop you from being you is YOU."

The bartender's advice immediately put Cody to the test when a couple occupied the stools beside him. Like a majority of the couples that night at the restaurant, the woman was Asian and the man was Caucasian. He should be happy for them, of course, but he couldn't help but feel a little envious. Were they genuinely in love or were they trophy lovers—she, the prototypical "Asian girlfriend" and he the "white boyfriend?" These thoughts shouldn't have been in Cody's head. But they were.

"Just remember," reminded the bartender as he passed by Cody. "Illusion."

It was then that Cody remembered a saying he once heard: The best magic doesn't trick you; it causes you to believe.

One o'clock. An hour after midnight.

Toby, his longtime feline companion, lay purring herself to sleep on his stomach. The cat had not a care in the world. The same couldn't be said for Cody; this was the time of night he felt his weakest. The redundancy of his life only amplified the fears that played upon themselves in his mind. His sanity was fragile. He started believing the supposed clairvoyance of his half-awakened dreams. His good friend Mindy would one day have twins. He saw what they would look like at the ages of three, nine, seventeen and twenty-five. It was like watching a nature show where the fast-forwarding footage of plant life made them appear to grow at super speed. That was one of the two common dreams he had. The other was so depressing that it woke him up every time he dreamt it.

"Daphne..." he muttered in his sleep.

In every incarnation of this dream, he was a guest at Daphne's wedding. The church where it was taking place was gorgeous; the weather outside was perfect, giving just the right amount of sunrays seeping through the windows. He looked at the bride's guests. All his former church friends were there. He tensed up when the organ started playing—Cody knew who would be walking down the aisle.

"Daphne!" he yelled out.

Family members of the wedding couple walked toward the altar; their look alternated between dream to dream since Cody didn't truly know their real life counterparts. Once they were seated appropriately in their sections, the hefty Asian man—the groom—confidently approached the altar. The soon-to-be-husband's side of the wedding was composed of Asian thugs, hooligans and gangsters. In these dreams they were always hollering around, firing their guns at the ceiling. Nothing they said was ever comprehensible. Idiots, dismissed Cody. The best man, bridesmaids, groomsmen, and a generic maid of honor were next to breeze themselves past him. Finally, the blushing bride-to-be walked in—Daphne Lee, at the pinnacle of her beauty, at the apex of her happiness. She was joined together at the altar with the hefty Asian man in upcoming matrimony.

"Don't do it, Daphne!" cried Cody.

He had reached the height of his insecurity. He could barely hear or see Pastor Willy Lu ceremoniously overseeing the marriage vows. Even in dreams, Cody could feel faint. He didn't care that it felt selfish to begrudge Daphne of her happiness. In truth, he already knew that it was a dream, but the dream was based on a reality where she was effervescent. The bad guy won. The nice guy, whom Cody designated himself as, finished last.

"You're wrong," a voice corrected him.

It was a familiar one, confined only within his dreams now. Yet it was still as powerful as ever.

"Nice guys," explained Jesus, "get their ass kicked for my amusement."

The violence of the punching and kicking from Jesus compounded when the rest of the wedding attendees joined in. The towering Marion held him while the diminutive Henry threw a barrage of haymakers. Ennis' kicking kneaded Cody's stomach until it was soft as dough. Felix. *Punch.* Deena. *Punch.* Zoey. *Punch.* Cody was discovering he could black out in his own dreams. When enough of them had gathered in their furious binge, Jesus retreated into the background where the mayhem was given remote encouragement. Finally, after a second wave made up of thugs and brutes had finished, Jesus ordered them to stop and handed the defeated Cody a whip. To his horror, the mob ushered in the innocent personage of Maple Washington.

"Beat this girl," Jesus ordered, pointing at the young girl.

"No, I can't. I won't," replied Cody.

"Do it," Jesus laughed. "It's okay. I'll let it happen. After all, her dad got away with it, didn't he? Hahaha!"

"No!"

"Fine," responded Jesus angrily, presenting a noose. "Then go hang yourself. Go ahead. I'll watch it happen like I watched it happen to your friend Jay."

The wedding day party cheered for the kill. Daphne cackled alongside her new husband.

"Do it," incited Zoey's little boy, Ryan. "Jesus doesn't love you. Nobody loves you."

"Yeah, listen to my son. Die!" screamed Zoey.

"See if Jesus gives a shit!" laughed Luke.

"Hang yourself! Jesus doesn't love you! Hang yourself! Jesus doesn't love you!" The crowd grew in volume as more people flooded through the chapel doors.

There were family members and friends. Ace. Mindy. Aunt Mei. Cody's mother and father were among the loudest to cheer for his suicide.

"Do it," replied his cousin Duke. "You're not an alpha male. Jesus loves alpha males. That's why everything good happens to me and everything bad happens to you!"

"Yeah," smiled the hefty groom, "I'm fucking Daphne."

"He's sticking his dick in me!" Daphne laughed.

"Bubblehead!" interrupted Mindy, "I only became friends to make money off you. HAHAHAHAHA!"

"NOOOOOOOOOOOOOOOOOOO!"

Cody crashed face first into his living room carpet. It was an unpleasant way of being disrupted from his nightmare, but he nevertheless welcomed the awakening. A mere fifteen minutes had passed since he dozed off, yet he was consumed in cold sweat. Toby approached him and gave him a soft head butt, her way of letting him know that she, at least, loved him.

"A dream," muttered a delirious Cody, petting his tabby, "just a dream. A silly dream. Fearful dreams."

Cody slowly made sense of his surroundings. Why am I hearing Spanish? he wondered, then finally remembering why he had intentionally left the TV tuned to the Telemundo channel. The sounds helped him sleep and his unfamiliarity with the language made it non-distracting. With enough consciousness recovered, he sought the notepad he had kept for almost a month. Upon finding and opening it up, he reached out for a pen to mark a twenty-third stroke to a page with twenty-two tally marks. Nothing. The pen had run out of ink.

"Son of a bitch," he cursed.

He lay upon his sofa for a few moments, contemplating whether or not to go upstairs for a new pen. He cursed himself, knowing he should've put some more of them in the living room. Cody had avoided his bedroom for twenty-two long nights; he knew once he was inside it, the temptation of the Internet would become irresistible. It was easy to stick with looking at work-related sites during his job—Kirk's cameras assured see that. But at home, Cody realized, the draw was too tempting, especially now that a new site called Facebook had grown popular. He cursed the day he ever joined it.

"Come," came a whisper from the direction of the upstairs bedroom.

He reminded himself that stairways didn't talk.

"Come," it repeated.

Cody couldn't turn his head away from it as he continued glancing at its direction. He wanted to know.

"You want to know," affirmed the stairway. "You need to know."

By the time he further contemplated resisting, he realized he was already upstairs; his legs had made the decision for him. Still, considered Cody, it took his finger to push his desktop's power button and at least he had control over that. Didn't he? The monitor turned on; the Windows interface greeted him. His finger apparently pulled a coup too. His body's rebellion continued when he found himself typing Daphne's name on the search button. He frantically tried telling his mind to block her profile. *Block her profile. Block her profile. Block her profile.* But there it was—her profile. *Damn.*

The streak ended at twenty-two nights. He couldn't overcome his addiction to her happiness, her life, her affiliation with her husband—the hefty Asian man.

"Andrew Huynh," identified Cody.

Daphne Lee was dead; Daphne Huynh was happy. So exhilarant was she that her perfect life was transparent through photos. Cody dug deeper and deeper into her Facebook profile. Why couldn't she have set it to private settings? he wondered. Inevitably, he clicked on one particular album that haunted him—her children. "Perfect," she wrote under one of her daughter's photos, "just like her daddy."

Four hours felt like four minutes; it took sunrise to break the spell. Finally, Cody logged off and made his way downstairs to the second-floor patio. The morning was redundant: hot, dry and predictable. Just like every other day.

If only a storm would come.

CHAPTER 14: LIGHTNING...THEN THUNDER

A few weeks later, the first drops of summer rain fell around three o'clock in the afternoon. Although it was merely a drizzle, many on campus welcomed it with open arms. Kirk celebrated the occasion by turning up the volume of his desktop speakers. Bad techno music blared throughout the department. Two more hours, counted Cody, two more hours before the working day ends. As he was tinkering on yet another spurious project, he had forgotten what it felt like to care. Apathy was torture—perhaps the worst kind. It was usually bearable through instant messaging distractions, but the volume of the techno hinted that Kirk would not be falling asleep.

Then, as if to prove Cody wrong, he suddenly turned his music down.

"Yeah?" Kirk answered his phone. "Hey, Ma."

It was always an amusing treat whenever Kirk's mother called him. Usually, it involved her having trouble with a household appliance and he wouldn't have a clue about how to fix it.

"No...no, press the orange button. Wait, which remote are you using? No, I told you it's the other remote. There's no orange button? Maaaaa..."

The phone calls also afforded Cody and the other workers the best opportunity to sneak in an unsanctioned break. Kirk imposed a three-trip maximum restroom rule because he believed an employee needed to go only that many times. This particular instance, believed Cody, the fat man was right. Cody had exceeded his three trips and he didn't really need to go. But he left anyway because Kirk wouldn't stop him with his mother on the phone.

"I'm going to take a break," Cody whispered, using hand gestures.

Kirk nodded and waved him away, resuming his conversation with his mother. "What? You forgot to open the garage door while you backed the car? Maaa!"

Cody appreciated yet another dose of temporary freedom. It was a far cry from his days in Rachel's office when he was able to walk in and out as he pleased. He missed those five-hour lunch breaks. It was possible he could report Kirk's many infractions or apply to another department, but apathy held him back. A sudden interruption from a sprinkle of rain was met with open arms. It was nice to have cool and crisp Houston weather. Since most of the students were in class, Cody easily became lost in thought while walking around the university. It wasn't until he saw his own reflection in the school store window that he snapped out of his musings.

"The University of Houston," he read out loud from one of the many plastered logos across the store.

Perhaps, realized Cody in a brief moment of clarity, he hadn't switched departments because he was tired of the university itself. He had worked there for so long that he accepted it. Would he be standing in this same spot, looking at his reflection again ten years from now? Twenty? Forty? His mother constantly reminded him of how lucky he had it. Working in a government job was easy and the benefits were excellent. This wasn't the pain his immigrant parents would understand. They worked hard so that he could be where he was today. But was this where he wanted to be? he wondered. What satisfaction was there in a life devoid of challenge?

Perseverance, the older Chinese generation liked to say.

An obsolete word, thought Cody, that had no relevance to the second generation. Making lemonade out of lemons was something to be proud of when it wasn't available in life's supermarket. But Cody's life had aisles and aisles of lemonade already made. He wanted more than lemonade. Life wasn't about lemonades. It was about variety, he thought. Cody wanted orange juice. Perseverance was merely surviving until the threat went away. It wasn't advancement. It was anachronistic endurance.

His thoughts were halted when an approaching figure accidentally bumped into him.

"Oh sorry, sorry," apologized the perpetrator.

Turning to face who had bumped him, he was met with a similarly aged Asian male. The guy was of average height, average build—even his face offered little detail for distinction.

"No problem, man," replied Cody. "It happens."

"Heyyyy. Aren't you—?"

"What?"

"Heh. HAH! It's been so long! You...you remember me, right?"

Cody wore a confused expression.

"Our teacher, Mrs. Frankfurter. Intermediate Chinese. Second semester," he said.

"Yeah," Cody slowly recalled. "The Chinese lady with the German name. She was a hard instructor. That was...wow, that was a while back."

"I was in your class! How could you forget?"

"You were?"

"Come on! Come onnnn!"

"Oh, uh...yeah, I remember," lied Cody. "...uh..."

"M..." helped the stranger.

"Mike?"

"No. Ma..."

"Matthew...?"

"Mar..."

"Martin?"

"—eeee."

"Mart...y?"

The stranger winked and pointed at him.

"Oh, haha. Er, nice to meet you again.......Marty," replied a penitent Cody.

"Wuh huhhuhhuh ha ha," laughed Marty.

Cody observed that he had a strange, yet non-threatening laugh.

"So what have you been up to, man?" Marty asked.

"Ah, just still working here. You know I work here, right?"

"Of course, you told me. Remember?"

"Yeah, I...maybe I did. I don't remember. But if you say so. Just doing the website gig. You ever follow up on Mrs. Frankfurter?"

"Dude, she died!" informed Marty.

"No way!"

"Yeah," sighed Marty. "It was tragic. You know how she was a former sniper in the Chinese army?"

"Uh-huh."

Marty made a gesture of a gun being fired.

"No way! The Commies got to her? I knew she wasn't ordinary."

Marty shook his head in despair.

"Damn, dude," continued Cody. "Sorry to hear that. Really liked her as a teacher. She was tough but fair. Who's teaching the Chinese class now?"

"Some Mexican guy," chuckled Marty.

Cody laughed. He couldn't remember the last time he laughed so genuinely.

"Yeah," Marty sighed. "First the beaners take over our restaurants, now they're teaching our language."

"Haha! Dude, harsh. Watch the language."

"It's like the Secret Invasion. I bet they're Skrulls," Marty said, referencing a popular comic book story.

"No way! You're a comic geek too!"

"Sigh. I thought I was the only one, we're a dying breed."

Cody eagerly shook Marty's hand.

"Hey, listen," Marty said, "I might need your help some time soon. I have a lot of jobs lined up, and I'm looking for a web designer. Maybe you could help."

"Sure, man! That'd be great," beamed Cody.

A loud roar of thunder abruptly interfered with their conversation.

"Holy shit! Did you ever think you'd hear that again?!" quipped Marty.

"No, man! I thought the dry spell would last forever."

"A thunder that loud could only signify the coming of a larger storm. It's going to be a big one. Wah-ha! Stay dry, Sean."

"Cody, you mean. My name is Cody Quan."

"Sigh," chuckled Marty. "Heh. Hah! Sean? I said Quan. You gotta check your hearing, man. Welp, I gotta go."

"Yeah, my supervisor must be pretty pissed by now," realized Cody.

"It's good seeing you again," Marty smiled.

They shook hands.

Cody and Marty walked their separate ways. As Cody headed back to his office, more thunder came. The storm intensified. Cody saw several people running in it, getting soaked from head to toe. They were 'persevering,' he laughed to himself, what foolish people. Cody went back to the store and bought an umbrella. He then proceeded to walk across the campus, staying dry from the weather.

"Rain," typed in MyMelodyBunny, "your art is getting gloomier."

The two bloggers could see one another from their respective webcams. Behind them were the interiors of their individual rooms, each reflecting divergent personalities. The forty-year-old Yuki Yee, also known online as MyMelodyBunny, was secretly young at heart, playfully convincing herself that she must have been Japanese in a previous life. Her compact New York City apartment contained evidence of her "weeaboo-ness." The decorations included giant Asuna and Spirited Away wall scrolls, an impressive collection of My Melody and other Sanrio-related dolls, a miniature bonsai tree, meditation gongs and, of course, the unmistakable Japanese red sun adorned on an ornamental giant fan. As an attribute to her outer appearance, though, there was also an orderly cleanliness to the arrangement. Fairly tall at her height of five-foot-six, the slim woman moved in a mature and exacting way, consuming energy only when needed and always in an efficacious manner. Yuki implemented an air of sophistication, which was complemented always by her unmistakable Manhattan accent.

"Well," replied RainYSkIEs589, "I haven't had much to smile about these days."

Rain's youth often lead her into overdramatizations. Living in a rented garage, her decor included a scattered assortment of pop culture posters, action figures, techware and other—often difficult to identify—objects. Chaos was the preferred atmosphere for the twenty-one-year-old Los Angeles student/artist/scriptwriter/blogger. All of that, of course, was appropriate to her nature because Rain was constantly bouncing around like a fly in a room. Multitasking was her way of life. In contrast to Yuki, Rain was short and stocky but full of constant energy. Where Yuki was conservative and orderly, Rain experimented with a colorful variety of clothes, gadgets and even hair dye.

"Well, I'm not saying it's a bad thing," wrote MyMelodyBunny. "It's just that it makes me notice your current mood reflecting on your art."

Her words took too long for Rain's attention deficit disorder to intercept.

"Hey," she replied, ignoring and changing the subject, "what do you think of this?"

She held up a sketch of a caricature with a large head, climbing the Empire State Building like King Kong.

Yuki shrugged on camera and typed, "It's still gloomy."

"How is it gloomy? It's Bubbleman. Cody would love this."

"Why'd you have to draw all these helicopters shooting at him?"

"Haha. Because he's a hazard."

"I think you need to draw his head bigger then."

"Haha! But then I would need a bigger sheet of paper."

Of course, the two took Rain's remark in jest; after all, Cody was the reason they had met in the first place. It was the result of an unexpected readership that grew out of Cody's blogging. Both had been actively following his writing, relating to the situation of being stuck in life's currentless oceans. Yuki had given up hope long ago on any ambition; she had resigned to starting a family of her own wasn't in the cards. Yet, she realized, there was so much left to do in life that she wouldn't pity herself. Traveling, eating well and making new friends—these things were attainable regardless of age. Rain, meanwhile, felt stuck because of her own indecisions. Yuki believed it was merely Rain's youth and, because the young woman possessed so much talent, her marooned situation would surely come to an end.

"Ugh!" Rain shouted, crumpling up the sketch and throwing it away.

"Hey, come on now!" protested MyMelodyBunny. "That was a good sketch! I can't even draw stick figures."

"It's not tha—" Rain starting saying out loud before she realized Yuki couldn't hear her through the webcam. She started typing, "It's not that. I should be working on my album. I came up with this song today in class, while I was working on my graphic novel."

Yuki watched her search frantically for something through the webcam.

"Can't find my damn guitar," typed RainYSkIEs589.

"Hey ladies," joined in Quanster7.

He had logged in through the webcam program. The three computers could see one another in a three-way video chat.

"Hello," typed MyMelodyBunny.

"Is Rain okay?" he asked.

"She's frustrated about deciding what to do again," responded MyMelodyBunny.

"It must be awful being so talented at so many things."

"It's not fair!" playfully whined MyMelodyBunny. "I suck at everything and she's great with everything!"

"Oh, who knows?" typed Quanster7. "Maybe someday they'll make a Scrabble game where you get to play everyone and you get to show how badass you are. It'll be called *Scrabbling with Friends*. Or something like that."

Yuki nodded. She was fantastic with words, seeing them visually as if they were subatomic particles. She had a sixth sense for noticing misspellings, dangling participles, comma splices and other mistakes.

"Hahaha. Yeah, that'll be the day. That would be great."

"It'd be impactful."

"Stop," corrected MyMelodyBunny. "There's no such word as 'impactful.' It's a common buzzword, created by marketing people in their endless quest to piece together mindless metrics."

"Grammar Nazi."

"Just trying to help. So what have you been up to?"

"Well...I had an epiphany today."

They both paused from their typing while they watched Rain seemingly scream obscenities while searching for her guitar.

"She lost her guitar again, eh?" wrote Quanster7.

"I don't have the heart to remind her that she loaned it to her friend last week. She must've forgotten."

"LOL. You're so mean, Yuki."

"Well, seeing how she was so mad at her friend before, it would trigger another bad memory she had forgotten."

"Ah, okay," he replied.

"So what about this epiphany you had?"

"I've decided to stop making lemonade and venture into orange juice."

"Huh? You're doing what now?"

"Remember I once told you how my friend Mindy and I had our own company?"

"Yeah, you went to jail. So this is about orange juice?"

"No, no. It's about not accepting things. I've been going through life playing not to lose instead of playing to win. It's the difference between the '02-'03 Rockets and the '93-'94 Rockets."

"Rockets pockets sockets. Speak in nonsports lexicon, please. Or at least in Harry Potterese."

"I've got to stop cruise-controlling through life, Yuki. I feel like I've died in my twenties, slowly marching toward my grave."

"So..."

"I'm thinking about taking out my retirement funds and

starting my own company with them. A big one. With employees and an office."

"Cody, that would be very brave of you if you did something like that. Most people, myself included, wouldn't have the guts to gamble it all away. May I ask what would your new company be about?"

"Websites. Think about it. There're all those mom-and-pop businesses out there with crappy sites. I want to give them five-star quality stuff for affordable prices. There's a market for that, you know."

Yuki's face displayed a serious expression. She knew Cody well enough to know his mind was stubborn when it was locked onto an idea.

"But you've never ran a company before. You're not even a business major. How would you know how to manage things? What about payroll and taxes?"

"Yuki, Yuki, Yuki...I haven't felt so alive about anything before. That's got to mean something, right? Today, I bumped into this guy on campus. He said he was a former classmate, but I don't quite remember him. Anyway, just talking to the guy made me realize how good it feels to be a person again. How good it feels like to have a fun conversation, not living life so monotonously."

"I'm...I'm not quite sure I follow. It seems like you're deciding out of emotions, Cody."

"I'm thirty-one now, Yuki. I don't have a family. I've got all this money saved up. It's now or never."

"But what about the recession going on? It's dangerous out there. Are you sure you think this is a good idea?"

"All the more reason it would work. People would be willing to spend if I can offer more for less."

Cody stopped typing. He was hesitant to say what he wanted to say next. But Yuki knew anyway.

"This is still about that Daphne girl, isn't it?" correctly guessed MyMelodyBunny.

"You don't understand, Yuki," he responded. "You don't know what it's like to be an Asian male in this society. I've been living the life of the model minority. The thing with Daphne, it's more than Daphne."

"Cody, were you looking at her Facebook page again? You promised you wouldn't be doing that!"

"I know, I know. I went twenty-two nights without looking at it. But I...I can't help it."

"So you're saying that she didn't like you because you weren't interesting, you weren't the bad boy, and now you've finally dealt with this fact and decided to act upon it, am I right?"

"Yes. In so many words."

"Well, it looks like your heart seems to be set on it. I don't think I can change your mind, Cody."

"It isn't just about Daphne though. It's about the plight about being associated with a certain stereotype. Look at me, I'm a web developer. I speak HTML. That's one of the most Asian dude things I could possibly do. I want to be something different. I want to be an entrepreneur."

"And you think that'll land you girls?"

"It's not just about girls. It's about respect."

"Cody, you really should think long and hard about this before you make the jump. I know this whole Asian male discriminatory thing is big with you, but you're slowly evolving into an irrational Angry Asian Man, and that shouldn't impact your decisions. I'm being serious here, as your friend. Think long and hard."

"Long and hard. LOL," typed Quanster7, decorating it with smiley emoticons.

Yuki drew a frowning face emoticon in response to Cody's sophomoric humor.

"Okay, okay," he continued, "I'll think about it. Mindy was right back then, you know. Why should I slave myself working to make other people rich when I could hire people to make me money?"

"I don't think it'll be that easy, Cody," replied MyMelodyBunny.

Rain could be seen popping back in front of her webcam.

"Arrggghh!" she punched on her keyboard, "OMG. Guess what guys?! I just remembered I loaned the guitar to that bitch ex-friend of mine last week! Shit! Motherfuck! Sucking ass!"

"Hey, hey. Cool it with the cussing. We've got a senior citizen here," typed Quanster7.

"LOL. Shut up, Cody," responded MyMelodyBunny. "I'll beat you with my cane!"

The three chatted online for the rest of the night. They were lonely drifters in the sea, but slowly they were beginning to feel a strong current.

The drizzle had now turned into a Texas-size downpour. It made a slow day at The Happy Lotus even slower. Quan Min-Lo shrugged it off because it gave him some free time to tinker with the restaurant's dry erase board. Since the hole-in-the-wall Chinese restaurant was located in the middle of Houston's Third Ward, the Happy Lotus was prone to a predominantly lower class African-American customer base. He wrote the word "Fried" in front of everything. If there was anything Quan Min-Lo believed as much as his homeland's superstitions, it was the reliability of stereotypes. All he had to know was someone's race, gender or nationality and he would figure them out in a second. Life was easy that way; the world was stupid for bogging into political correctness.

"<What bad luck, the news didn't even predict the rain>," chimed his working waitress and sister-in-law, Hannah Wong.

"<When did you start trusting the news?>" winced Cody's father. "<Ever since they switched the white weatherman to a black one, the weather has been all wrong. I warned you of that.">

"<Huh?>" she asked.

"<Well, it's obvious, isn't it? That black weatherman got the job because everybody felt sorry for him! If they didn't give him that job, the black people will sue. They will riot! They will kill us all! That's why they gave him that position. They thought it would be dry and sunny for the next few weeks, and the current weatherman took a vacation, so that's a chance to give the job to a black man and say 'hey look, we kiss your ass, black man. Please don't rob us.' Understand? That's America, okay? So now the news is wrong and it's raining and no one's coming to my restaurant. Black man equals bad luck. Bad luck to my restaurant! Bad luck to you because you have no tips today!>"

"<Oh>," replied the simple-minded Hannah, "<I think that makes sense.>"

She wasn't the brightest of Cody's maternal aunts, though the Quan family had to provide a job for her when she gave birth to her daughter Megan in America. Mr. Quan had suspected she did so intentionally to grant herself a quick citizenship. Smart move, he thought, for a dumb woman. Unfortunately, Hannah was a slow worker who, as The Happy Lotus' lone waitress, worked far too inefficiently.

"<Why are you standing still?>" Cody's father cursed at her. "<Wipe some tables, refill the soy sauce bottles...you're still working!>"

Suddenly the attached bell from the front door chimed. Both Mr. Quan and Cody's Aunt Hannah looked up, seeing an unexpected person.

"We have Chinese customers?" Hannah muttered in surprise.

"Oh!......Diana!" recognized Mr. Quan in English.

An old childhood friend of Cody's, Diana Li remained exactly like his father remembered her. She was the twinkle-eyed goody-two-shoes girl, with her identifiable bright smile. Had so many years gone by? he wondered. Diana should be in her early thirties by now, like his son. Yet, her highly successful career as a corporate public relations director hadn't changed her uplifting personality at all.

"<Hello, Uncle>," she said, using "uncle" in a loose sense; he wasn't literally her relative. "<How've you been?>"

"<Same as usual. Same as usual>," smiled Mr. Quan. "<We haven't seen you in years!>"

Hannah wasted no time and interrupted, "<This is...?>"

"<A family friend>," Mr. Quan explained, a bit irritated by her disruption. "<Her mother and I used to wait tables together. She was such a little girl back then. Twenty...twenty-seven years it's been, I think.">

"<My name is 'Diana'>," she introduced herself to Cody's aunt in perfect Cantonese.

"<Wow!>" admired Hannah, "<your Chinese is perfect! Not a hint of an accent! And you were born here?>"

"<Yes, in the States. I'm originally from Hawaii>," she explained. "<It's a bit slow for you guys today, isn't it? Is it the weather?">

"<It is what it is. We just have to persevere. You picked a good time to visit. So how've you been?>" asked Mr. Quan, signaling for Hannah to get her some tea.

Diana described what she had been up to; there was a lot to catch up about. The conversation lasted for thirty minutes—the two talked about her job, past stories and the state of her family.

"<Tell your parents that I want to take them out for dinner in Chinatown>," offered Mr. Quan.

"<Of course, Uncle. How's Cody been by the way?>"

"<Tsk>," the middle-aged Quan snapped in disappointment. "<My son refuses every girl that I find for him. I don't think he wants to be married. He's too shy. He needs to be more like his cousin Duke. Duke is more assertive. More masculine.>"

"<Heehee. How do you know he isn't hiding a significant other?>" laughed Diana, thanking Hannah as she returned with the tea.

"<His mother and I check on everything in his life! He can't hide a relationship from us! I'll know. Trust me.>"

Diana politely laughed. There was a slight pause in their conversation. Cody's father knew her visit was more than just small talk. She must have needed something.

"<Uncle...the reason I came today is because...I need a favor>," she began.

"<Yes? Sure, sure...anything! Your mother and I go way back.>"

"<Oh, don't worry. It's a small favor. I've got a cousin who just immigrated from Hong Kong. She's still in college. I was wondering if she could maybe find a small part-time job here in your restaurant. Just a couple of dollars a day would be enough for her to buy some books>," Diana insisted.

Hearing this, Cody's aunt felt a little nervous. She knew the little restaurant was slow enough already. A second waitress would further diminish her tips.

"<Well>," slowly answered Mr. Quan, "<Cody's aunt here is our only waitress. And she works every day except Thursdays, when we're closed.>"

"<Please, Uncle. She really needs it.>"

"<Sigh. Well. Okay, okay. Well...okay...she can maybe share some tables with Cody's aunt.>"

Hannah Wong started opening her mouth in protest, but she was interrupted by Diana's jubilation.

"<Thank you, Uncle!!! Are you sure?!!>"

"<Of course! Cody's Aunt Hannah wouldn't mind!>" he assured.

"<Can I bring her in? She's actually in the car. She's kind of shy.">

"<She is? Wow. We made her wait. Yes, yes. I'd like to meet her.>"

"<Okay, one second, okay?>"

As Diana headed back to her car with an umbrella, Cody's aunt took her brother-in-law aside.

"<I don't think it's a good idea for this girl and myself to share tips together. I barely make enough as it is, and Megan is about to be in college. As a single mom, how can I support her?>"

"<But this girl needs it. Okay, okay. Fine. I'll...I'll just...I know! I'll take it out of my pockets. You can show me how much tips you've made and I'll double it since she's taking your half.>"

"<That's not the point. I—>"

The bell from the front door clanged again. This time, Diana returned with a guest. As Diana closed her umbrella, a tiny, meek girl walked in. She had very thick glasses and a bowl cut.

"<Uncle>," introduced Diana, "<this is my cousin Kiki Tang.>"

The nervous girl snorted a laugh.

"<It's good to meet you>," greeted Mr. Quan. "<What part of Hong Kong are you from?>"

"<Kowloon Bay, Mr. Quan. Emmm, yeah, emmmm.>"

"<Please, call me 'Uncle.' So you're here to study? Where do you take your classes here?>"

"<HCC, but I'm only doing it for the credits and it's cheaper. Then, maybe I'll take a few classes at UT and finish my Master's there.>"

"<Wow, Master's? You know, my son works at UH. Maybe he can show you around campus.>"

Kiki let out a snorted cackle.

"<Emmm, but I have no affiliation with UH>," she insisted. "<All my core classes can be handled at the community college level, Mr...I mean, Uncle Quan.>"

"<Oh, you know. Just to make friends!>" he insisted.

"<It's really okay, Uncle. I don't want to be a burden...>"

"<No burden, no burden! Hey, how about this. You can start working next week immediately. Cody's auntie will show you how to wait tables.>"

"<Thank you so much, Uncle>," Diana said in her sweetest voice.

They made more small talk until a few customers began showing up for early supper. Cody's father could barely hide his delight. The young girl was studious, polite, Cantonese and her animal zodiac sign even complemented Cody's—he figured this out after he learned her age. Wedding bells were chiming inside the middle-aged man's head. It was followed by the imagined sounds of a mahjong tournament, seven-course traditional Chinese meals, red envelopes and Cody's smiling grandfather.

"<I approve!>" blurted Mr. Quan.

"<What'd you say?>" asked Hannah.

He could answer with only a nod and a highly satisfied smile.

The wedding reception two weeks later was rushed, spectacular in some parts, but overall, too little food for too many people. The older Asian relatives grumbled about how it wasn't a traditional Chinese-style dinner; the buffet was a bad idea. Those who stood early in line stuffed their plates with more food than they should have gotten. Some even took two or three plates at once. The banquet hall was filled up to the point that it became standing room only. Not only did the bride and groom invite relatives, friends and work colleagues, but they also invited their hairdressers, third-degree friends of friends and random people they had chatted with at the supermarket. Then there were the wedding crashers.

"Cody!" screamed the bride.

She was a beautiful sight to behold in her white dress, perfect hair, makeup and expensive jewelry.

"Get out of the way!" she said, pushing him aside to make room for the wedding cake.

"<Don't worry about her",> said the groom, Minston Chun. "<She's just being irritable on our wedding day. You know how it is.>"

Cody's playboy cousin had finally married. After a seemingly endless series of women of all ages, colors, nationalities and background, he had chosen Wanda Nguyen to be Wanda Nguyen Chun. Wanda was much younger than Cody while Minston was far older. The couple was almost twenty years apart in age. What was even more unique was that Minston didn't speak much English while Wanda didn't speak any Cantonese. Love, they claimed, was their ultimate communication.

Cody could care less about their reason. He hated weddings. A bachelor like him couldn't be invisible for long. There were constant bombardments of "why are you still single" questions and offerings of blind dates that he knew weren't his type—anyone chosen by prodding relatives wasn't his type. He scoffed at the popular belief that weddings were the best place to meet potential dates. Not in Chinese weddings, dismissed Cody. For one thing, he realized, families watched potential pairings with hawklike intensification. When a girl accidentally looked at his direction, Cody's aunts and uncles immediately analyzed their match potential. His father gave him a disapproving glare—that girl is Vietnamese, he communicated with merely his eyes, I don't want my son marrying a Vietnamese girl. They're crazy. And they're probably in gangs.

"<Good evening, everyone!>" welcomed Minston, covering his ears as the microphone emitted a piercing screech.

"Good evening, everyone!" translated one of the groomsmen.

"<Thank you for showing up to our wedding! Get yourself something to eat from the back. There are king crabs, sushi rolls, sashimi, filet mignon, clams, Cantonese noodles, Vietnamese noodles, Shanghai noodles, curry chicken, ham, shark fin soup, stuffed mushrooms, rosemary meatballs, egg rolls, spring rolls, hors d'oeuvres, fettuccine alfredo, crepes, har gows, shu mais, jalapeno corn muffins, baby back ribs, eggplant rollentino, veal marsala, pecan pie, blueberry pie, coconut ice cream, chocolate ice cream, strawberry ice cream and egg tarts>," finished Minston.

The translator cleared his throat. "There's, uh, a lot of food in the back. Just be sure to get some before it's all taken."

A mass exodus of wedding attendees immediately got up and extended the already long buffet line, resulting in a jam. Some of the elder relatives grumbled about ditching the wedding for Chinatown. Among the people standing in line was Cody. He stood observing various members of his family, particularly Duke who was proudly showing his girlfriend, Annebelle, around to everyone like a prized possession. Duke greeted each and every congratulation with a silent and pretentious stare.

"Wah-hah! Hey!" interjected the person in front of Cody.

"Whoa, hey!" Cody smiled, recognizing a recently familiar face. "Marty! What are you doing here at my cousin's wedding?"

Marty slapped his knee and gave out a hearty chuckle.

"I was, heh, I was just about to ask you the same thing, Cody!"

They shook hands like longtime friends.

"Minston's my cousin," explained Cody.

"My wife works with Wanda at her bank."

"You're...you're married?!"

"Well, heh, yeah! Remember? I told you that the last time we met two weeks ago!"

"You did? I don't remember—"

"Yeah, of course I did! Come on! Don't get all old man on me here, Cody!"

"Oh, yeah. Yeah! I guess you did!"

"Wahuhuhuh. What did I tell you? Early Alzheimer's. So you've been considering about us working together? I've got a few projects lined up and I could really use a web developer."

"Sure. I don't see what's the—DUDE, did you just see that guy grab FOUR plates?"

"Sigh, Asian people," Marty shook his head, "you know what I mean?"

"Man, this buffet thing sounded like a good idea when Wanda told me about it, but now it's a complete disaster."

"Yeah, too many people. I heard they even invited their mailman. It's crazy!"

"So what were you doing in UH that day? Are you still a student there?"

"Me? Heck no! I'm a graduate from the Art Institute, remember?"

"Wait, didn't you just say you had a class with me in UH?"

"Well, wa-hah! I'm from both the Art Institute and UH.

Haha!"

"No way! That's freaky man, me too! Class of '98?"

Marty slowly nodded with a smile.

"Cool!"

"Hey, you two! Move forward or get a room!" pushed a man from behind them.

He looked like a character from the X-Men comic books.

"Saber—" began Cody.

"—tooth." finished Marty.

They both laughed.

"The Adam Kubert version of Sabertooth," clarified Cody.

"With a little Jim Lee too, I think."

They spent the next fifteen minutes in line pointing at random people from the wedding, giving them look-alike pop culture matches.

"What about him?" asked Cody.

"The Asian Egon Spangler from Ghostbusters."

"Ah, good one. Old man with a hat right there?"

"Mmm, wah-heh, Darkwing Duck."

Cody smiled and pointed at Duke from across the banquet hall.

"And what about that dickhead?" he pointed at his cousin. "The one with a stick up his ass. Who does he look like?"

"Ricky," replied Marty, "Ricky the Steamboat Dragon."

"That...hahaha...that doesn't even make sense! Hahahaha!"

"Sorry, everybody!" informed one of the venue staff. "We're out of food!"

A large grumbling of complaints of Vietnamese, Cantonese, Mandarin Chinese and English erupted from the crowd.

"Let's go to House of Bowls!" declared someone's uncle.

Minston angrily walked up to the manager of the venue.

"You say good food! Enough for everyone! Why not?" he yelled in broken English.

"Hey, hey! Don't blame us!" replied the staff. "You said there'd be a hundred people. There're over two hundred tonight!"

"Fuck, man! You blame me? You hole! Asssss hole!" cursed Minston.

He then hurried over to his DJ.

"<Hurry, get everyone to the dance floor. Play that 'left, left, right, right' song!>" instructed Minston.

"<You mean 'The Cupid Shuffle'?>" inquired the DJ.

"<Whatever. You're the expert. Do something to take their minds off the food problem. Damn, I need a cigarette!>"

Sheer pandemonium erupted. Angry relatives offered Wanda a condescending lesson about planning beyond her means. Meanwhile, the greedy guests who previously hoarded food were now ironically being mugged for it. A divine miracle in the form of "The Cupid Shuffle" saved the day. The catchy beat drew the guests to the middle of the dance floor like lemmings to the sea. Old and young, male and female, angry and not-so-angry joined together to crudely follow the instructions of the lyrics. *To the right, to the right, to the right, to the right, to the left, to the left, to the left, to the left, now kick, now kick, now kick, now kick...*

"<I love this song!!!>" declared Cody's father.

...now walk it by yourself, now walk it by yourself...

Minston and Wanda gave a sigh of relief; the wedding had been saved by the modern day hokey pokey.

Outside of the banquet hall, Cody and Marty took solace among the smokers. Neither smoked, but it was a preferable torture than the generic dance music that was publicly imposed on them thousands of times. The light drizzle and breeze were also a nice welcome from the smothering atmosphere inside.

"So, hey man, I know this sounds crazy, 'cause we barely met, but I'm really thinking about starting my own website company. I saved up enough to get our own office, equipment, employees.......everything. It'll be a blast," Cody told his new friend.

"Okay. Heh...okay. Tell me more," listened Marty.

"'Cause I'm thinking, look at us. Smart, charming talented young Asian-American men. Wasting away our lives. We could be captains of our own destinies, man. We could get a fresh recruit of designers from the Art Institute. Get an assembly line system going. Get a hot-ass secretary. It'll be fun!" exclaimed Cody.

"Yeah. Well, wu-hah, yeah. We shouldn't be wasting our lives. We should be captains of our own destiny! Totally agree."

"Marty," Cody said with a stern look, "I want you to be my business partner."

"Wah-huh! I'm flattered, but I don't have that kind of money, I—"

"Don't worry about the money! I got enough for the both of us. I'll pay for everything! Money's not the issue here! You get a fifty-fifty split in power. What do you think?"

"Well, I...hah! Heh...sure, man...you know...sure! Of course, we'll have to get this thing legal and what not."

"Yeah, man! Of course!"

"Wah-ah, why don't we use my attorney?" insisted Marty. "I trust him. He'll write up all the legal documents and we can get things started."

The bromance was off to a good start; straight men who were best friends were rarer than gold, thought Cody. There wouldn't be an ulterior reason tainting it. Things would be equal, things would be understanding and they were on the same side. He felt an instant kinship about Marty—he was the kind of best friend worth succeeding with.

They shook hands.

"Dude...yeah! Let's do it! Welcome...partner," said Cody.

As he said it, a strong lightning bolt struck dangerously close to the venue. It briefly illuminated the surrounding area like a natural light switch. Inversely, the banquet inside suffered a power failure, which resulted in screams of panic. A moment later, an audio eruption arrived in the form of thunder. It shook the ground so violently that various car alarms blared in the parking lot, sounding like the different instruments of an orchestra. Marty and the smokers covered their ears from the noise. Cody, however, paid no attention to it.

CHAPTER 15: PAYING IT FORWARD

Cody's grandfather looked at his grandson and wondered if he understood the concept of "paying it back." It was the old Chinese retirement plan—a Confucian-based tradition where the younger generation spent a lifetime taking care of the old until they, too, became old. Then they were taken care of by the newer generation, a newer generation that obeyed them with unquestionable respect. This was especially necessary with the immigrant experience. The survival of Cody's grandfather and father depended on Cody's advantage of knowing America's language and culture. Unfortunately, Cody's grandfather had discovered Americans tended to discard the elderly like used batteries. His grandson was no different. He acted like a prince—unresponsive to the needs of senior family members, yet always looking to take as much as possible.

Still, thought his grandfather, regardless of role reversals and the dissolving of customs, he loved Cody because blood was thicker than water. This, in turn, had transformed him into a new kind of Chinese grandparent—one who was kind, patient and understanding. He had never beaten or scolded his grandson, even during times when Cody needed an obvious berating. Even if Cody had to be coaxed into having a weekly dinner with him, his grandfather didn't mind and didn't take it personally. Spending time with his grandson was all that mattered to him. He knew which hole-in-the-wall restaurants that Cody loved—the kind where Cody wouldn't know how to order. The kind of restaurants where the best dishes weren't on the menu, where one had to have a certain affiliation with the Chinese community to request them. And Cody, despite outer appearances, wasn't Chinese enough to know that.

"<Eat! Eat!>" insisted Cody's grandfather.

"<Full am stomach can impossible>," explained Cody in broken Cantonese.

"<Then take some home! I know you can't cook Chinese food very well. How is my favorite grandchild supposed to succeed on an empty stomach?>"

There was something natural and genuine about their bonding. Cody's relationship with his grandfather was an amity where actions spoke louder than words.

"<How's work going?>" he asked Cody.

"<Fine is going, grandpa>," Cody answered.

"<Good. Good. It's your seventh year now, right?>"

"<Yes.>"

"<For twenty years, I worked for an umbrella company in Hong Kong and I was proud of it! I never missed a day of work and whatever my boss told me to do, I was obedient in doing it. You should embrace your longevity. Always be obedient and do whatever your boss tells you to do. You take care of your job, and your job will take care of you.>"

Though his grandfather meant well in giving advice, Cody didn't have the heart to tell him how much he disagreed. Being stuck working in the university for twenty or more years was the last thing he wanted; it certainly wasn't a badge of honor for him. There was no desire to end up like his coworkers—routine government employees who stayed until retirement. It wasn't either the American or Chinese dream; it was cowardice.

"<Grandpa...>" Cody began.

"<Yes?>"

"<...start new my company I want.>"

"<What?>"

"<Start...new...my company. I want.>" Cody repeated in broken Cantonese.

"<You want to start a new company? Why would you want to do that? You already have a great life. It's a government job. It's safe.>"

"<Wasted potential my.>"

"<Potential. You have already achieved such a high climb! Leaving your success would not be a good idea>," advised his grandfather.

His grandfather slowly put his chopsticks down and looked at him for a moment.

"<You are my lifetime's hope. When I survived the war, when I worked for twenty years at that umbrella factory, when I immigrated to New York scrubbing toilets in restaurants, and then when I came to Houston as a cook...it was done so that one day you will have the opportunity to get a good job. And you've done that. You have a lifetime government job. Why do you want to throw it all away?>"

Such a deep question, thought Cody, demanded a greater flexibility with words. It wasn't something he could answer with such a limited vocabulary. Fortunately, the sincerity in his eyes did not betray his feelings to his grandfather. Cody had no idea how truly lucky he was. In previous generations, a youth would have been chastised for wanting something from the elderly. It didn't matter anymore, realized his grandfather. They were in America, and Cody was American. It was his nature to take without full appreciation. This didn't make him a bad person; it just meant that Cody was simply always looking forward instead of behind.

"<Grandpa>," Cody slowly asked, "<this company I money need. In case.>"

He did not know that his grandfather had spent six decades to amass his savings. It was money derived from backbreaking labor and basic government aid.

"<Why do you need so much money? You should just do it alone. Start out small. Earn it>," his grandfather said.

"<But partner. I have.>"

"<You have a partner? Who is your partner?>"

"<A friend new. He's Chinese too. Worry you don't.>"

"<Don't worry just because your partner's Chinese? Haha. Of course I worry! Chinese people can have bad intentions as well. What does he do? How will he help you?>"

"<Sales>," Cody replied.

"<Sales...>" his grandfather echoed.

The feeling gave Cody's grandfather an unpleasant trip down memory lane. During his umbrella factory days, a colleague presented him with a partnership scheme. It involved putting money up front for a business that was "bound to make them rich." Cody's grandfather trusted his instincts and said "no"—even though rejecting the colleague's aggressive advances was difficult to do so. Consequently, he was spared. It turned out to be a scam. The colleague stole a lot of money from a lot of people and disappeared for good. This was a lesson he wanted to bestow upon his grandson, but Cody preferred to hear what he wanted to hear. He knew it would be a bad idea, but it didn't overshadow Cody's unhappiness if he replied "no." The old man cursed himself for giving in; it was a selfish mistake he consciously made.

"<Okay>," his grandfather hesitantly answered, "<I don't have much, but I can ask other relatives from Hong Kong to contribute.>"

Cody's face lit up. It was worth the hefty price, thought his grandfather.

When they returned to his retirement complex, Cody's grandfather did not immediately leave the car like he usually did. Instead, he grabbed Cody's arm and spoke. If he couldn't stop himself from doing something foolish, he thought, at least he would try and give Cody some wisdom.

"<I, your grandfather, am doing this out of love. If you want money, then I will find a way to get you your money. But know the difference between blood from family and blood from a friend. They're not the same. I hope you realize this difference.>"

Cody silently dismissed the advice as unnecessary paranoia.

"<You have made me so proud. So proud>," he continued. "<I don't need to feel any prouder. I wish you would just start a family instead. I don't know why you need to do this. You should be happy with what you have. I worked hard and your parents have worked hard so that you can have what you already have. I will wonder why it wasn't enough. But your happiness means something to me and if this is what makes you happy, I'll find a way to give you this money. I just hope you know what you've chosen.>"

With those words, he made his way out of the car. Cody watched as the old, withering eighty-five-year-old body of his grandfather slowly made its way past the automatic front doors. It was pride that kept Cody from feeling shameful about taking instead of giving.

"He got paid too much money!" someone in the room exclaimed.

"Well, he should," scoffed another. "He's Chinese."

"What does him being Chinese have anything to do with it?"

"Don't you see how many Chinese people are watching these games now? Seventeen million dollars a season wasn't enough! They made millions more off of him! It was a bargain!"

The two debating fans were among a boisterous crowd. There, in the Toyota Center, amidst a sea of No. 11 Houston Rockets jerseys, was the public photo op with injured basketball player Yao Ming. Fans were assigned numbers indicating when they would be allowed to have photos taken with him. There were rumors that his career was close to over. Indeed, he looked sad and uncertain up close in person.

"Marty!" shouted Cody, happy to have found his new best friend. "Come on, I want you to meet my parents, dude."

"Hohhh, man, sorry I'm late. There was an incident at Panera Bread."

"What? What happened at Panera Bread?"

"Psssh. Haha! You wouldn't believe, heh. There was a robbery."

"No shit!"

Marty slowly nodded his head.

"Sigh. I know, dude," Marty exclaimed. "I can't believe my bad luck either. Hah! Can you believe that? This guy wearing a ski mask came in asking for money from the cash register. But guess what?"

"What?"

"He tripped while he ran out!"

"Damn, that's crazy, man. Glad no one got hurt. How could someone just trip up like that?"

"Wu-hah! He had help."

"Help?"

Marty pointed at his left foot. Cody was speechless that his new friend had the guts to stop the robber by tripping him.

"Well," replied Marty modestly, "I would've been much more nervous if it wasn't for my martial arts training. Pshew!"

"You know martial arts?"

"Since I was a kid."

"<Hey!>" interrupted Cody's father. "<We're about to go next! I've been looking all over for you!>"

It was comical seeing his father in a Yao Ming basketball jersey two sizes larger than him. Cody had told him not to purchase one until the store carried his father's size, but Mr. Quan had bought a jersey anyway.

"Dad," introduced Cody, "I want you to meet my friend Marty."

"<Oh, Mr. Quan, it is such an honor. Such an honor, sir>," bowed Marty while shaking his hand.

"<You're Cantonese!>" remarked Mr. Quan.

"<Actually, I was born in 'Detroit'>," Marty clarified.

"<But you speak it so flawlessly. It's like you were born and raised in Hong Kong!>"

"<You humble me, Mr. Quan. Hoo-ha! I'm sure there's an accent in there somewhere. Heh. I give all credit to my wife. She's from Shanghai, but she speaks to me in both perfect Mandarin and Cantonese, heh heh ha!>"

"<Ah, a Chinese wife from China!>" remarked Cody's father. "<See, Cody? Your new friend has taste! He gets a smart and pretty wife from China. He doesn't chase these Asian-American women with their back talk. It saves you a lot of trouble.>"

A Toyota Center employee barked out the Quans' waiting list number. Cody's father had an idea.

"<Do you like professional basketball?>" Mr. Quan asked Marty. "<Why don't you take my ticket and meet Yao

Ming?>"

"<Ah, haha. Ah-ha! No, no, no. This is your day, Mr. Quan. I appreciate your generosity, but I'm already lucky enough to be invited here. Heh.>"

"<Come, I insist—>"

Cody's mother came storming towards the three of them.

"<WHAT THE HELL IS TAKING SO LONG? THEY'RE WAITING FOR US!>" she yelled.

"<This is Cody's new friend>," introduced Cody's father. "<His name is Marty. Look, he's Chinese!>"

"<I can see that>," Cody's mother crisply replied. "<Come on, let's go!>"

The giant's height was even more overwhelming in person than it appeared on television. Cody struggled to comprehend how Yao and he could be from the same species. During the brief photo shoot, they found China's living basketball legend cordial and self-effacing. The height differences didn't seem as noticeable after some friendly conversation.

"<Yao's parents raised him right>," declared Mr. Quan.

Cody left his father and mother to meet Marty at a local coffee shop near the Toyota Center. There were business plans to discuss.

"Okay," began Cody, sipping a crème brûlée. "So I've decided to start us off as five people. You, me, a secretary and two designers fresh from the Art Institute."

"Uh-huh," replied Marty, eating a bagel.

"This, with our predicted estimate in rent and amenities, takes us to roughly $22,500 we need to match per month. Do you think you, as sales, can get us that much income every thirty days?"

Marty took a long look at Cody's numbers. The planning was done in meticulous detail, color-coded and cleanly sorted. His attention, however, was primarily focused on the word 'secretary.'

"No. I can't do this," Marty replied, "unless I have help."

"Help?" asked Cody.

"Wuh, well, yeah. Um, heh! It's not fair that you get a hot-ass secretary and I get no one right? Hah!" winked Marty.

"Well, yeah, I'd definitely get a hot girl for the job, of course. But the main reason I said we need a secretary is because we'll probably be fielding a lot of calls and emails. We have to make sure that the clients approve the design and functionality of the websites."

"Heh, oh yeah, heh. Ah, well...I mean, that's a lot of sales I need to get! I need a...a mediator, man. Someone to join me in sales so that I can be more efficient in what I do. You know, heh-uh?"

"Yeah, you're probably right," agreed Cody. "Okay, let's add a sixth person on the payroll then. A...what'd you call it...a mediator? But that means you'll have to increase your sales quota."

"Psssh," smiled Marty, "come on, haha, I got this, Cody. I'm good at what I do."

"Okay. Okay, I trust you, man."

"Heh. Ha!"

"Oh, one more thing. I get to name the company. I have chosen to call it Mosaic Design Studios. In honor of the former business a friend of mine and I once started."

"Okay," nodded Marty, who didn't quite get the reference.

The coffee shop waitress came to check up on them.

"Okay, you guys want any more coffee? Any more bagels for you, sir?" she asked.

"No. Phewwww. Six of them...heh...that's enough for me! What about you, Cody?" asked Marty.

"No, I'm not much of a coffee or bagel person," Cody replied, looking at his sheet of paper with the estimated number crunching.

"Well, guys, I'll come by and give you your checks! Split?" asked the waitress.

"Oh yeah, heh, split it, please," Marty replied.

Once the waitress headed back for their checks, Marty hunched over to Cody.

"Eh, heh, Cody?" Marty asked. "Got a bit of a dilemma here."

"Yeah. What's up, man?"

"I...I kinda...sighhhh...this is...this is so embarrassing for me to even say, but...heh...ha!...I forgot my wallet. Can you—"

"Dude, no problem. I'll cover you. We're friends, man. But why'd you go ahead and tell the waitress you wanted to split the check?"

"Uh, you know, I gotta save face. Hah! I'm so forgetful sometimes. You know my wife, Xia, she was, heh, telling me to feed the dogs this morning while I was tending to the garden. Then, heh-ha, I remembered I had promised to meet you here. And halfway to downtown I thought, whoa, heh, I forgot my wallet! Heh."

"It's okay. It's just coffee and bagels, man," waved off Cody. "I mean, you did stop a robbery today, after all. You're a hero!"

"Thanks, buddy, sighhh," Marty chuckled at himself, shaking his head.

"Alright, guys," the waitress came back, "here's your check, and here is yours."

"I'll...I'll be paying for his too," informed Cody.

"Oh?" asked the waitress, "I thought you wanted to split the checks."

"We, uh, heh, just had a little discussion," answered Marty. "And my friend felt bad because I paid for his coffee the other day, right Cody? Right? Right? Heh. Ha!"

Marty secretly tapped one of Cody's feet with his own.

"Sure," Cody played along.

He plopped down his debit card.

The most famous chef in Hong Kong was not a chef at all. Chef Bernie "Sky" Mo became an international sensation when his cup noodle franchise, Chef Mo's Big Wok Ramen, transformed itself into a household sensation. Never someone who particularly enjoyed the spotlight, he nevertheless became a good sport with his fame. He wouldn't decline a photo op or refuse replying to the thousands of Facebook fans who messaged him—even when they numbered into the millions. He accepted that particular consequence for his unforeseen fame; what irked him was the stream of loan requests he kept getting. Bernie's reputation as a good-hearted and nice man made him a target for opportunistic friends and family members alike. It was enough to turn the once extroverted business man into a recluse.

Luckily, his fortune enabled him to assemble a personal condo of solitude. Living space in the grand city of Hong Kong was already incredibly expensive. He counted his blessings to have many homes, including entire buildings, when so many people couldn't afford just one. Even married couples continued living with their parents. Putting that appreciation in perspective, Bernie was glad he had a place alone. It was inspired and designed like a Japanese home, decorated with shoji room dividers, tatami mats, oil warmers and various calligraphy. It was the perfect setting to achieve a zen-like state of peace.

Yet, even that didn't make him immune to investment petitions, for in his mailbox was a handwritten letter. *Who knows this address?* he wondered. The loft was in his wife's name and it was off the books. One look at the sender's name, however, gave him the answer: his brother-in-law Quan Min-Lo. Bernie knew the man somehow had talked his wife into it. How else would Min-Lo know where to personally contact him? It wasn't that he disliked Min-Lo; his brother-in-law had a good heart. Concurrently, though, Min-Lo was also impulsive and foolhardy. Before he opened the letter, the bogus chef had an inkling as to what it was about. He had heard rumors of Min-Lo's son, Cody, starting a business.

The letter read in Chinese:

"<Mo,

Hope this letter finds you in good health and in good luck. When will you be returning to Texas? I have since found several more gun ranges that you may like. Let me know when you're coming back to visit. We'd be glad to have you again as our guest. We can tour the west side of Texas this time, especially San Antonio. You'd love the River Walk and the Alamo. Plus, the Mexican food there is quite nice, even though I don't prefer it. It looks like diarrhea, but it's considered popular. At any rate, I'm sure you've heard the gossip from our wives and their side of the family. It's true. My son is starting a new company. I didn't think he was serious at first, but then I met his partner, a fellow Chinese guy similar to his age. In fact, they're both Year of Snakes. As I've mentioned to you before, the company will be about websites. They're very in-demand now. Even the local funeral homes are wanting them. With a Chinese partner who has a Chinese mind, I'm sure this will succeed.>"

Bernie temporarily put down the letter and collected his thoughts. He knew what was coming up. He continued reading:

"<And that's when I realize—why settle for winning cents when we could be winning in dollars? Thousands upon thousands of them. My son has put in his entire retirement savings for this, and my father has given what he can as well, but I believe with proper financial backing, he will likely succeed exponentially. You know I'm a humble man, and I would never ask for a loan unless I was positive it would succeed. I've consulted several fortune tellers on this, and all have foretold his guaranteed success.>"

The rest of the letter discussed details of the estimated profits and a timeline for returned payments with interest. Then, finally, he saw the bottom line—the substantial total amount they wanted to borrow. Bernie Mo sat cross-legged on the floor and meditated with his thoughts. It was immediately apparent to him that the math did not make sense. This partner of Cody's was either one hell of a salesmen or his nephew was a victim of gross exaggeration. After much contemplation, the chef decided to give Cody a chance; perhaps, the young man's judgment of character was better than his father's. After all, Bernie wondered, what if Cody wildly succeeded? He couldn't pass up being a part of it. Risking things and going for the win was what made him successful; pulling back from a potential business deal countered that philosophy. Even if it did require a hefty financial accommodation.

Bernie got up and found a few clean sheets of stationery. The Chinese he wrote was crisp and beautiful. Hong Kong natives, he liked to say, kept the traditional way of writing the language. He would never succumb to the butchered look of simplified Chinese the Mainland people were learning. The reply to his brother-in-law was short and to the point. He would soon deposit the amount of the requested loan into Cody's business account. It was in good faith that it would be returned. Mostly, Bernie wished his nephew the best of luck.

Luck was a big part of Marty Ho's life.

The thirty-one-year old made his decisions based on his superstitions. In accordance with the luckiest Chinese number, he was obsessed with the number eight. His shirts had eight buttons, he counted to eight before opening doors, he told everybody he was born in '78 instead of '77, he took months to choose a phone number with almost all eights. Conversely, he was also captivatingly fearful of the unluckiest Chinese number: four. He refused to accept change for purchases of four dollars or multiple of four. He wouldn't do anything between four o'clock and five. He never said words like "quartet," "quarter," "quart," "quartz"—even if the last one had nothing directly to do with numbers. Those weren't the only Chinese superstitions he subscribed to, of course.

"Whoa, shit!" he shouted.

He was angry at himself for not seeing the red-and-blue car earlier. It was a fatal color combination, not only for him, but also for his loved ones. All red is fine, even welcomed, he believed. Same for blue. But the two of them together were enough to send Marty into a nervous breakdown. He needed the car to pass by him.

"Wahhh-ahhhh, damn it, hurry up, hurry...up... huh-ah, pass me, you old man!" Marty begged.

Not letting chance decide for him, he took action by pulling himself to the side of the road. It took seemingly forever for the red-and-blue car to drive by. After a few seconds, the gasping salesman closed his eyes and took a deep breath. *Feel the chi. Feel the chi.* Once he was assured the universe was aligned again, Marty resumed his driving. Suddenly, a large ringing noise was heard all around him; it was from the hands-free phone system in his car—or as he dubbed it: "the Batmobile."

"Uh, hello?" shouted Marty.

"<Hey, when are you going to collect the check? It's almost the end of the month>," blared a female voice.

It was his wife, Xia Xiang.

"<Just in time!>" he nervously laughed. "<I'm heading to my meeting now!>"

"<Yeah? Is this one of those meetings where you get paid?>"

"<Wah-ha! Of course, sweetie. This guy...why, let me tell you...this guy, he's a doctor. I think we'll be able to pay all of our bills AND get us that Bahamas vacation.>"

"Wow, really, bay-be?!" Xia exclaimed in English.

Marty smiled. He loved it when he had his wife fooled hook, line and sinker.

"<Ahhh, would I settle for anything less? Heh. It took me months to get him to like me>," proclaimed Marty.

"<Is this the doctor guy from the masquerade party last month?>"

"<Masquer—? Oh, hah! No, not that one. No, no. This one was the mayor's invite!>"

"<Mayor's invite? You didn't tell me you went to something like that. Why didn't you take me?>" his wife asked.

"<Haha. You forgot? Don't tell me you forgot we talked about this.>"

"<What'd we talk about? I don't remember this.>"

"<Sigh>," Marty teased, "<it's because you're always so busy. Heh heh. Always stressing. You forget the little details.>"

"<I guess I do...>" Xia agreed.

"<I only had the one invite. I begged them to give me another, but they said no. You know how politicians are. You know I'd bring you in if I could.>"

"<Yeah. Well, there'll be other opportunities, right?>"

"<Hooah, ffft, of course! There's three more coming up! You're always on my mind. Even when I close my eyes I see you...oop! Look! I'm there with the client.>"

"<The rich doctor guy?>"

"<Heh. You guessed it right. Hawha! I gotta go now, sweetie! I love you, okay?>"

"<Okay! Come back home with a check! Our electricity is about to get shut off!>"

With that, his wife hung up. Marty parked his car and whistled his way across the parking lot. The building he walked into was a modest one. It featured three stories with one tenant on each floor. He made his way to the one on the first floor, the one with the sign that read "Homer Flacco, Attorney at Law." There, sitting inside the waiting room, was Cody.

"Sup, dude," greeted Cody, who was reading an old issue of Sports Illustrated.

"Sighhhh," Marty replied, shaking his head.

"What? What's up?"

"I don't know. It's just...I'm so excited, I guess. I'm nervous! Heh. Ha!"

"I know, man! I'm excited too. Can't wait 'til the day I can tell my asshole supervisor Kirk to stick his fist up his own ass," grimaced Cody.

"Heh...yeah. I mean, no, no, Cody. No. Not that kind of excited."

"What...what do you mean?"

"It's just, like, a month...you know, heh, a month before we start Mosaic Design Studios, that's when we need to, you know, haha, start getting clients, you know?"

Cody thought for a moment.

"You know," said Cody, "that does make sense."

"Heh heh, I know, right? Wouldn't want to feel pressured into meeting the quota from day one, haha. Give me thirty days to prepare and it's better, weh? Wahah?"

"But that's...not too long from now, Marty."

"I know, Cody, I know. But I care about the company. I care about it so much."

"Thanks, man," smiled Cody. "I knew I was right into making you my partner."

Marty shook his head with a humble smile.

"Alright," continued Cody, "thirty days before opening day you should get some clients. Okay. Go for it, dude."

"Uh-hah. Yeah. Sigh. It...it sure would help though... if, heh, if I didn't have to worry about my own problems while I was doing it."

"Well, we've all got to make sacrifices. I'm still doing my job. But we got to do what we got to do, right?"

"Sigh," Marty said, looking at Cody with a puppy dog expression. "It's different when you have a family to raise."

"What do you mean? You've got a kid?"

"Ha! Heh. No, buddy, no. Just me and the wife. But that's considered a family, right? Heh. Well, ffft, I don't know if I can handle the job while providing for her too."

"Provide for her? I thought she worked with Wanda at the bank."

"She does, but she makes next to nothing. She's just a loan officer, Cody. Heh. Ha! Breadwinner. That's me. Sigh. It's such a tough title to take," Marty said it while looking at the floor, shaking his head for effect.

"Hey, I got an idea," Cody suddenly said.

"Yeah? Wuh...what is it?"

"Why don't you just take your salary a month in advance."

"Hooohhh, sigh. Well, does that mean I'll get August's salary for July and so on?"

"Yeah."

"Er, mmm, eh. But that would mean I didn't really get

compensated. Eventually we'll bump December to November's salary, so what will I get for December? Nothing?"

"True, but..."

"Come on, heh, we got all this dough lined up. Didn't you just tell me your rich uncle approved a lot of money this morning?"

"Yeah."

"Wah-ha! So! For the sake of our company, wouldn't it benefit us best if I were, weh-hah, to give us a head start and I'm able to already cover for my family? That would allow me to put all my focus on us. Heh? Ha? You know? Hah hah heh?"

"You're right, man. It would give us a boost if we had all these clients lined up for the new employees. Whatever you need to clear you from distractions, man, I'm all for it."

Marty winked and offered him a fist bump. Cody returned it.

"Can we do it in cash?" Marty requested.

"What do you mean?"

"My first salary. It's close to one month before our opening already. Come on, Cody. Hah hah! I need it today. Bills are waiting to be paid and all."

"What's wrong with a check?"

"We don't even have a bank account yet for our company, dude! Heh."

"What about a personal check?"

"Come on, heh. Cash, man."

Cody scratched his head, but decided to give his new friend the benefit of the doubt. "Okay, we'll go to an ATM after this."

"Hehaheehhh, thanks, Cody," Marty grinned happily, knowing he would have the money tonight for his wife.

Echoes of resonating footsteps from the polished wood floors could be heard approaching them. They were from a balding middle-aged man wearing a gray Armani suit.

"Cody, this is my attorney, Homer Flacco," Marty introduced. "Homer, this is my best friend, Cody Quan. Heh heh. He's a really good guy."

"Nice to meet you, Cody," greeted the lawyer. "Why don't you guys come to my conference room and I'll have all the paperwork set up for you."

On their way to the conference room, Cody quietly held reservations about Homer. Everything he did was fast—perhaps too fast. He took two quick steps for each normal one that Cody or Marty took. His speech pattern was also unnaturally fast, even faster than Cody's. It was almost like Homer disliked revealing more than what people were meant to see. Then again, Cody thought, what attorney wasn't secretive in one way or another?

"Please, have a seat. You guys want anything to drink?" offered Homer.

"No thanks," replied Cody.

"Coffee for me. Heh heh. Two creams and a sugar," chuckled Marty.

Homer buzzed the front desk secretary.

"Hey, can you please get us one coffee with two creams and a sugar. And also, I'll have a Diet Coke," ordered Homer.

"Wow, 'Diet' Coke? You, uh, you look fine to me, Homer, heh," complimented Marty.

"Nah, I just gained a couple of pounds over the weekend. Wife and I had our anniversary. Ate a lot of food. I'm a sucker for ham," explained the attorney.

The secretary came in with a cup of coffee and a can of Diet Coke.

"Well, eh, heh, you sure look fit to me! Wouldn't even have noticed, hah," flattered Marty.

"Oh, Marty. You salespeople are such charmers. Now, let's get down to the details of your business, shall we?"

Homer went step-by-step explaining the terminology of their limited liability corporation. He explained how it protected the two of them from having clients and banks seize their assets should they decide to break up the company. Then he explained the various payroll taxes and whether these were paid by the employee or employer or both. Finally, the attorney ended it by explaining their legal titles.

"Wait, wait, wait," interrupted Cody while he was looking at his copy. "This says that Marty is the president of the company. Not me."

"Oh, heh. That. Pssh," laughed Marty.

"Why am I the vice president?" asked Cody.

"Well, Marty told me that you both agreed to it while I was preparing these documents for you," explained Homer.

"No. We...never had a discussion about this," Cody replied.

"Come on, man! Don't you remember?" Marty asked.

"When?"

"At the coffee shop, heh-ha?" Marty winked and pointed.

"No."

"Dude, sigh. I really think you're getting senile. Sigh. Well, hefff, hahh, look, you got Treasurer and I also got Secretary. You can't get all the cool titles, ah-hah?"

"It's...really not a big deal, Cody," assured Homer.

"See? It's just titles. Heh. Semantics," insisted Marty. "Come on, Cody, heh, weh-ha, you're really going to make a deal out of something so insignificant? Haha. We can list us both as CEOs on our business cards. That's what people will see."

"Okay, okay," dismissed Cody, "let's move on. What else do you got, Homer?"

"That's really it. Just sign where I marked an 'X' and we're good to go."

Cody and Marty both signed the paperwork. There were stacks of forms and documents. Once they were finished, Homer congratulated them.

"Oh and one more thing, gentlemen," he said. "Should you both have any disagreements in the future and decide to break up the company, I will need to get you guys together and draft how to divide assets and responsibilities."

Cody laughed. "Why would we fight? Look at us. We're practically joined to the hip!"

"Well, how long have you guys known each other?" asked Homer.

"A couple of months," replied Cody.

"You never know what happens a year from now, guys. That's life."

"I doubt anything bad will happen," smirked Cody.

With that said, he broke out his checkbook and paid the attorney.

CHAPTER 16: CROUCHING SERPENT, HIDDEN AIR

It had been several years since Cody's father had successfully played matchmaker. Since then, of course, Mr. Quan hadn't stopped trying; his son simply had eluded his chosen prospects. This time, however, Cody gave in; over the years, he had had bad luck finding a girl on his own. That disconsolateness made it worthwhile for another try with his father, Cody thought, hoping there was a one-in-a-million chance his dad had gotten it right. To his disappointment, upon arriving at the dim sum restaurant that Saturday afternoon, he execrated himself for having the nerve to hope—sitting across from him was the nerdiest and most socially awkward girl he had ever met.

"<Hi, I'm Kiki! *Snort kak*!>" she greeted.

I want to run away.

"<What'd you say?>" Kiki asked.

"<Hey>," muttered Cody. "<Hi.>"

At first, he squinted at her, hoping her appearance would improve through concentrated eyesight. He tried to make sense of her strange bowl cut, which was probably a botched attempt at a halo. It didn't take long for him to be distracted by her heavy glasses that frequently slid down her tiny nose. She had lousy posture, constant fidgeting, poorly attired color combinations, and worst of all, a nauseating laugh that was half a snort and half a cackle.

To add insult to an already bad date, he discovered they weren't alone. Cody's family and Kiki's family were "coincidentally" at the same restaurant, sitting at the table next to them. He should've known his father would try something like this. Their "date" was soon to be a Facebook status.

"SAY CHEESE!" ordered a laughing Mr. Quan. He

took a few photo snaps with his phone's camera. Kiki cackled and made a V for victory sign. Two clicks later, their date went viral. "Having fun?"

"Not really," muttered Cody.

"Just having the fun! Just friend, OK?" advised Mr. Quan in broken English.

"Dad, why are you speaking to me in English? You never do that."

"What you mean? Your dad always say English to you!" his father replied.

Cody gave his father an unimpressed look; he was very used to the passive-aggressive back pedaling.

"<I swear>," Mr. Quan protested, "<I didn't know you two would be here! It's just a coincidence that we came here too!>"

"I should've known better than to assume a normal date," Cody muttered to himself.

"<Haha, it's OK, ummmm>," Kiki interjected. "<We're here. We might as well enjoy it!>"

"You know, my cousin Ace would probably like you a lot," quipped Cody. "Too bad his student visa expired and he had to permanently return to Hong Kong."

His father heard the key word.

"<Yes, yes! Hong Kong! She's from Hong Kong! Ask her about Hong Kong!>" advised Mr. Quan, returning to the other table.

Cody rolled his eyes. "So, what do you like to do?"

"Ummm, well, I like to study. *Snort-keekee-snort!*"

"No, I mean, what do you LIKE to do for fun? Not what do you HAVE to do."

"Studying."

Cody took a deep breath and then responded, "Anything else?"

"Oh, I like to listen to music...especially when I study!"

Kiki continued blabbering about school, the courses she was planning to take, how well she did on her TOEFL, techniques to help read chapters faster, questions about credit hours, grades she received from her past, what days she went to school, her favorite subjects, her favorite teachers; the school-related topics seemingly ran without end. It was almost a welcome distraction when Kiki's younger sister ran over and interrupted her.

"<Sister, look what I bought from the ninety-nine cent store!>" the kid exclaimed, showing Kiki a bracelet.

"<Can I sit next to you guys? Is that your new boyfriend?>"

Kiki let out a big snort-filled laugh, "<Hahaha-*snort*-ha! We're just talking!>"

"<OooOoOooh, 'talking'>," teased the younger sister.

Kiki's face turned red.

Cody's father frantically dialed his cell phone.

"<Hello?>" answered Cody's mother on the other end.

"<Where are you?>" he asked.

"<I'm almost there! Your father wanted to buy rice cakes from Six Ping Bakery! I couldn't talk him out of it!>"

"<Well, hurry! They're all here!>"

"<I wish you would stop doing this to our son>," Cody's mother said over the phone. "<He can find his own girlfriend.>"

"<That's what I'm afraid of. Hurry up and get my father over here!>"

Cody sat in silence, eating his shu mai. He had grown tired of his father suppressing the modern times, treating the year 2009 like it was early 20th-century China. A little common sense would dictate that dowry accommodation discussions were a thing of the past. A very extinct one too.

"<Hey, your dad said you work in a university. Do you have any interest in academia?>" asked Kiki.

"No," dismissed Cody in English, "it just pays the bills."

"<You should be honored to work for a school. All that education. All those books.>"

In Cody's mind, there was no point to continue the conversation. When he saw his father introducing his grandfather to Kiki's parents, he couldn't take it anymore. Without so much as a good-bye to her, Cody left Kiki and made his way outside of the restaurant. Mr. Quan immediately chased after him, catching up with his son outside.

"<Hey, where are you going? The bathroom is that way!>" informed Mr. Quan.

"<I'm not going to the bathroom! I'm getting out of here>," explained Cody.

"<No no no, we're so close!>"

"Close to what? Your dream marriage, dad?"

"This not a dreaming!" protested his father in bad English. "She perfect for you!"

"Perfect? If you like that Kiki girl so much, you marry her then!"

"Just be friend! Come on!"

"This is an arranged marriage proposal, dad. I'm embarrassed! Do other Chinese families still do this?"

"<Don't be so disobedient! You should be thanking me I found you such a good friend!>"

"Friends...yeah right," replied Cody, before walking farther away.

Disappointed, Mr. Quan walked back into the restaurant. He returned to his chair, defeated.

"<Eat your chicken feet>," insisted his wife with a sly smile. "<They're getting cold.>"

"<Ah-huh, my dear Aunt Juicy, let me get those luggage bags for you, huh>," bowed a humble Marty.

His dear Aunt Juicy stood fanning herself with a folded Hong Kong gossip magazine. It wasn't particularly hot, but from the moment she exited the doors of Bush Intercontinental Airport, she hated the late mid-summer heat. Her son, Guy Tsing, stood dumbfounded in the passenger pickup area as he watched his cousin do all the work. Marty took several of their suitcases and placed them in the trunk of his beat-up

Oldsmobile. His wife, Xia, sat patiently in the "Batmobile's" passenger seat, watching the events unfold from the side-view mirror. Once the luggage was situated, Guy made his way to the backseat and immersed himself in his iPod music.

"<Huff...hah...phew>," let out an exhausted Marty.

"<I want to sit in the front>," requested Aunt Juicy.

Marty observed his wife's disapproving expression from the passenger- side mirror. He knew she would not agree to move herself away from her seat.

"<Well, heh, Houston isn't like Chicago, Aunt Juicy>," replied Marty nervously.

"<What do you mean by that? I'm your elder, I want to sit in the front>," she repeated.

"<I...ah...sigh...the sun in Houston...it makes this glare. And a lot of people get skin cancer sitting near the front of the car>," explained Marty.

"<Are you sure?>"

"<Well, yeah. Heh. I'm surprised you didn't know. It's all over the news.>"

"<Maybe you're right...I haven't followed the news in a while. I've been reading too many gossip magazines instead.>"

"<Heh-ha, well, it's up to us younger folk to inform you of what we're told.>"

"<Is that so? Well, then, why is your wife sitting in front? Aren't you afraid she'd be exposed to these cancerous sunrays too?>"

"<Well>," Marty whispered in hush tones, "<your health is a greater concern to me. She's young. You know? She can take it.>"

His aunt gave him an understanding stare.

"<Eh? Haha? Heh?>" he ushered, opening one of the back doors for her. "<Your chariot arrives, Auntie.>"

Small talk kept the mood light and peaceful throughout their ride home. It eased Marty's initial nervousness—not an unusual feeling from him due to his heightened sensibilities. He knew Xia was difficult to deal with, stubborn in her own way. On the other hand, his auntie was immensely assertive.

"<Can you turn up the air conditioner?>" whined Aunt Juicy. "<It's hot.>"

The air conditioner was a level below full blast. He knew his wife wouldn't stand for it getting colder than that. A quick glance at Xia's challenging glare confirmed that her stance remained unchanged.

"<Uh, well, uh, sure>," Marty replied.

You dare? Xia turned her head directly toward him in silence, amazed at her husband's audacity.

"<Why thank you, Marty!>" smiled his aunt. "<You know, you're such a good, obedient boy.>"

"<Heh, huh...heh!>" he chuckled.

The voice of Xia's mother ran through her head. *Why'd you marry this loser?* Her husband was like a puppy dog, eager to please and wanting a pat on the head. He was cowardly too, always taking the path of least resistance. It might have been a bit easier to forgive Marty if he hadn't placed so much pride in those traits. He seemingly enjoyed being a tool—a submissive puppet who made them lose face. How many people have laughed behind their backs? The former Shanghai beauty queen felt she deserved better. Why did she marry this loser indeed?

"<Oh, whoa, oh no! Sigh, heh>," Marty expressed.

"<What? What is it?> asked Aunt Juicy.

"<The knob on the air-conditioner...it's...it's broken! I can't turn it up any higher>," he lied, pretending it was stuck.

That was enough to turn Xia 180 degrees on her opinion. Now her husband was clever and fast-thinking, dissolving tension with passive-aggressiveness. Marty had a way of ensuring drama didn't surface. Perhaps he was protecting her, she reminded herself, in his own indirect little method. Then again, he had always done so when they had fought too. He used his sympathy-generating techniques against her. It was a little overwhelming to think he was incapable of forthrightness when the time called for it.

"<Hey, I think someone is calling you>," Aunt Juicy interrupted.

"<Huh? Wha-what?>" asked Marty.

"<Your phone...I see it flashing and vibrating.>"

Marty fumbled around, searching for it with his hands. He had left the phone in the drink holder.

"H-Hello?" he answered.

"'Sup dude? It's me, Cody."

"Heh! Oh, hey! Heh! HA! Ha...ah...haha. Hey, what...what are you doing?"

Xia raised an eyebrow, "<Who's that on the phone with you?>"

Marty shrugged.

"So yeah," Cody continued, "I just wanted to know if you could hang out tonight, man. We could shoot the shit, talk more about our upcoming company. Oh! And guess what? I've got Street Fighter IV! This guy I know called Herman Shu is coming over. If you make it early, like, around five o'clock, we could play it together. I got lots of beer too. Shiner Bock, good ol' Texas beer."

"Wah, well, yeah, sure...I mean, my cousin from Chicago is here. He might be a burden," warned Marty.

"<I said>," repeated Xia, loud enough for everyone to hear, "<who's that on the phone with you?! >"

"Just bring your cousin!" insisted Cody, "the more the merrier. And we could go for Mexican food afterwards. Let's do this, man!"

"Okay, sure. I'll come," Marty responded.

"<Come where? Where are you going?"> asked his wife. "<It's my shopping night with you, remember?>"

"Badass, man," commented Cody. "Well, you know where the CVS Pharmacy is at by Piney Point? Meet me there. My house is close by."

"Yeah, sorry to hear about that, I'll see what I can do. Tell your wife she has my condolences," Marty replied.

"Huh?" asked a confused Cody. "Sorry about what? I don't have a wife. What are you talking about?"

"I'm losing power. Gotta hang up," said Marty.

He quickly ended the phone call.

"<Sigh>," he said, slowly shaking his head.

"<What's going on? Is something wrong?>" asked Xia.

"<You know my friend from Remax?>"

"<The guy with the one arm?>"

"<Yeah. Sigh. He just blew up his other arm.>"

"<What?! Then how did he call you?!>"

Marty stuck out his tongue and pointed at it.

"<He dialed by using his tongue?>" exclaimed his wife. "<That's incredible!>"

Her husband slowly nodded his head. "<Sigh. You know how it is>," replied Marty. "<Poor guy can't catch a break. Well, hah-heh, I really want to visit him tonight, but I did promise you that I'd—>"

"<No no no. This is important. You should see how he's doing. I can be with your cousin and Aunt Juicy.>"

"<Well, heh, I have to take Guy too. I mean, he's got to see what tragedy looks like.>"

"<I agree!>" interrupted Aunt Juicy. "<Take my son. Let him know how lucky he has it.>"

She looked at Guy disappointedly. Her son was lost in his own world, immersed in the latest top-40 junk songs. Guy felt no hesitation pulling off imaginary butt-grabbing moves while gyrating his shoulders and hips. His mother wished he had more sense of responsibility, a hint of maturity and above all, an obligation for obedience.

Just like, she thought, Marty Ho.

The new Street Fighter was much more difficult than Cody expected. He enjoyed the classic Street Fighter II of his youth; perhaps he was getting too old to deal with the complexity of modern games. It also didn't help that the most obnoxious person on the planet was shouting at him in his living room.

"Use the Metsu Shoryuken!!!" screamed Herman Shu.

"I'm trying! How the hell do you do it again?!" asked Cody.

"Down swing forward down swing forward all three kicks!!!!!!"

"Down swing what?"

"YOU LOSE!" informed the video game.

Cody had lost the match.

"Agh! Ugh! Aghhhh! WHAT IS WRONG WITH YOU?" screamed Herman.

Herman was from Cody's Fellowship Communion Baptist Church days. There was never a sensible reason for Cody to keep in touch with Herman all these years. Perhaps Cody found some strange sympathy in himself to be Herman's only friend; nobody else could tolerate the guy. He was known to be very loud and, worse, very inconsiderate of personal space. Herman was a habitual line stepper. Cody was reminded of that when he heard loose springs bouncing around behind him.

"Stop jumping on my couch, you prick," Cody commanded.

"But you know how to do the Metsu Shoryuken, don't you? You understand that you have to slide your thumbs in a fast motion and—"

"I don't give a shit about the Matshu Dookey! Stop jumping on my couch, asshole!"

Herman ceased and slid down to where his friend was sitting. He sidled up real close to Cody and playfully gave him a massage. Cody immediately swatted Herman's hand aside and scooted away.

"Come on!" protested Herman. "Why can't I touch you?"

"You sure you ain't gay, dude?"

"No!....okay, seriously, about the Metsu Shoryuken, it's done similar to the regular Shoryuken except—"

Herman's explanation was suddenly interrupted by the doorbell. With a sigh of relief, Cody got up and anticipated who would be on the other side of the front door.

"Marty!" greeted Cody, "so glad you could make it!"

"Heh heh heh. Ah-ha...heh!" chuckled Marty.

"Is that your cousin?" asked Cody.

"Oh hey, I'm Guy..."

The buff third-string Division III quarterback casually gave Cody a warm handshake. He enjoyed claiming his similarities to a particular character from his favorite television show, *Jersey Shore.*

"...aka the Asian Situation," he pointed and winked at Cody.

The three of them took off their shoes and went upstairs where Herman was playing Street Fighter IV on the Playstation 3 console. Herman pretended to be so focused on the video game that he ignored Marty and Guy greeting him. They watched as Herman lost to his computer opponent.

"I HAD IT! I HAD IT!" screamed Herman. "Did you guys see that? The Tatsumaki Senpukyaku fails me every time!"

Guy took the controller and fiddled with the game.

"Hi," Marty offered Herman a handshake. "I'm Marty."

Herman ignored him and screamed at Guy, "Oh my GOD! Use the mid-kick combos and tap it with fireballs! Don't you know how to play?!"

He wisped the controller away from Guy and started playing the game himself.

"Soooo...eh, Guy," inquired Cody, "Marty tells me you're quite an athlete."

"Bro, I wouldn't say that, but, yeah, I play a little quarterback."

Guy made a football throwing motion, celebrating successful catches by imaginary receivers.

"Wow. How much can you lift?" Cody asked.

"I'd say three-hundred-fifty pounds or so benching, max."

"Damn," laughed Cody. "How many Hermans does that translate to?"

"Haha, I don't know, bro. A million?"

Herman shot Guy an angry look. He dropped the controller and walked up to Guy, sizing him up. Both Marty and Cody laughed as the bony Herman gave the football player a stare-down. He then surprised everyone by casually dismissing Guy.

"Pssh. You couldn't handle me," claimed Herman.

"Whatever, bro. I don't even think you can beat me in Street Fighter," Guy joked.

"What?!" challenged Herman. "I'll tell you, aside from being a master singer, dancer, philosopher and intellectual prodigy, I'm also trained in the art of Jeet Kune Do. Whoooooo-ahhhhhh!!!!"

Marty and Cody both looked at one another, laughing hysterically.

"Really?" asked Guy with an amused smirk.

Herman started making snake punch motions in the air.

"Well, heh, actually, that's not Jeet Kune Do," corrected Marty. "Those are snake style kung fu techniques."

"WHAT DO YOU KNOW?" challenged Herman.

"Wuh, eh, I happen to know because I, eh, know martial arts, heh," Marty replied.

Herman looked at him up and down and then did more kung fu poses. He spread his legs wide and extended one hand forward with the other upward.

"What's this style called then?" tested Herman.

"Ah, hmmm heh...that...looks made-up," Marty answered.

"It's called Communist Scorpion!"

Cody and his two new friends burst into laughter.

"I'm serious!" claimed Herman. "I could end your life in two seconds with this move! Be glad my secret master made me vow never to use it."

"Sure, bro," laughed Guy.

Accepting the challenge, Herman immediately leaped at Guy, clinging onto him. His bony arms flailed about, landing punches that didn't seem to affect the gentle giant.

"Hey, hey!" Cody shouted. "Don't go breaking my furniture!"

Both Cody and Marty whisked Herman away from the quarterback.

"Oooooh!" moaned Herman. "Lucky I took it easy. I don't believe in hurting other Asians."

"I've seen children bigger than you," responded Guy.

"Ladies, ladies," Cody chimed in, "let's keep this discussion civilized. Herman, don't try and monkey fuck Guy again, alright?"

Herman responded by doing invisible Street Fighter-type uppercuts into the air.

"I'll take that as a 'yes' from Herman," nodded Cody.

There was a brief moment of silence.

"So, what do you guys wanna do tonight?" asked Guy.

"I dunno, I'm kinda hungry," Cody replied. "What about you, Marty?"

"Shhh, ehh, heh. I don't know. You said Mexican food, right? Up to you, heh."

"Alright, let's do that then. There's a great restaurant a couple of blocks down from my house."

"Cool," agreed Guy. "What about afterwards? We've got all night, bro."

Cody thought for awhile and then he smiled.

"Afterwards," chuckled Cody, "Herman can teach us some martial arts."

Usually during his evening shift at eleven o'clock, the manager of the CVS Pharmacy near Piney Point took his smoke break. It was a strategic time, one that protected him from the highest traffic of drunks and loiterers. It was the highlight of his shift, the last moment of peace he would receive for the rest of the night. This time, however, he observed a strange sight behind the dumpster area. As he calmly absorbed the effects of the nicotine, he made note of the four shirtless Asian men jumping in the air, high-kicking it in partially acrobatic moves. The bony one, he observed, seemed to be their leader; he was yelling at them at the top of his lungs. The CVS Pharmacy manager dismissed them as harmless and decided to enjoy their actions as entertainment. Once his ten minutes were up, he stomped his discarded cigarette and returned to the store.

"I want you to focus on me," demanded Herman. "See my stomach? Breathe in and breathe out."

His belly shrank and expanded in rapid motion.

"Okay, like, so when are you going to teach us some cool shit? Show me a move, bro," requested Guy.

"You're not ready," Herman replied dismissively. "You haven't grasped the concept of the golden rule yet."

"Okay, and what's that?" asked Cody.

"The golden rule," revealed Herman in a low tone, "is to know that martial arts isn't really an art.......it's a science."

"Martial science," contemplated Cody.

"Exactly! Think about it," Herman said.

"Okay, so now that we know that," Guy concluded impatiently, "show us a move."

Herman adjusted his thick glasses. He then made a space for himself and did a strange combination of jump kicks, spin kicks, wild punches and finger pokes. It was done in such a blur that none of the others comprehended what he did.

"Wooooooohhh, aAAaaahhhh," finished Herman.

"Heh, hah! Ahaha! That was so fast I didn't catch on, heh," Marty said.

"Yeah," egged on Cody, "do it again. But slower."

Herman repeated his attack.

"Fist of North..." he explained, "then...to Claw of Shark...then...Force of Tai...Love of Chi..."

He started spinning over and over.

"And now," he concluded, "Crouching Serpent, Hidden Air!"

It took a lot of willpower for the others to resist laughing. Cody couldn't continue his restraint anymore; he fell to the ground howling hysterically. It was amazing how Herman was oblivious to his own humiliation. Cody concluded he was either too naive or didn't care. Cody decided to find out which one it was.

"So show us how to defend ourselves, Herman," he said, picking up a stick on the floor. "Let's say this stick is a knife and I'm robbing you. How would you stop me?"

"<Hah. Look challenge stick me defy?>" replied Herman in broken Cantonese.

"What?" laughed Cody.

"Learn to speak Chinese!" tsk-tsked Herman.

"You don't seem to speak it very well yourself."

"<What? Laugh you me that is touch heart?>"

"Uh, ok. Anyway. I'm a robber and I have a knife. I'm telling you to stick 'em up and give me your wallet. What do you do?"

"What time of the day is it? How many people are there?" asked Herman.

"You're alone in an alley, and Guy, Marty and I are surrounding you."

"But they're not surrounding me, they're in front of me."

Cody rolled his eyes and gestured for Guy and Marty to form a triangle surrounding Herman. They obliged.

"Okay," Cody said, "there. Now you're trapped. I got a knife—"

"That's not a knife. It's a stick."

"—I know. Pretend it's a knife. So, you're trapped and we're telling you to give us your money. What do you do?"

"Depends on the wind resistance."

"Stop stalling, dickwad. You're being mugged. Who the fuck cares about the wind?"

Herman closed his eyes and started singing.

"It's so hard...to say...goodbye...to yesterdayyyy..." he sang.

"What? Why are you singing Boyz II Men? Hey, pay attention," demanded Cody.

Herman then lunged at Cody by grabbing his wrist. Cody ended up poking the stick at Herman's chest.

"Dude," Guy observed, "he just 'stabbed' you."

The three of them laughed at Herman again.

"But I would've decapitated him first!" Herman insisted. "I would have, look, I would have pinpointed the acupuncture nerves of Cody's wrist and sent his heart exploding after a few steps."

"Heh-wah, like, uh, Kill Bill?" quipped Marty.

More laughter.

"No! Not like Kill Bill!" Herman protested.

"Can't you think of something original?" chuckled Guy.

Herman spun around and tried to attack Marty. Marty dodged him like a matador, sending Herman tripping onto the alleyway pavement. The three laughed at him again.

"Okay," threatened Herman as he picked himself back up, "you want me to take the kiddie gloves off? Is that what you want?!!!!!"

"I'm sorry," laughed Guy, "you were holding back on us?"

Herman ruffled his own hair and growled. He closed his eyes and began hopping around.

"OooOOAAAaa," he moaned.

The sight of his boney, shirtless body along with his serious expressions made him look ridiculous. He pointed at Marty.

"Wah-huh. Me?" Marty asked, pointing at himself with an innocent look.

Herman gestured with his finger for Marty to approach closer.

"Ah heh heh," chuckled Marty.

In a speedy, yet clumsy motion, Herman got on the ground and tried to sweep kick Marty. He ended up missing him, even though Marty hadn't moved.

"Hahahaha!" laughed Guy.

"Ooohhh waaaaa!" shouted Herman.

He approached Marty, poking at him with short kicks.

"Ah ha, stop it, heh...eh...stop it...heh..." Marty flinched.

"Ahh yaaa waa yaa!" Herman continued.

Guy thought it was enough. The big guy calmly walked behind Herman and constrained him from the back. Herman, however, continued flailing his arms and legs at the air.

"Alright, okay. Calm down," suggested Guy.

"Lucky, you're so lucky..." Herman said.

Cody went over to Marty and checked on him. Marty was slouching over and breathing hard.

"You okay?" asked Cody.

"Heh...ah...sigh...he got me in a few places," Marty replied.

"Why'd you let him beat you up like that? I thought you knew martial arts."

"I, wah-huh, I took it easy on him," explained Marty. "You know, it's like beating up on a retarded person. I couldn't do that, you know? Heh?"

Cody turned around and walked toward Herman, who was still being held by Guy.

"Well, Herman," taunted Cody, "you couldn't stop a fake mugging. Guess your little martial arts need a little work, eh?"

He playfully jabbed Herman with the stick from earlier.

"Stab! You're dead," laughed Cody.

"SHORYUKEN!" shouted Herman, stepping on Guy's toes.

"Bro, can you please not step on my new shoes?" requested Guy.

Herman gave him a head butt, using the back of his head. The move surprised Guy and stung him on the bridge of his nose. The impact caused him to loosen his grip, making it easy for Herman to squirm loose.

"You have potential," Herman said, pointing at Guy. "I can train you into becoming a master."

"That was a cheap shot!" Guy claimed.

"Like it?" asked Herman smirking. "It's called Reverse Fortune Cookie."

"I'll turn you into a reverse fortune cookie," threatened Guy.

"Ooooh aaaah!" challenged Herman.

He started throwing random punches and kicks in the air, alternating between Guy, Marty and Cody.

"Toisan Fireball!" he shouted, swinging at Marty.

"Uh hah! Ah!" Marty protested.

"Romance of the Three Kingdoms!" he shouted, kicking Cody.

"Damn it! Stop!" pleaded Cody.

"Su Su Gai!!!" he shouted, flapping his arms around at Guy.

The pattern continued. Chaos ensued. Herman appeared to have a thousand arms, swarming at the other men like locusts invading crops.

"Okay, bro, ow, ooh, it's... not... funny anymore. Stop it, ow, before...you get...hurt," Guy warned.

"Water Meets Wood! Hong Kong Feet!" continued Herman.

Among the turmoil, Marty was given the least attention of the barrage. He, too, was secretly feeling aggravated by Herman's behavior. It was rare for him to feel enough hostility where he felt compelled to take direct action—it was tempting, no doubt. Instead, it took an overwhelming need to save face that turned him toward an alternative solution. Marty decided to be suggestive in letting someone else do what he wanted done. As Herman aggressively thrashed himself at Guy and Cody, Marty waited until the right moment when both their eyes were closed. Once the opportunity presented itself, he clenched his fist and gave his cousin a hard right to the jaw.

"OW! DAMN!" shouted Guy. "OKAY, THAT ONE HURT!"

"Monkey Tail Spin! Bamboo Wall!" continued Herman, oblivious to Marty's interference.

"I DON'T GIVE A FUCK THIS TIME."

Without restraint, Guy gave Herman's groin a nice swift kick, sending the frail young man onto the pavement with pain. He added complementary kicks to voice his displeasure.

"WHAT DO YOU THINK OF THAT, HUH? WHERE'S YOUR FLYING DRAGON UPPERCUT NOW?!"

"Heh, wah-huh, whoa, Guy, heh, hey, calm down," Marty advised.

"He hit me! Hard! Right here.......in the jaw!" Guy said, pointing at the side of his mouth.

Cody walked up to Herman and kicked him too.

"That's for hitting my friends!" Cody explained.

"Heh, huh-ha. Come on, Cody. Let's take a breather. Heh?" Marty said. "Violence never solves anything. You guys really have to control your temper. Heh? Ha? Haha?"

Marty helped Herman up.

"Sigh. I guess I'll be the mature one and end the fun, wuh-eh," he said.

"I have to...I have to go to the bathroom," mumbled Herman.

"There's one in the CVS," informed Marty.

He helped Herman up and patted him on his back. They watched as Herman limped his way around the corner and disappeared toward the front of the pharmacy.

"Man," Guy commented, "how'd you meet this douche bag?"

"Church," answered Cody.

"For real? Haha."

"Sigh, you really shouldn't get so carried away, Guy. You're three times his size," said Marty while shaking his head.

"He really hit me. That last punch...it wasn't like his other punches..."

"I'm sure it wasn't that bad," replied Marty.

"Let's leave him," Cody commanded. "What a loser."

The three friends headed back to Cody's apartment with Herman already erased from their minds. They discussed plans for the upcoming weekend and fantasized about the pretty women they were going to hire.

At two hours past midnight, the CVS Pharmacy manager was lucky enough to sneak in a second cigarette break. It was a rarity for him. It seemed like the late-night customers were scarcer than usual. Before he could light his cigarette, however, he heard a soft whimpering behind the dumpster. Curious, he approached it and saw Herman, whimpering alone with a blank stare in his eyes.

CHAPTER 17: LOOSE ENDS

"<Perfect>," Cody's Aunt Hannah commented, "<just like the American catalog pictures from my childhood.>"

For a moment, all she could notice was the two-story, red-bricked town house in front of her. To an objective eye, the home was modest and unassuming; to Hannah, it was Monticello itself. It was a lifetime reward for penny-pinching and countless overtime hours at the Happy Lotus. Never having to live in another person's house again was an idea she could get used to. At the crossroads age of fifty-two, the single mother required only a few things to make her life complete: a house of her own, her teenage daughter Megan and love. At the present, she was around all three.

Megan didn't share her mother's optimism. Growing up in the information age only accelerated her maturity; the independent eighteen-year-old had sought out a wealth of information online. It was enough for her to know that her mother was getting a shabby deal. Worse, the real estate agent who was snake-oiling Hannah had charmed her heart as much as her wallet.

"<But mom>," reasoned Megan, "<this particular home is priced almost twenty percent more than its market value. There's nothing special about it. I'm sure we could find a better deal elsewhere.>"

"<Nonsense>," Aunt Hannah dismissed, smiling at the man responsible for the laudable find. "<What does a kid like you know about homes anyway? Tell her how foolish she is, Mui.>"

Patrick Mui had sold fewer homes than any other realtor in Sugar Land, Texas. He was, by definition, unsuccessful. Megan had never understood what her mother saw in him. Everything about him looked recycled—from his patched-up hobo-looking jacket to his taped-up glasses. The middle-aged loser with the salt-and-pepper hair had nothing physically, financially or personality-wise going for him. Surely her lonely mother couldn't have sunk so low?

"<Well>," laughed the duplicitous agent, looking at Hannah's eyes, "<your mother has good instincts. The exorbitant markup was based on its popularity. Where you see just a number, your mother sees its magnetism, its concealed desirability, its...magic. Some things, dear girl, are beyond the logic of price alone.>"

Hannah found it impossible to camouflage her blushing.

"<Come>," Patrick said, taking a hold of the flushed woman's hand. "<Let me lead you both around the house one more time.>"

The tour failed to convince Megan the house had hidden charm. In fact, she realized, it looked even more vulnerable than the first time they had inspected it. Vulnerable also reminded the teen of her mother—the loser salesman had her melting like putty. They stopped at the upstairs bathroom where Patrick paid an unusual amount of attention to the individual air conditioner unit.

"<Remember these in Hong Kong?>" he asked, pointing at it.

"<Oh, I do, I do! That was decades ago though. They used to blow the stink right back at me!>" Aunt Hannah laughed.

"<I'm sure glad we don't have to squat anymore.>"

"<Hahaha! What are you talking about? They helped improve our leg muscles!>"

They have chemistry, Megan admitted to herself, I'll give them that. Then again, Patrick coincidentally related everything to her mother. Either the stars astonishingly aligned in their favor or, more likely, he reacted with lie after lie. Her mother was just as guilty of it too; nobody falls for people like Patrick Mui, she realized, unless they willingly let themselves.

"<My dear daughter>," Hannah insisted with a noticeable giggle, "<why don't you venture around on your own? See if you like the guest room. That would be your room. Mr. Mui and I will be checking the living room downstairs.>"

With her natural tendency towards obedience kicking in, Megan did as she was told—even at the expense of possible trouble. The two adults were heard laughing on their way downstairs. The lanky teenager distracted herself by imagining how she could furnish the small guest room.

"<Oh, Patrick!>" Megan heard her mother's voice, "<that's silly!>"

Meanwhile, in the empty living room below her, Hannah lay on some of the plastic boxes. It was her makeshift sofa.

"<I'm so tired>," she sighed. "<All this walking up and down the stairs. I love this house. I just love it. Too bad Megan's stuff is so heavy; we'll need to carry it upstairs. At our age, our muscles easily cramp. Especially the arms and legs.>"

"<Speaking of leg muscles...>" suggested Patrick, leaning to massage one of Hannah's thighs, "<...perhaps yours could use a little tender care.>"

"<Oooh>," Aunt Hannah giggled.

"<Mom, I have choir rehearsal in thirty minutes!>" Megan interrupted from upstairs.

Aunt Hannah leaned over and gently pushed Patrick off her.

"<Yes...yes, I suppose we must get going>," she said. "<I love this house though.>"

"<So is that a yes on the purchase?>" asked Patrick with eyebrows raised. "<You should claim it soon if you decide. A lot of people were looking at this house. I can't guarantee that you'll get it. You'll have to act fast.">

"<Really?>"

"<Yes, you and this house fit like a hand in a glove. I knew it was meant for you the moment you saw it.>"

"<You know what? I felt the same thing!>" Aunt Hannah said in amazement.

"<Then what's there to hold you back?>"

"<Mom>," reminded Megan, "<let's go.>"

"<Your daughter>," he observed, glancing at the upstairs direction,"<she's seventeen by now, isn't she? Shouldn't she have her own car to drive?>"

"<Ah, you know, giving a teenager a car is just asking for trouble, perhaps—>"

"<She should work for it then>," continued Patrick. "<That way she can find something useful with her time.>"

Megan came downstairs and approached them with a frown.

"<Monkey>," he said.

"<Pardon?>" asked Aunt Hannah.

"<Your daughter is Year of the Monkey, isn't she? She's seventeen. Monkeys have mischievous personalities.>"

"<Haha. You sound like my brother-in-law, Min-Lo. He's very superstitious>," laughed Aunt Hannah. "<But I don't believe in any of that. I say if it feels good and you want it, go after it.>"

"<Of course. Life is short.>"

Patrick Hui gave her calf muscles a tight squeeze. Megan rolled her eyes as her mother exaggerated a swoon.

"<Come on, Mom...>"

"<Yes, yes>," Hannah brushed her daughter aside as she got up, "<I suppose she's right. We do have to go. I had a great time today, Mui.>"

They left the house together. Patrick watched both her and Megan as they walked toward their navy blue Toyota Celica. It was a good day for him, knowing he had sold his first house in ages—but perhaps just as important, he also won his first heart in ages.

Now all he had to do was conceal it from his wife.

"I haven't seen you in days," typed MyMelodyBunny.

Yuki's tiredness was evident on webcam; she had been waiting for Cody to go online for most of the night. There was a noticeable change to him, but it wasn't necessarily for the better. Though he might have embraced his newfound confidence, she liked her Internet friend better when he was his humble, doubting self. Before then, they were kindred spirits, two souls behind the looking glass understanding one another. She knew there would be a day they would drift apart, but she had hoped it wasn't she who would be left behind. Now that Cody was busy planning for his new company and constantly hanging out with his new friend Marty, she wondered where their friendship fit in. She hoped their time together hadn't completely dissipated.

"I've been busy," answered Quanster7.

"How's the company coming along? It's called Mosaic Design Studios, right?"

Cody seemed distracted or disinterested in talking with her; she wasn't sure which one it was.

"Marty's been fantastic," Quanster7 typed, ignoring her question. "Let me tell you. He's already started looking for clients a month before we start. I like having a partner who's as passionate about succeeding as I am."

"I see. So everything's all set up?"

"Oh yeah, we've found the perfect office. It's right in the middle of the Sugar Land Town Square. My office view is fantastic. I can see the mayor's office from my window. LOL."

"So everything's ready? Furniture, legal documents, employees?"

"Eh, well, we're probably going to IKEA next week. They have fantastic furniture for affordable prices. As for legal documents, we've already taken care of that with Marty's lawyer. For employees, we're going around notifying people about our job openings."

"Marty's...lawyer?"

"Yeah. His name is Homer. Seemed like he knew what he's doing."

"I'll bet he does. Why couldn't Marty get a neutral attorney? One that neither of you knew?"

"Because," Cody felt annoyed, "he just trusts this guy, okay? Why should we go to someone we didn't know? That's just ridiculous."

"I'm sure there're a lot of attorneys capable of helping you out, Cody. Any one of them would know how to file proper paperwork for new businesses."

"Yeah, but it's less hassle going with someone that we know."

"You mean someone that HE knows."

"Why are you so paranoid, Yuki? Geez. Guess I shouldn't tell you we're using his I.T. friend too."

"Well, I'm just playing devil's advocate here," she typed. "For all I know he's really this great guy as you say he is, but it's always best to err on the side of caution."

"He IS a great guy, Yuki, and I wish you would trust me on this."

"Well, I mean, hey, it's your business, not mine. I'm just looking out for you. We haven't talked in awhile. I just...I just missed the way we used to talk."

Yuki wished she hadn't typed that. She didn't like revealing emotion. It was important for people to see her as a strong, independent woman. Telling someone they were missed was fluffy and sentimental. At best, it was awkward as platonic friends; at worst, it was an inappropriate statement.

"Yeah, I miss you too, Yuki."

"Who said I missed you? I just said I missed the way we talked."

She smiled, knowing it gave her a loophole for her momentary display of weakness.

"And wouldn't talking to each other require me?" Cody said. "Wouldn't that, by extension, mean you miss me?"

"Yeah, yeah. Don't flatter yourself, Cody Quan."

Cody smiled. Yuki was proof that when one good friend moves along, another one takes her place. Of course, she and Mindy were very different people. Whereas Mindy was openly emotional, aggressive and insensitive, Yuki was reserved, independent and respectful of emotional space. She was the perfect companion for Cody after the fiasco with his former church. Their friendship was good for her as well. Yuki had recently slammed past the forty-year-old wall. Grey hairs, farsightedness, an aching back; how did the years go by so fast? she wondered. Cody, being much younger than her, had an energy that excited her. His bits and pieces of naïveté made him less pessimistic; it kept her feeling young—even when she wasn't.

"I want to tell you something," typed MyMelodyBunny.

"Yeah?"

"The anniversary of my mother's passing just came."

"Oh, shit. I'm so sorry, Yuki. Here I am always telling you about my upcoming company and you've got real pain to deal with."

"No, no. It's nothing like that. I mean, I accepted it. It is what it is. It's just, I don't know. I guess that's how life is sometimes."

"You know, you should hold on to my number. Let me give it to you."

"Please don't give it to me. It's just..look, Cody...why is it with men it's always about fixing things? I'm just telling you all this because I want to share it with you. That's all. I just wanted you to know that I was a little bummed that night and that it's okay. It's only natural because I loved the memory of my mother."

There was a slight pause between their typing.

"Yuki? Can I honestly ask you about something?"

"Sure."

"Why do you still call yourself a Christian?"

"Because we're both baptized, Cody. And that makes us Christian."

"No, it doesn't," typed Quanster7. "In fact, you walked away like I had. That's how we first met in these blogs, remember? 'Dear Alice'?"

Dear Alice. Cody had forgotten the name of that advice columnist for years. He had forgotten the question Yuki submitted; he remembered only commenting on it because he considered Dear Alice's advice poorly given. It was amusing how important people come from the least important moments.

"That isn't related to the Christian thing," explained MyMelodyBunny. "It wasn't Dear Alice. It was your entry about a rant to all your 'fellow Christians.' You told them you had quit because they were hypocrites. You asked them to change their ways, be less judgmental, be more active in philanthropy, that sort of thing. I agreed with you and said I left for the same thing. That's why we became blogging buddies. It was...admirable."

"So, then, why do you still believe?" asked Quanster7.

"Because when we're baptized, we are told that we're Christian for the rest of our lives."

"But we both gave it up. We can't still be something we no longer believe."

"It's not that. It's hard for me to explain."

"Well," he typed, "regardless of whether or not you're just trying to share, you should take my number anyway."

"Cody, it was your idea not to take each other's phone numbers. It made it safe that we didn't cross into each other's worlds, so that we can talk about each other's lives without fear. That our confessed secrets wouldn't come back and haunt us."

"Yes, but what if it was an emergency and suddenly we needed to talk to each other?"

"I can handle it. It's never that bad, Cody."

"Well, what if it was me that needed to talk with you?"

"You can handle it too. Besides, we also have Rain."

Cody typed himself groaning. He then added a frowning emoticon.

"What are you groaning about?" asked MyMelodyBunny. "I can see you making a pouty face on webcam."

"Rain...she's a nice person. But I wouldn't go to her in my greatest time of need."

"So you choose the old woman instead."

"Stop calling yourself that."

"It's true, Cody," she typed. "I'm old enough to be your mom."

"LOL. No, you're not. You're just a decade older. Maybe an older, wiser sister."

"ROFL!"

"Besides, it's not how old you are, but how old you feel. Your real age inside seems to be younger. Much younger."

"That's sweet talk to an older woman like me. Thanks."

"It's true."

"Well...I guess we're the same age then, if you put it that way. Still, I do like the term 'cougar.' It sounds menacing, Cody."

"Well, Ms. Cougar, it's getting late there in the Eastern Time Zone, isn't it?"

"Yeah. I'm feeling droopy. Let me know how the company goes."

With that said, Yuki disconnected herself from the webcam. This was how two close friends say farewell. No words were needed. They simply understood.

———

"Let's only hire white chicks," suggested Guy.

It was seven o'clock the next evening. He placed an unlit cigar between his lips, the one he bought from the shop next door. Reflections of Hooters waitresses were seen from the surface of his sunglasses.

"Sigh...Guy, stop posing with that cigar. You look like a douche," observed Marty.

The quarterback ignored his cousin, distracted by the sea of blondes and brunettes walking past him. Their presence had made him twist his head from side to side; it was so frequent that he feared it would come off his shoulders.

"Check out this one," Cody insisted, handing a resume over to Marty. "Web and graphic design skills. Three years professional experience. Knows a bunch of useful software and his samples look incredible. Human Resources from the Art Institute highly praised him."

Marty skimmed through the resume with a disapproving look. The name on the resume indicated the person was most likely male. Men, he believed, were hungry for power. If he and Cody were to be president and vice president respectfully, they needed to be free from male employees who could potentially usurp their authority.

"No," he replied, shaking his head.

"Why not? He seems to be very useful. We could—"

Marty shook his head again.

"How about this one then," Cody asked, pointing at a resume with a female name. "Waverly Jong. Oooh, aside from her design background she's also a former chess champion. It hints she's übersmart."

Marty shuddered at the idea of an overly intelligent woman. The last thing he wanted was someone who questioned him.

"Hey, huh, what about this one?" Marty insisted, pointing at a resume of his choice.

"Hmm. A Flash specialist. Patricia Aguilar."

"Yeah. Lots of sites done in Flash these days. Fancy graphics, wah-ha."

"No, Flash is going to be obsolete. You can't update it easily. I don't think we'd need a Flash specialist."

"Um, well, that's not what I heard."

Cody grew defensive. "What? Where'd you hear that? You don't trust me?"

"No...no! Heh. I mean, no, I trust you. It's just, heh, I wanted our company to get the best. Sure, Flash graphics are a hassle, but I'm sure our employees will respect you enough as a leader to make changes."

Cody didn't seem so sure, especially on any mention of leadership.

"I don't know," he said, "fancy or not. Flash is a hassle. We could make similar effects with Ajax. That's why I'd rather hire that guy over this Patricia girl."

"Wuh-eh. But we could charge extra if the clients want Flash changes," Marty insisted.

"I don't know, dude."

"And she could be a hot one, heh. Every Patricia I know is hot. Ever known one that wasn't? Eh? Ah heh heh."

"Actually," interrupted Guy, "I know this ugly chick named Patricia."

Marty quickly lifted his right foot and gave Guy a silent but impactful kick.

"Ow, bro!" howled his cousin, "I mean, this Patricia was an Asian chick. We don't count Asian chicks, right, guys?"

"Wuh-eh, yeah, I meant other girls," said Marty.

"Interesting rule," Cody commented.

"Heh, just think. Heh. An office full of hot women." Marty waved a hand around the Hooters restaurant.

Cody laughed.

"Ah? Huh-ah? Ehhah?" winked Marty.

"Hahaha! Damn, you're right. You're so right," Cody said, lifting a bottle of beer.

The three of them clanged their bottles and finished them, bottoms up. They imagined coming to an office every morning, greeted by an all-star lineup of beautiful women. Each gave the other a nodding approval, knowing they were thinking the same thing.

"One redhead..." said Cody.

"...one brunette..." replied Guy.

"...and, wuh-eh, one blonde," finished Marty.

They looked around the man's paradise and exhaled. Life was going to be good from now on, they predicted. The ease with which the gorgeous women made them feel assured their confidence. Indeed, amid a succession of greasy buffalo wings and pitchers of beer, the men drowned themselves in an euphoria of testosterone. Marty's own confidence boost gave him encouragement in snagging their table's waitress. She was everything he secretly crazed for: tall and leggy with long blonde hair flowing down to her waist.

"Anything else for you guys?" she giggled. "Would y'all like any more beer?"

"Nah, babe," flirted Guy, "don't think I need beer goggles to appreciate looking at you."

The big guy tilted himself on his stool, pretending to puff on his unlit cigar. Marty gave it a slight nudge, sending his cousin toppling toward the floor. Their leggy blonde waitress let out a hearty laugh.

"Ah-heh, whaoh! You've got to forgive my cousin," apologized Marty sarcastically for his cousin. "All that porn he watches makes him socially awkward."

Guy slowly picked himself back up.

"It's okay," she continued giggling. "I wasn't bothered by his comment at all. It's natural for us to be hit on in this job, heehee."

"Wah, er, HAH! I'm sure you must love it all the time then, heh, ha! Haha! Wa-huh, I mean, I would sure love it if I got hit on by everyone in my job. Men or women! Yuh-hah?"

She giggled in agreement. "Tee-hee-ha!"

"By the way," Marty offered a handshake, "eh, don't you hate it when people forget to introduce themselves? I'm Marty. Marty Ho. The goofy big guy that fell down is my cousin Guy, and this, heh, is my best friend, Cody. He's a good guy."

"Nicky. Nicky Zeigler," she answered, shaking his hand.

"Wauh-hmmm. Zeigler," echoed Marty.

"Yes. Guess the origin," Nicky smiled.

Marty nodded.

"You already know?" she laughed. "Get the hell out of here!"

"Heh. Eh..."

"Australia!" blurted Guy.

"No...it's European," she hinted.

"Poland," guessed Cody.

"No..."

"Alaska!" Guy shouted.

"Guy, that's not in Europe," chided Marty.

"France," guessed Cody again.

"Nope."

"Sighhhh. I guess I'll just have to say it..." Marty shook his head.

"What is it?" laughed Nicky.

Marty smiled.

"You know it, don't you?"

Marty nodded.

"Oh my God!" laughed Nicky, "how did you know 'Zeigler' was a German name?"

"Ah heh heh heh!" Marty laughed. "Well, don't let me keep you from this happy job. Lots of people need to be hitting on you. Sigh. Hufff...heh!"

Nicky hesitated to move on. Her fluffy demeanor had now turned into a serious one.

"Actually," she confessed, "I hate this job."

"Wah? Whoa?!!!" Marty appeared surprised.

"Yeah. Some days I could use a little more respect."

"That's right!" exclaimed Guy. "You tell 'em--"

"Mm-ah, that's a coincidence, Nicky," interrupted Marty, "because Cody and I here happen to be starting our own company."

"Really?!"

"Yeah! In fact, wah-eh, we're here at Hooters to celebrate it."

"Heehee! Congrats!" she smiled.

"Yeah, but, sigh, well, we are missing a few pieces..."

He smiled, knowing he had his prize. It was only a matter of time before she said yes to accepting a job interview, possibly by the end of this conversation.

"Few missing pieces?!" she gasped. "Do you think you have room for me? I'm good with people!"

"Well, eh, ahhh, I would, but heh, it's a job that's constantly out of the office. You'd have to dress up a lot, meet classy people, I mean...sales...it's, heh, not something I want to burden you with..."

"No, no!" Nicky insisted, "let me know if you guys need help! I can charm the skin off a rattlesnake!"

"Hell!" blurted Guy, "It would be so awesome if you could join us! We—"

"Oh shh! Mmah, shh!" hushed Marty. "Heh-ha! You have to excuse my cousin. He gets too excited with the opposite sex—"

"Yes!" replied Nicky, "I'll definitely do it!"

"Oh. Eh, wow. Haha! Well, um, eh, what do you think, Cody?" nodded Marty.

"I don't know," Cody hesitated. "We'd have to formally do a job interview first."

No big deal, thought Marty. All he had to do later on was set the fix and she would be hired, regardless of whoever else applied. After that, he excitedly realized, he could talk her into doing anything with him as his sales assistant.

"Sigh," Marty responded, looking back at Nicky. "I guess he's right. Look, why don't you give me your phone number and we'll set you up for an interview. Eh? Aheh?"

"Oh, SHIT you guys are the best!" she said, covering her mouth. "Sorry for my cussing. Can't do that in front of my new employers now, can I?"

Marty chuckled. Mosaic Design Studios had now added its first employee. She was blonde, bubbly, gorgeous and, most important to him, probably more attractive than anything Cody could find as his secretary.

A few days later, Kirk Santiago awoke in the middle of his afternoon hangover. He knew drinking on the job was prohibited, but no one dared to squeal on him. The distinct sound of humming computers gave him an indication that something was wrong. Very wrong. Sweeping a pile of empty Oreo boxes from his desk, the overweight supervisor leaned his face closely at his enormous monitor. One by one, he inspected each of the workers' desks. *Cubicle one.* Check. *Cubicle two.* Check. *Cubicles three, four and six.* Check. *Cubicles eight and nine.* Check. Wait a minute, he muttered to himself. *Cubicle seven was empty.* That was Cody's desk.

"Where is he?" bellowed Kirk, storming out of his personal office.

He walked up to the intimidated intern from cubicle six, who looked clueless.

"Did you see where the Asian guy went?"

Before the intern could say no, Cody came back, snacking on a donut.

"Why did you leave your desk?!" demanded Kirk.

Taking his time to answer, Cody finished his donut and licked the leftover frosting from his thumb.

"I was hungry," shrugged Cody, adding, "you fat fuck."

"What?! You know you're supposed to tell me whenever you leave the office!"

"Well...Kirk...I figured you suffered a heart attack and died."

"I was sleeping!"

"Sleeping, eh?...With a bottle of Coors in your hand. Don't you know you could get in trouble with that? It's against university policy. Tsk tsk."

The fat man looked at Cody up and down. He couldn't believe Cody's bold new attitude. Had he paid attention from the past three weeks, he would have noticed Cody's change. Instead, it came to him as a surprise and an enigma.

"Don't test me," he threatened Cody. "I have friends in high places you didn't even know I had!"

"I thought that was crabs, dickface."

Kirk approached himself inches away from Cody, staring at him eye-to-eye.

"Trying to get yourself fired, my friend?" challenged Kirk. "Where are you going to go? You'll never get a good referral from anyone in this university for as long as I'm here! And I'm going to be here for a long, long time. The rest of your life, at least. You can't survive away from this nest. Where will you go? No one will ever hire you in this town again!"

Without breaking eye contact, Cody dug through his pockets and produced a folded letter. He placed the letter into his supervisor's hands. Kirk slowly looked down, then back up at Cody.

"What's this?" Kirk inquired.

"My two week notice."

"You're leaving town?"

"No. I'm leaving UH."

"But you're staying in town?"

"Yeah."

Kirk laughed. "Are you deaf? Didn't you hear me? Who would hire you? How would you get referrals from us?"

"I don't need any. I'm tired of this charade. I'm tired of the bamboo ceiling. I'm tired of it all. I'm starting my own company, tweedleballs."

"Heh...heheheh...hehehehehahaha! Yeah? Then why wait two weeks? Get the fuck out of here, Jackie Chan!"

Cody smirked and walked over to his desk. He had already backed up all of his projects, burning them onto coordinated CDs. He removed the Dilbert calendar from his cubicle wall and packed the rest of his belongings into a large cardboard box. Kirk walked up to Cody's desk and threw a small box next to him.

"Fits your little penis," he laughed.

"Funny comment coming from a fat man that can't find his own dick."

Cody placed his packed belongings onto a dolly, making his way toward the exit.

"You'll be back," predicted Kirk.

Cody let out a long, emancipated laugh.

"No, I won't," he smiled.

It was well-known that Kirk made a nightly habit of attending the pack of dive strip clubs along Telephone Road. Even though he was a frequent visitor, the owners continued to dislike him with a passion. For one thing, the butterball was cheap; the dancers hated his stingy tipping. The other reason was that he was loud with poor alcohol control. It was that carelessness, however, which helped a peculiar unlicensed van find him tonight. By the time he had exited his final dive strip club, Kirk was too intoxicated to hear the approaching footsteps.

Stumbling with his balance across the makeshift dirt parking lot, the drunken fat man needed to relieve himself. He bumped into a large steel object, something that turned out to be the side of someone's parked truck. Kirk, however, thought it was a metal bush. As he unzipped his pants and searched himself, he realized that Cody was right about the difficulty of him finding his penis. His soon-to-be-kidnappers waited patiently behind him as a steady stream of urine was heard splashing on the ground. *Tappppppppppppppp. Tap tap tap.* Once the ordeal was over and his pants were back in place, the two ski-masked figures grabbed him and forced him into their van. Through his intoxicated state, Kirk was able to make note of the discrepancy in the size of his captors. One was a big guy, strong in build; the other was short and light—suspiciously about the same size as Cody. Before he could observe more, he was blindfolded with a piece of cloth, had his arms secured together with rope and was tied onto the backseat.

"Drive!" ordered the smaller kidnapper, after slipping into the front passenger seat.

The van burned rubber and headed toward the I-45 South Freeway where they would later head up the Beltway 8 Tollway and eastward toward La Porte.

"Hey, bro, is it 225 West or 225 East?" asked the larger kidnapper.

"East."

"Are you sure? Because I could swear the map said 'west.' Let me check the GPS on my iPhone—"

"Can you please not talk so much? We want to be a little mysterious here."

"Sorry, man."

"Cody?" shouted Kirk. "Look, I know it's you, Cody."

The smaller kidnapper turned his head toward the larger one.

"I thought you duct-taped his mouth!" he inquired.

"Yeah I did!" protested the larger kidnapper. "It must've came off. He was kinda greasy, dude."

"I'd recognize your voice anywhere, Cody," Kirk claimed. "Where are you taking me?"

Cody cleared his throat. He attempted a deeper voice to disguise himself.

"You're going to be quiet and do as we say!" boomed Cody.

"Hahahaha!" laughed Kirk. "What are you...Batman? Was that Batman's voice?"

A long moment of silence followed the question.

"Shit," teased Kirk, knowing he had guessed correctly. "This is pathetic. Is this your revenge plan? I'm gonna so put a lawsuit on you when we get back."

"Oh, yeah?" replied Cody in the same hoarse and deep voice. "What proof do you have?"

"Who the fuck else would do this?"

"You don't have any witnesses, Kirk."

Cody and Guy decided to keep quiet for the remainder of the trip. Kirk, meanwhile, continued asking questions or insulted them with crude comments. Once they had finally arrived at the Houston Ship Channel, the van weaved its way onto a non-disclosed dock. Soon there was a complete stop.

"Where am I? Tell me!" demanded the blindfolded Kirk. "This fucking sounds like the Ship Channel. What the fuck do you think you're doing, Cody?"

Kirk heard various people speaking in Taiwanese. He felt pairs of hands grabbing him; this time it was a lot more hands than just the previous kidnappers. The new kidnappers made the overweight man waddle for a few steps until they led him inside a large shipping container that was sixty yards in length. Cody had known the owner of this port since his days of buying forged home decor. He slipped two thousand dollars in cash to the lead stevedore.

"Damn it! No! What's going on?" asked Kirk. He was now nervously sweating.

"We're sending you to Taiwan," growled Cody in a deep voice.

"What? Are you fucking serious?"

They were, he realized. More conversations in Taiwanese between the stevedores could be heard. The blindfolded fat man swallowed deeply when he heard the shipping container being closed. A few moments later, he felt the container being hoisted by a crane and loaded onto a large cargo ship. The defiant sound of a loud foghorn blew; Kirk began wetting his pants even though he had peed a short while back. It would be quite some time before the ship would arrive in Taipei. Until then, the stevedores planned on keeping him alive, feeding Cody's former supervisor a steady diet of water and ramen noodles.

CHAPTER 18: PURCHASES

Jack Tsing was the black sheep of his family. His worth was based on the people he scammed. His close friends jokingly labeled his flimflamming as his full-time job. He didn't have bank accounts or money in his pockets; instead, he charmed others into covering for him. He reflected on those scamming skills proudly as he looked at his latest masterpiece. She was half-asleep next to him: a beautiful Japanese exchange student whose name he struggled to recall. Miko? Machiko? Mahoko? It didn't matter. For the past five months she had paid their rent, food, entertainment expenses and alcohol habits. Her name might as well have been Yen, because she was money.

"Mr. Jack?" whispered his temporary meal ticket, "can they please be a little more....... quiet?"

She was referring to another one of those parties she and Jack often threw outside of their rooftop swimming pool. Jack never understood why she made such a big deal out of them. If her rich parents in Japan were going to splurge on one of the most expensive Houston penthouse suites, they might as well throw as many parties as they could. Besides, he thought, the parties made them—at least him—very popular. Jack knew he wasn't the handsomest guy, but he had a talent for rubbing people the right way. He often wondered if it was something inherited from his cousin Marty. The difference, he believed, was that he didn't bother deluding himself that his scams were benefitting others.

"Mr. Jack...please," Miko/Machiko/Mahoko repeated, interrupting his chain of thought.

"Sure...hey, uh, Mik—Mach—honey, have you seen my pants? I was sure they were somewhe—...eh, who cares. I'll just go out there naked. I don't give a fuck."

Jack grabbed a cigarette and his lighter, making his way past a living room full of empty vodka bottles and other trash. The sliding glass doors did not do a good job of muffling the sound of the thumping music from the pool party. There must have been at least a hundred guests. When the drunken partygoers caught glimpse of Jack coming out, they greeted him with loud "woohoos" and "fuck yeahs." Walking with a notable swagger, he lit a Marlboro and puffed it with a smile.

"Hey Jack!" shouted someone from the party, "we're hell outta pot!"

"Yeah? Then fucking buy some fucking more, damn it," Jack replied, facing the crowd. "Can we get this guy some cash so he can buy more weed?"

"I've got a twenty..."

"Fifty bucks here..."

"Yeah," Jack encouraged with a cigarette dangling from his lips." Pass a cup around like a collection plate from church."

A styrofoam cup was handed around until it returned to Jack. He counted the bills.

"Thirty...forty...sixty...THERE," Jack declared, handing the money to the designated marijuana courier," five hundred and sixty dollars. Go get us something nice."

"Yeah! Go Jack!" shouted a random person from the crowd.

Jack continued strutting around in the nude, taking a few breaths in before making his announcement like a king. The partygoers were waiting for him to speak.

"Ladies and gentlemen!" he began, "we start out as babies, thinking that the world...THIS world...revolves around us. Then...then we learn that life isn't like that. And that's why we cry. That's why we get mad. Because we're told to think we can't do what we want to do."

Someone handed him a bottle of Crown Royal. He took a long sip.

"But I say," he continued, "fuck all that shit! I'm gonna do what I fucking want! No responsibilities! No consequences!

Let others clean up our mess! 'You Only Live Once'! Y.O.L.O., motherfuckers!"

"WOO-HOOOOOOOO!"

He had a crazy thought.

"Someone hand me that garbage bag full of trash right there!" ordered Jack.

With lighter in hand, he set the garbage bag on fire.

"OH SHIT!" someone shouted in admiration.

"I'M GONNA BURN THIS MOTHERFUCKIN' PLACE DOWN!" Jack screamed, "Y.O.L.O. MOTHERFUCKAS!!!"

The trash and traces of remaining alcohol from the near-empty vodka bottles gave immediate life to the fire. This was unexpected, he thought, I was just going for effect. Realizing he had to think of a fast solution, Jack headed back into his apartment and came out through its front door. The burning trash bag illuminated the dim hallways. Panicking, Jack made his way to the building's public laundry chute and tossed the burning bag into it.

"Hey you!" scolded a witnessing tenant. "What are you doing?"

"Y.O.L.O.!!!!" screamed the intoxicated and naked Jack.

Twenty minutes later, fire trucks surrounded the expensive apartment complex. Amid the chaos were screaming residents, including a petrified Miko/Machiko/Mahoko. More were coming out, thanks to the brave firefighters who risked life and limb for their safety. The particularly devastating fire devoured most of the high-rise, resulting in millions of dollars of property damage. Police found many eager witnesses willing to describe Jack Tsing's appearance.

Meanwhile, hiding inside the bathroom of a nearby gas station, Jack frantically dialed his brother's number for help. It had been awhile since Guy heard from him, and it was never a good thing whenever Jack called.

"Come on answer...answer..." Jack pleaded.

"What do you want?" answered his little brother. "What kind of shit are you in now?"

"Deep shit. Don't tell mom. Where's Marty?"

"I'm in a car with him and Xia. Why haven't we heard from you in years?"

"I need you to come to this address I'm about to text you. It's a gas station. I'm hiding in the bathroom stall. Bring a hoodie sweat shirt and some pants. I need to conceal my identity."

"Dude, what the fuck?"

"Just do it!"

When local law enforcement arrived at the gas station, the employee at the cash register decided the facial composite sketch looked enough like the naked young Asian man who had stormed into the men's restroom. The police officers rushed into the stalls, finding only one of them locked and a visible pair of feet near the bottom of the stall door.

"HPD!" screamed one of the officers with authority.

"Huh?" came a voice from the stall.

"Come out with your hands up!"

Without another moment of hesitation, one of the officers gave the stall door a hard kick, shattering the lock. The door swung wide open, revealing a middle-aged Indian man sitting on the toilet, paralyzed with fear.

"That ain't him," observed a policeman.

"No shit, Sherlock," replied the officer who had kicked the door.

Jack had just made his way out, running among the shadows. He was wearing his newly-acquired hoodie sweat shirt from his brother Guy. Together, the two Tsing brothers snuck away through the back streets where Marty's car awaited them. Jack let out a long sigh of relief when he made it into the backseat. His cousin Marty was driving while Marty's wife Xia angrily glared at him from the passenger seat.

"Okay, first question, how the hell did you get into a gas station naked?" asked Guy.

"I don't know. I just did. The employees didn't stop me though."

"I ask the second question!" insisted Xia in her buttery Shanghainese accent. "You responsible for fire?"

"..." Jack was speechless.

"Oh fuck, bro," Guy realized. "You did that shit? That was you?!"

Xia lost her cool. "You stupid milky boy! You set fire to building, eh?!"

"Now, weh-uh, let's all settle down here," Marty said. "Jack, what happened?"

"I fucking...uh, God...okay, I fucking got a little crazy and set a trash bag on fire. It was full of leftover vodka bottles. I then tossed it into the laundry chute."

"You're kidding me!" Guy said, looking at his brother in awe.

"No. No, I'm not. I'm fucking not. Look, the cops are after me. You guys gotta hide me."

"I should let mom decide that!"

"Ah, damn, you guys haven't told her, have you?"

"Heh ha...heh!" laughed Marty. "Just calm down, shhh. How could we've told her if we didn't know what happened?"

"Yeah, that's true," replied Jack. "But what am I going to do now? The girl I was staying with probably wouldn't want anything to do with me anymore."

Marty had a worried look on his face. It dawned on him that he would have to look after his troublemaking cousin. "Well, eh, don't you have any other friends you can stay with, Jack?"

"Come on, Marty! You're family. You guys gotta help me lay low for the next few months."

"You're so in deep shit," predicted Guy. "Mom's gonna tell Dad back in Chicago and it's over for you, bro."

"Fine then, tell them!" responded Jack. "See if I give a shit! Just cover for me."

"Heh heh, Jack, just...please...calm down..." pleaded Marty.

"You're going to have to help us then!" Guy blurted.

Marty looked at the quarterback incredulously, frustrated that he couldn't keep Mosaic Design Studios a secret. "Wah, no, Guy. Eh, Guy? Don't tell him—"

It was too late.

"—Marty and his best friend are starting their own company! Marty is the president. You're going to help us, bro," splurged Guy.

Marty's heart dropped.

"What?!" shouted Xia. "Own company? What own company?"

"Nuh-wah, er, ah, Guy was just saying...um, that is, freelance-wise I am figuratively my own company, um—"

Xia recognized that tone; her husband was being deceitful again.

"Don't shit-talk me! I will slap you!" she threatened in broken English.

"Sighhhhh," Marty huffed.

"Man," said Guy, "I can't believe you hadn't told your own wife this the whole time. You and Cody planned the company for months."

"MONTHS?" exclaimed Xia. "And who is Cody?"

"Well, uh, you know how I said I had a surprise for you?" explained Marty.

"Yes?"

"Um...surprise?" Marty chuckled nervously. "Ah huh ha? Ah heh heh ha ha? P-Please honey, let's speak in *zhong wen*."

She was glad to oblige. English frustrated her anyway.

"<Why didn't you tell me this?>" she said, growing madder. "<You always lie to me! Don't think I'm stupid! I can bring up divorce papers again if I have to. How much money are you putting down for this business? What is it about?>"

As the couple conversed back and forth in Mandarin Chinese, the two brothers began discussing the upcoming company. The more Guy spoke of it, the more Jack grew excited about the freeloading opportunities. This new partner of Marty's, Cody Quan, seemed wealthy from how his brother had described him.

"I want in!" Jack demanded.

———

The next few weeks passed in a blur. Cody not only dared to dream; he felt entitled to it. As he and Marty's family were doing a massive office shopping spree, his vision of the office kept getting bolder. He wanted custom granite floors, walls with flowing water, giant monitor touch screens. The other guys had similar thoughts, but it was the lone woman, Xia, who kept their purchases realistic.

"You cannot waste the money," she claimed. "You need to save some."

They settled for self-assembled furniture from IKEA, Super Target and Sam's Club. Marty talked his way into the Apple Store, at least. Even with the pressure from Xia to keep the budget low, Cody insisted on splurging whenever she wasn't around.

"Don't worry about it!" he kept saying. "Money's not an issue."

Indeed, he had never seen so much in his bank account before; it was easy to forgive him for thinking there was an infinite supply of funds. Just when he, Marty and Guy had grown exhausted from splurging, they went out and splurged some more. There were new wardrobes and fancy restaurants, cool gadgets and company car leasing. Marty enjoyed taking Nicky Ziegler out for shopping and dates—it was part of her job interview, he claimed.

All that fun eventually gave way to work. Once the construction company had finished their office's setup, the two best friends and business partners began blueprinting which furniture went where. Cody sighed and smiled as he envisioned the area where his lovely future secretary would be. *Hello, Mr. Quan,* she would greet him. *Hey baby, you're a sight for sore eyes*, he would respond to her. *Want a massage? Why don't you tell me all about it, Mr. Quan?* He could hardly contain his excitement; it was all going to happen very soon.

"Self-assembly office furniture coming through!!!" barked Guy.

The big lug's booming presence curtailed Cody's daydreaming. His mind was back in the office where a makeshift crew was putting the IKEA purchases together.

"This is the job your I.T. man did?" pouted Herman as he inspected the computer cables. "You should have asked me to do it. I'm the master at I.T.!"

"The hell you are," critiqued Guy. "The only thing you master is masturbation."

Guy bellowed at his own joke, believing it was more clever than it actually was.

"Real classy," commented Herman.

"I'm all about class," Guy said, chugging a carton of milk.

The office was like their own tree house—a place to call their own. There was no boss, no clock, no meddling elders telling them what to do. Everyone was happy and in good spirits. Even Marty's cousin, Jack, whom Cody had just met that same evening, contributed without complaining. The self-assembled furniture was put together in an efficient time frame, enough to call for an early dinner of shrimp fried rice and sticky buns, courtesy of Cody's father at the Happy Lotus.

"No...yer, ah...no..." Marty was hovering around the desks, looking for various other ways to arrange the furniture.

"What is it? What's going on?" asked Cody. "Come eat with us, man."

"Probably a luck thing," muttered Guy. "Hey, we got any more sriracha sauce?"

Marty muttered random comments about poor feng shui and the number of desks. When he started arranging the desks himself, Cody approached him and placed a hand on his shoulder.

"Hey, it's okay. You're from Detroit, man," Cody said. "We don't believe in that old world superstition here."

Marty wasn't hearing it; he was too lost in his own irrationalities.

"We can't have the desks facing north. It...doesn't it

look like a classroom format to you? We want them to face us. This way. East."

"Okay, well, duly noted," Cody shrugged. "We can do that after dinner."

"No, it's...heh, well, we got to do it now. It's like a running faucet. We're pouring bad luck into our office."

"Jesus, you're like my dad."

Cody walked back to the others and continued eating with them. Every once in awhile, he turned around and observed Marty's obsessive compulsiveness. He seemed possessed, revealing a vulnerable, superstitious side to him.

"You know what this place needs?!" Guy declared, clearing the air of awkward silence. "A little Akon!"

He began playing an Akon song on his new Apple laptop. He set the volume to maximum, turning the office into a club. Guy grabbed a sticky bun and began dancing to the music. He swung his hips and rubbed his nipples, lip-synching to the lyrics.

Girl, I can't notice but to notice you... noticing me...

"Mmmahhhuhhhh-auh! Baby baby baby!" sang Herman off-key. His words were not a part of the song.

"And you know what else this place needs?" added a smiling Jack. He took out a large bottle of whiskey from his backpack. "A little Southern Comfort."

"Hey! Where you get it?" inquired Xia.

"Swiped it with Marty's Mosaic Design Studios credit card. I knew they'd use the Sugar Land Town Center zip code for their verification," he said proudly.

"What?!" she gasped. "You steal it from my husband?"

"Hey, I slipped it back to him," shrugged Jack. "All's good."

He began pouring shots into disposable plastic red cups, handing one to each of them.

"Come on, Marty!" he insisted. "Leave the feng shui shit alone for a moment and join us."

Marty had single-handedly finished moving all of the desks to face eastward, although he still wasn't satisfied that there were four of them. Four. Death. This was a bad omen.

"Dude!" ushered Jack.

"Mm-ha, okay, heh," Marty obliged, joining them.

Jack began with a toast, "To a great and—"

"TO ASIANS KICKING ASS AND NOT TAKING SHIT FROM ANYONE!" interrupted Herman.

Jack glared at him in silence. The toast started over again.

"To a great and prosperous beginning," said Jack, "and a special thank-you to Marty for starting this company."

"Well, uh, heh, it's not just my company..." smiled Marty, looking at Cody.

Cody smiled back, thinking he was given credit.

"...it's also made possible by all of you helping my company," Marty finished instead.

Cody's smile quickly turned into a confused frown.

"*Gan Bei*!" screamed Xia, which meant 'bottoms up' in Mandarin Chinese.

"GUN BOY!" imitated Guy in bad Chinese.

They all drank their cups in one gulp.

"Eh, Jack?" observed Marty. "This, heh, this tastes like apple juice."

"Yeah, apple juice..." Xia agreed.

"Shhhh..." Jack winked.

They watched as Herman walked toward the other side of the room. Jack signaled for the rest to be in on the joke as he poured a bigger portion of whisky into another cup. He walked up to Herman, offering a second shot.

"You...you think I can't handle this?" Herman shouted. "I drink straight vodka, son! I'll outdrink all of you!"

Jack repeated the shots until Herman became drunk, half shouting and half singing barely recognizable Michael Jackson songs. Cody and Jack led their wasted friend outside where he began serenading the people around Town Square.

"Why? Why?" Herman lunged himself toward a woman holding shopping bags. "Tell them it...tell them that it's human nature...I like it this way!!! Hic."

"Get away from me!" the woman cried, hitting him with her shopping bags.

From the second-floor office window, the rest of Cody's friends laughed at Herman.

"This so mean!" Xia protested. "But so funny!"

"You are not alone...oooooh ahhhh," Herman sang, grabbing a black security guard. "Mr. Black Guy Police Officer! They don't...they don't care about us!"

"Oh, shit," muttered Jack, who walked back to the office. "That cop is going to arrest that fucker."

"Nah, he'll be okay, it's just a security guard," observed Cody.

They witnessed the security guard talking with the intoxicated young man. Then Herman did something unexpected—he pointed at the direction of their office window.

"Shut off the lights! Shut off the lights!" ordered Cody.

Marty quickly shut them off. From the window, they witnessed a drunk Herman leading the guard toward their building. Minutes later they heard knocking on the office front door. After two more knocks and no response, they heard footsteps walking away. Minutes later, Jack slowly opened the door. In front of them, they found a nearly passed-out Herman outside. He was rubbing his genital area.

"Well, bros," quipped Guy, "I guess he really is the master of masturbating."

"Hey," suggested Jack, "let's drag him somewhere."

"A horse stable," laughed Cody.

"Gay bar bathroom," brainstormed Guy.

"I know!" laughed Jack. "How about—"

"No no no!" lectured Xia. "This too much joke already! You take Herman to his home now!"

"Aw, come on, Xia..." protested Jack.

"NOW!" she ordered.

The boys collectively wished Marty's ball and chain hadn't tagged along; she was never any fun. Following her demands, they carried the unconscious Herman to Marty's Oldsmobile. Once in, Cody led them to Herman's residence—the one he shared with his mother. With little regard for subtlety, Guy repeatedly nudged and tapped his face.

"Hey! Wake up, bro!" urged the big guy.

"Hunh?" uttered Herman.

"You're home, Herman," explained Cody. "Go home."

The intoxicated debauchee stumbled outside. The others watched from the car as he looked around and then took off his pants. Herman then proceeded to squat in his neighbor's flower bed and answered nature's second calling.

"Dang!" observed Guy. "He's like an animal!"

"Why he not use his house bathroom?" wondered Xia.

"I dunno," Cody shrugged. "Guess he didn't know people were watching."

"Let's get out of here," Jack suggested.

The Oldsmobile drove off, leaving Herman to do his business.

Time froze the next night when Sonia Rodriguez walked into the lobby of the Sugar Land Marriott hotel. The bellboys collided with one another, trying to be the first to offer help. This, of course, was natural for one of the most beautiful young women in Texas. Whoever claimed that beauty was subjective hadn't met Sonia. She had a perfectly symmetrical face, an irresistible voluptuous body, smooth tan skin, alluring eyes and a Cindy Crawford mole. Most of all, Sonia boasted the one important feature that men primarily care about: a perfect pair of colossal-sized breasts. Her low-cut dress shirt accentuated that asset. Complementing it was a skirt that looked like business wear except for its unusually short length. Her attire was slightly unfitting for a job interview, but she didn't think her potential employers would mind.

"Sonia!" Cody fought himself from slobbering. "So glad you could make it!"

Their location for the job interviews was suggested by Cody; the hotel lobby near their office building was so much cozier and spacious. It also allowed the fun of surprise once their new employees saw the office on their first day of work. Sonia was curious to find another though less-attractive girl sitting along for the interview. The idea of interviewing rival candidates together was Cody and Marty's way of having girls grovel over them.

"Hi, I'm Sonia, nice to meet you," she smiled, shaking the other girl's hand.

The other girl contrasted her; she was dressed conservatively professional with portfolio in hand. By all means, she exemplified class, but that probably escaped the notice of her two enraptured interviewers. Sonia knew she was going to destroy this young woman.

Cody started the dialog rolling. "Since we've got a lot of interviewees today, we're conducting our interviews with two of you at a time."

"Mm-huh, let's start," nodded Marty. "What do you feel that you can contribute to this position?"

"Well—" they both began, then stopping to let the other go first.

"No, no. You go ahead," insisted a smiling Sonia.

The other girl gladly accepted.

"Well," she began, "as someone who has had vast experience doing secretarial work, I offer not only proven skills directly related to the job but also additional skills that would benefit the goals of the company. These skills, as stated on my resume, include extensive knowledge of all of the Microsoft Office products, Adobe Acrobat, Quickbooks, Peachtree, general HTML and MySQL database languages."

She sat upright, impressed with herself. The two men frowned.

"And, heh-eh, what about you Sonia?" smiled Marty.

"Well," Sonia grinned. "As for me, I've been known to give a fax or copy machine a nice swift kick whenever it was needed. And maybe I'm not as tech savvy as Ms. Microsoft Excel here, but sometimes what a customer really needs is a calm, warm voice. A voice that makes them feel like they're cared for. Caressed. Touched."

Guy's jaw dropped. Cody and Marty immersed themselves into her charm.

"Any more questions?" laughed Sonia.

"Well, uh, yes, certainly," stumbled Marty. "Heh. Ha...haha. Okay, wuh-heh, what would you say are your greatest strengths and weaknesses?"

Both girls hesitated to answer before the other.

"Why don't you go first, Sonia?" insisted Cody.

"Oh, this one's easy," she laughed. "My greatest strength is that I know what my weaknesses are. And then I turn them into strengths."

The three men nodded to one another in agreement. It became clear to Sonia that what she said made sense to them even when she didn't. Cody gestured for the other girl to respond.

"I guess how I would describe my strengths," the other girl began, "would be my ability to time manage and multitask. When I'm given a deadline, I aim to finish my tasks way before the given time limit. This way, there's plenty of room for fact-checking so that I'm ensured that everything is done right. And, above all, help maintain an overall positive image for the company. As for my weaknesses, my drive to succeed may sometimes override my calmness. I understand that while everyone in the company will want to do his or her job, sometimes I have to remind myself that everyone's passions manifest themselves differently."

"Wow," Guy said, still thinking about Sonia's answer. "Changing weaknesses to strengths so that there are no more weaknesses. That's deep."

The busty vixen tilted her head and winked at him.

While Marty conducted the rest of the interview, Cody found himself mesmerized by Sonia's allure. She was the one in his previous daydreaming—the one who asked how his day went and gave him a massage. The faceless secretary in his fantasies now had a face. It was more than enough for him to make up his mind about hiring her.

"Okay uh, that, well, that concludes our interview for today," Marty nodded. "Cody and I will, heh, uh, evaluate who we think is best for the, uh, job and we'll let you both know."

"Well, it was so nice meeting the three of you," Sonia said in a sweet tone. "It would be a shame if this was the last time that we met."

"Oh, trust me. It won't," chuckled Guy, ogling her with his eyes. They had almost forgotten they had more interviews for the secretary and mediator positions. A whole lot more. There were forty women in all, most of them pretty and all of them giving the three men their utmost attention. Cody was on top of a pedestal, happy to wield so much power and persuasion. If only Daphne Lee could see me now, he sneered to himself. The river of beautiful women came to its end two hours later when they reached their final interview. The guys discovered it was possible to overdose on the opposite sex.

"So," asked an exhausted Marty of their final two candidates, "how would you breast evaluate success?.......I mean, heh-ha, best evaluate success, heh."

"Success," repeated the latest interviewee, "is something that I strive for no matter what I'm doing. Whether if it's in your office or simply going out and running in triathlons. I want to be the best. It's how I'm wired. And nothing would please me more than to win with your new company."

Perhaps, thought Cody, it was the fatigue in him, but the woman who said that stood out. She was absolutely ravishing, with movie star looks, perfect almond eyes, smooth skin and perfect long black hair. And, of course, lovely breasts—that detail was inescapable to him. However, those details alone, at least for a night filled with beautiful women, didn't make her stand out. This particular young woman also possessed a keen intellect and articulation. He took a look at her resume and reminded himself of her name once more.

April Finley.

When the interview ended, the three men walked over to Starbucks. They had experienced a well-found high, realizing it was possible to consistently enjoy the company of beautiful women. Each was eager to share their experience.

"So," Cody started, stirring his coffee with a swaggering expression, "what do you guys think?"

Guy could barely wait for Cody to finish before responding. "Oh my God!!! I could fuck that Sonia girl in half! I mean, did you see her tits? Did you? Did you?!"

"Guy," Marty pleaded, "heh-ah, keep it civilized, ok?"

"I'm serious, bros!" Guy continued. "I had a boner the whole time!"

"Ugh!" Cody flinched. "Marty? What do you think?"

"I think...sigh...it's too bad I already made a deal with Nicky Ziegler, heh."

"It's not too late," mentioned Cody. "She didn't sign anything."

"True," Marty replied. "But, I'll look like the bad guy. I can't do that. What would she think of me? Sighhhh."

"Who cares what she'll think of you? Choose whoever you want to choose," reasoned Cody.

"I can't...I just...huh-ah...I just can't."

"You liked that April girl, huh?" pried Cody.

"Oh maaaan, April," interrupted Guy, "I'm so gonna whip my dick out tonight and think about her. First thing I'll do tonight!"

Cody and Marty continued to ignore the quarterback's overt self-romancing.

"Well-yuh, yeah. Heh. HA! But. But no...no, no...I can't ask for a second sales assistant. That...that would affect our, heh, quota. No," Marty said.

"Which one do you like more?" inquired Cody.

"Sigh. I'll just...I'll just stick with Nicky."

"You didn't exactly answer the question, Marty."

"Well, they both have different strengths. Heh. Can't say which one I like more. It would be good to have both. It would certainly, muh-uh, triple our sales, heh heh ha."

"No, we can't have both," replied Cody.

"Mmm, you sure? I mean...heh...you sure?" Marty started getting defensive. "Dude, it's...that is to, uh, say...it's not fair that you have three girls and I only get one. Three to two...that's all I'm saying, Cody. Heh...you know? Hah? Wuh-ah?"

"Three girls? I thought I get to choose our secretary. That's it."

"Mm, well, what about the two designers?"

"Marty, we're a design and web company!" explained Cody. "I'm choosing those two based on individual skill. It's one thing to have hot girls as our secretary and sales assistant, but the designers will be sitting behind a computer all day long. No one will care what they look like."

"Except for you."

"What?"

"No, um, heh. Haha, it's okay, Cody. Shhh. Heh, ffft. I get it."

"Get what?"

"I saw that Flash specialist when you were interviewing her the other day. Come on, Cody, she's a looker, heh. HA!"

"What do you mean?!" asked Cody. "You were the one who recommended her at Hooters. You said we should hire a Flash specialist."

"Okay, whatever, huh...it's okay, heh. HA! Wuuuhhh...hah!"

"Guy, isn't that what he said that day?" Cody asked, looking at Marty's cousin for confirmation.

"Well, to be honest," Guy admitted, "I wasn't paying any attention, bro. Too many hot Hooters waitresses when we were there."

"See?! Huh-heh, you've got some selective memory, Cody. I, hah, I never said that. Seriously."

"I swear, I wasn't picking that Patricia girl out for looks," Cody protested. "And, if it makes you feel better, the other designer I chose isn't a looker at all."

"Oh-ah, don't tell me you picked that ugly flat-chested little Asian girl," Marty said.

"Hey, Lydia is very skilled. You should have seen her portfolio! It's important to have someone with experience to help Patricia out."

"Sigh. Well, I guess. You still have two hot girls. It's not fair."

"They're not MY hot girls. They're OUR hot girls, Marty. You can still talk with them."

"Well, I'm just, heh, it's about fairness. We're partners. Okay, I, eh, I guess I'll be the mature and understanding one and let you have two. Sigh. I really wanted that April girl too. But, in the interest in preserving our budget..." Marty shook his head in sadness.

"Geez, Patricia is pretty and all, but I wouldn't call her hot," Cody reasoned.

"Hey!" Guy proclaimed, "I've got an idea! Why don't we remove that ugly designer and replace her with April! We can teach her how to design, right?"

"It doesn't work that way," Cody scoffed. "It's a skill you develop."

"Right. Develop. We can train a hot girl to design, can't we? I mean, how difficult could it be?" asked Guy.

"No. Just no. We're trying to actually succeed here. That means getting people who can do the job."

"Just sayin', bro," Guy shrugged.

It was getting closer to the start of the first day. Cody and Marty excitedly spoke about the good times they anticipated for their company. So far it was smooth sailing. And now, it was time for celebration.

The following Saturday evening, the assembled staff, close friends and family of the new company celebrated at The Oceanaire. They had reserved a large table with the best view of the five-star restaurant. Each business partner was on opposite ends of the table, sitting next to the ones they were most associated with. Cody sat next to Herman and his longtime friend Mindy Cheung, whom he hadn't seen in awhile. Marty sat close to his wife, Xia, along with his cousins Guy and Jack. The middle part of the table was reserved for the new employees: Sonia, Nicky, Patricia and Lydia. Marty, in a classy new Banana Republic suit and tie, lifted a glass of red wine to toast the occasion.

"Wuh-ha, several months ago, Cody and I found out that we were pregnant." Marty let a few seconds for the laughter to die down, then continued. "Mm-huh, no not that kind. We were about to give birth to an idea, and that idea, heh, is born today."

Sonia began clapping. The others followed with polite applause.

"And here we are," Marty grinned, "reality."

Louder applause came, joined with whistles, hoots and hollers.

"<FEEL GOOD SPIRIT WE LIFT>!" screamed Herman in incomprehensible Chinese.

Their jubilation caught the attention of several patrons, who viewed their table with curiosity.

"Er, hah, yes, Herman. Yes," Marty sheepishly replied.

"OHHHHH, LET'S STAY TOGETHERRRR," sung Herman, "...LOVIN' YOU WHETHER, AHH-EHH, WHETHER TIMES ARE GOOD OR BAD OR HAPPY OR SAD AHHH..."

"MAN, SHUT THE FUCK UP AND LET HIM TALK!" Guy hissed from across the table.

Herman slumped back down into his chair.

"Heh heh...ah heh heh...thank you, er, ah Guy," Marty cleared his throat and resumed. "Yes, uh, we're very lucky to have you all here. I spoke with Cody and we both agreed that, haha, that you all are our best choice in who we wanted. And without further ado, Cody, do you, ah, have a few words you'd like to say? Ah-heh? Haha?"

Cody finished off his red snapper and slowly got up, wiping his mouth with his napkin. He thought for a moment about what he would say, looking at each and every one of them. This was the moment he had waited for all his life. King of his castle. Captain of his own destiny. He lifted his glass of cabernet franc and said the first thing that came to his mind.

"I really don't have anything to say," Cody toasted. "Good luck to us all."

The rest of the evening, they ate imported oysters from the East Coast, freshly cooked lobsters and other fine seafood delicacies. Mindy looked at Cody with a twinkle in her eye.

"Bobbie, I am so happy for you!" she kept repeating.

His longtime friend poured herself another glass of wine and uncharacteristically devoured it. Mindy then entertained Sonia and Lydia with stories about how she and Cody met. With each retelling, Mindy clutched Cody's hand and warmly smiled at him.

"So, like, yuuh," Sonia asked, replacing the word "yeah" with "yuuh." "Are you two a couple?"

"Hahahahaha!" laughed Mindy. "What?! Of course not! I am married! With twins!"

It was a deliberate opportunity for her to whip out her little girls' photos and pass them around like business cards. Sonia and Patricia oohed and awed at the adorableness of her children—it was even enough to get a word out of the shy Lydia.

"How precious... how old are they?" she asked.

The pixie-like Thai-American appeared different from the other girls. She wasn't nearly as attractive or assertive. Cody could only best describe her so far as invisible, though she boasted one hell of a design portfolio.

"They are both just two-and-a-half years old," proudly answered Mindy. "Cody's the godfather! He and I are best friends!"

"Wow, Cody!" admired Sonia. "You're popular. You've got so many best friends here at this table. Mindy...Marty..."

"No, no," corrected Mindy. "He only has one best friend: me."

The other side of the table could care less about best friends and babies. The Tsing brothers and Herman took liberty in their obvious pursuit of Nicky. It didn't take them long to discover the blonde bombshell's alcoholic threshold was four glasses; Jack didn't even have to resort to his usual spiking. Once she informed them of her past as a gymnast, the boys encouraged her to show them her flexibility. Nicky easily obliged their whims, flexing both legs over her shoulders in her chair. This resulted in an assemblage of gawks and disapproving stares from the people at nearby tables. At the north end of their table, Marty's wife looked on with a censured frown. This was the sales assistant her husband had chosen? Xia thought. She dismissed the former Hooters waitress as a feebleminded airhead. Guy's reaction, however, hinted at his disagreement.

"Holy, yes! That's so damn awesome! That's what I'm talking about!" he expressed.

Jack calmly lit a cigarette and offered one to Nicky.

"Uh, no thanks. I don't smoke," she declined. She unfolded her legs and made herself upright again.

"Come on," insisted Jack. "Life is short. Y.O.L.—"

"Um, excuse me, sir," interrupted the restaurant manager, "but you can't smoke here."

"Of course I can!" Jack said, looking up at him with a smirk.

"No, it's state law," corrected The Oceanaire manager. "Besides, this is a classy establishment. Not a drinking hole in Midtown."

"Sigh," puffed Jack, looking at his cousin. "Hey Marty, pay the man."

"Hoah-wuh?" Marty asked.

"I wanna smoke a fuckin' cig. Pay this asshole so that I can!"

"Sir," the manager replied, "I assure you that bribes won't work at The Oceanaire."

Jack rolled his eyes and dumped the cigarette into his glass of water. Satisfied, the manager walked away.

"Teehee! You're so baaaaad," admired Nicky. "I thought Asian guys were supposed to be submissive and good at math."

"I am good at math," Jack agreed. "You plus me equals a family of three."

"Maaaaan," Guy added. "Submissive? Look at us. This is a new world, baby! Asian men rule!"

With the dinner ending, Cody was given the check. Disregarding any existence of a budget, the new boss asked the waiter what the tipping record was. When the waiter halfheartedly revealed the number, Cody wrote twice the amount on the check. Afterwards, the newly forged Mosaic

Design Studios crew left the restaurant, waiting outside for their valet cars to arrive. With their expensive and classy attire, they looked ready to conquer the world.

"Remember, everyone," reminded Cody, "ten o'clock sharp Monday morning."

Their first day of work.

CHAPTER 19: GRAND OPENING

The first day didn't go as Cody envisioned; funny how things are always better in the mind, he thought. He had imagined it beginning with a full-body workout before sunrise, followed by a steaming half-hour-long shower to help him meditate over the rousing speech he had prepared. Upon reaching the office, he imagined, he would find his employees standing in a line with a respectful salute. At ease, he'd tell them. Then, with complete certainty and confidence, he would deliver unto them the most gut-wrenching, morale-inducing speech in the history of speeches. It would be right up there, he fancied, in the Mount Rushmore of Public Speaking alongside of Douglas MacArthur's *Farewell Speech*, Martin Luther King's *I Have a Dream* and Abraham Lincoln's *Gettysburg Address.*

Reality, however, had a different plan.

In the early morning hours of the company's opening day, much of the furniture still had to be assembled. There were plenty of desks, but no chairs. Worse, the computers didn't work properly and neither did their network connectivity. The company's first morning lay in the hands of the volunteer crew. Marty's I.T. friend and Herman, who expectedly talked more than he worked, scrambled to get the computers working. Xia, who had sacrificed some much-needed sleep, perspired heavily as she assembled the rolling cabinets. She proved herself to be more effective than Guy, whose blundering repeatedly caused him to reassemble things. Marty and Cody tended to most of their own desk equipment. Jack was totally useless, mostly walking in and out for cigarette breaks.

"Shit!" exclaimed Guy.

"What?" Cody asked, looking in the big guy's direction.

"Sighhhhh. I see—" observed Marty, "—the chair you made is backwards."

Guy grew livid. "Bro, how the hell can I understand these IKEA instructions? They don't have any words in them!!!"

"That's the point, isn't it?" countered Cody. "They're supposed to be so easy that even an illiterate simpleton can understand them."

"Yeah, but I still don't get it," Guy whined.

Xia, wiping sweat off her brow, tossed a bag of White Rabbit candy to him.

"There! More sugar...help you think...maybe it make you smarter!" she laughed.

"White Rabbit candy?" observed Guy. "Isn't this the crap where you eat the wrapping paper too?"

Cody began feeling very frustrated as he noticed the hour hand of the clock reaching five. He appreciated the others helping, but he was annoyed at the ones who lacked urgency. Guy seemed to enjoy the attention he received screwing up. Herman could work faster if he stopped yapping. Jack was completely undependable. And Marty, he realized, seemingly approached the situation without awareness of exigency.

"Argh!" yelled Guy. "Now this lamp is backwards!"

"Eat more White Rabbit candy!" Xia advised again.

"Let me do it," Cody demanded, pushing the big football player aside.

"What do I do now?" the quarterback asked.

"Go find your brother," answered Cody. "We need more manpower. And switch to a different song—we've been hearing that crap over and over again for the past thirty minutes."

"Dude, I love Taylor Swift!" Guy defended.

"Fuck Taylor Swift! Don't you have anything other than top-50 hits?"

"Play my Shanghai hop-pop! Real hip!" Xia recommended.

Without waiting, she fiddled with Guy's Apple Macbook and added her own songs in there. Within moments, the office intercom blared with Chinese rap music. Cody walked around assisting the others on various tasks, pushing them to speed up. Marty, in particular, was working too slowly.

"Please, Cody, heh, don't...heh heh...don't rush me," he pleaded.

"We're opening our doors in under four hours. We need rushing," Cody bossed.

"I'm, haha, I'm going as fast as I can! Heh-ha!"

"Why are you taking so long anyway?" wondered Cody. "I've already put five chairs together, the printer desk, the supply cabinet, our desk chairs and multiple drawers."

"Sighhhh. I guess it happened again then, heh-ha," Marty said, shaking his head. "Just my bad luck, you guys got all the good ones and I happen to have the defective chairs and cabinets."

"Are you sure?" asked Cody suspiciously. "What's so defective about them?"

"Heh-ha! Hey, guess what?" Marty said, ignoring the question. "They should sell special insurance for people like me. Bad luck insurance, I'd call it. Heh heh ha!"

"That's funny, but seriously we have to—"

His sentence was suddenly interrupted by the loss of power in the entire building. Herman could be heard slipping and falling in the darkness. Somebody let out a loud fart; probably Xia, guessed Cody. They heard the door open.

"Dude, what's going on?" they heard Jack asking.

"This was no accident," theorized Marty's I.T. friend. "I think we're pushing the computers too hard. Herman, don't tell me you placed all the plugs into one socket."

Herman got vocally defensive. "DON'T BLAME ME MAN! YOU TOLD ME TO—"

The power immediately resumed; everyone could see one another again.

"Guy, put your shirt back on!" insisted Cody. "Man boobs aren't in season."

"It was hot," the big guy pleaded, covering himself.

"W-What's that noise?" winced Jack.

The power surges began beeping like an army of crickets. Soon, their decibel levels reached an unbearable high, inducing panic among the volunteer staff.

"Oh my God!" screamed Xia. "My ears hurt!"

The temporary I.T. manager fumbled for an explanation. "I...I'm trying, but the power surges are designed to chime during times of emergency, which—"

"I DON'T CARE!" screamed Cody. "JUST FIND A WAY TO TURN THEM OFF!"

Without waiting, he grabbed the closest power surge protector to him and unplugged it. To his horror, Cody discovered that it continued chirping. The rest of the volunteer crew tried a similar tactic, producing the same result.

"Fuck, bro, what do we do?!!" Guy wondered out loud. "Marty? Any ideas?!!"

"Muh-uh, we could...um...uh..."

"Ah, screw this!" Cody threw up his hands. "I'm hungry. Let's grab a bite at Waffle House."

No one disagreed. The power surges were left beeping in the office during their pursuit of food at the popular diner. They entered the nearest Waffle House in a dejected and offensively pungent state.

"How many, sir?" asked the hostess.

"I am a woman," corrected Xia. She looked at a window reflection of herself and flinched.

"Oh, sorry!" the hostess corrected.

"It's okay. Tonight, I am ugly."

The party of seven was taken to the farthest booth from the windows in an effort to prevent scaring potential customers. None of them blamed the diner's precaution; they truly looked awful. Most of them ordered eggs and pancakes. Marty's I.T. friend, however, ordered a full meal of chicken fried steak. His nap immediately afterwards was inevitable and so was the increasing visibility of his armpit stains.

"Dude," flinched Guy as he noticed the I.T. friend's sweat. "I am not carrying him into Marty's car."

"Yes, you are," Cody flatly opposed. "You're the biggest one out of all of us."

"Don't worry about him!" declared Herman. "I can finish networking the comps. Besides, this ass was in my way."

"Your ass is in the way of your face," Guy countered.

"Guy, that...that doesn't even make sense," Jack scoffed. "Anyway, it's not like you guys are going to make it. First day and your company doesn't even have working computers. Real good impression, guys."

"Shut up before we send you to jail!" hissed his brother.

"Ahahahahahaha!" Xia bursted out laughing.

"Fuck you, Guy," Jack sneered, taking out a cigarette. "Shit, my lighter's missing. What the hell..."

"Good!" Xia exclaimed. "No chance for you to do another fire!"

"Fuck you too, man-bitch," growled Jack. "No offense, Marty."

"Mm-huh, eh, watch...watch your language, Jack. That's my wife."

Cody slumped his shoulders. "Jack's right. This wasn't how I envisioned our first day. I can barely stay awake."

"Well, uh-ah now, heh heh," Marty patted Cody. "Don't say that. Heh. Eh? Come on...heh...we'll be alright. Ha-uh-hah."

"No, we've got to be ready to roll on our first day. You've already got all these clients lined up for us," reasoned Cody. "We can't fall behind."

"Mmm...huh," understood Marty.

"Speaking of which—," paused Cody. "Can you tell me who some of these clients are? The ones you had a month to get?"

Marty paused and thought.

"Well, uh, heh," he nervously laughed. "Wouldn't want to spoil the surprise, Cody."

"A month head start. I bet a superstar salesman like you must've gotten twenty by now."

"Guh-huh-ha, oh yeah, I've got us a big name too."

"<Really?>" perked Xia. "<I'm your wife and I didn't know?>"

"<I told you!>" insisted Marty. "<You just forgot!>"

"You always say this!" Xia switched to English. "'You forgot, You forgot.' Oh. Maybe...maybe you the one doing forget, huh?"

"Yeah," joined Jack. "I don't remember you mentioning this big name client either. So who's the big name, cuz?"

"Sigh. Pout. Sighhhhh." Marty looked at the ground and shook his head.

"Come on, man! How come we're finding this out after you tell the new employees? Tell us first! Who's this super client?"

Marty closed his eyes and twirled his head. Then huffed a long sigh.

"Why can't you guys just wait?" he pleaded.

"What? Who is it? Come on," pushed Cody.

"Yeah, bro," joined Guy. "Who is it?"

Their voices turned into a cacophony of pleas and random guesses. Marty felt pressured to give an answer.

"Um, ah, huh, ah..." he stumbled.

"Tell me!" Xia ordered.

"H...," Marty blurted the letter again. "H..."

"Holy shit......Home freakin' Depot," guessed Guy.

"It's Hustler, isn't it?!" excitedly screamed Herman. He jumped up and down. "Oh man oh man oh man!"

"Herman, sit down. You're scaring the senior citizens," Cody pointed out.

"Honda, History Channel, Hugo Boss," Jack listed.

"H-E-B Pantry," Cody guessed.

"I know!" beamed Xia. "H-Mart!"

"Er, ahhh." Marty nervously looked around the table. "Yes, er, heh yes! It's H-Mart. Once again, my, eh, beautiful wife is right. But, heh, shhh. Ffft...heh...shhhhhh."

They oohed and aahed at Marty's revelation. H-Mart was the Korean supermarket juggernaut in Houston.

"Fuccccck," Jack marveled. "Hey, you think you can hook me up with those hot Korean chicks that go there? I swear they all look like Hyori Lee."

"H-Mart," reflected Cody. "Marty...you're the fucking man!!!"

The whole crew came alive with excitement. Cody rushed to give his best friend an approving handshake; Marty had delivered. He cursed himself for doubting him. It was the perfect news to tell the new employees. With newfound excitement, the passengers enjoyed a refreshing atmosphere during the car ride back. They were given a friendly greeting by the morning sun, which gave the blasé Texas landscape a beautiful red hue. Cody stopped Guy on one particular song he discovered fiddling with the radio knobs. He didn't know what the name of it was, but the beat had a nice rock-and-roll rhythm—a perfect soundtrack to the scenery. As his left arm was catching the wind from the driver-side window, Cody basked in the excitement of anticipation. A couple more hours and he would be a boss. How would it feel? What would he say? He'd remember this day for the rest of his life.

When the doors of Mosaic Design Studios opened and the girls arrived, things remained far from perfect. However, Cody was determined to make it so. Amid competition from the chirping surge protectors, he gathered his staff in the conference room and let out the earth-shattering speech he had memorized and saved up for just this moment. What came out instead was a collection of bumbling and stammering, partly including a few sensible points within. He was learning the hard way that public speaking without practice was difficult. The girls looked at him, patiently observing his lack of eye contact and constant fidgeting. He also spoke fast, nervously fast.

"—and without further ado," the new CEO concluded, "we have lots of things coming up busy ready for you yeah coming up so be ready big, big things, I mean, clients, which is to say one of them we got was H-Mart and other important customers who we depend on to spread a good rep perhaps I've over-talked and without further ado, wait, I already said that, well, without further ado, Marty will fill you in on how to fill out your W-2 forms and gather your information about W-2 forms of which information will be gathered."

Cody took a well-deserved dose of air. His heartbeat was racing a hundred miles an hour. Marty took over, calmly explaining the instructions for the paperwork. This gave Cody a chance to collect himself within the privacy of his office room. Guy followed him.

"Hey, yo, you okay?" the big guy asked.

"I'm fine," insisted Cody. "I just...didn't imagine I would sound like that. Thought I would be a little more General MacArthur-like."

"Huh? Who?"

"American History. World War II." Cody gave up. "Never mind."

"God, look at Nicky and Sonia," fantasized Guy. "They could both blow me all day long."

"Hey, could you, like, not say that kind of stuff so openly? This is a real company. This a real work environment. Jesus...don't make me fire you, man."

Guy ignored him and added, "You think Sonia's tits are real?"

Cody looked at the jock in disgust and walked back toward the main office. He was in awe of how patient Marty was with them. His partner was a natural at dealing with people, and they seemed to respond better to him. Cody thought it was too bad that they arranged for him to be in the office while Marty was out with clients. But then again, Cody realized, it was a good opportunity for him to learn leadership. Daphne Lee had always criticized him for a lack of it.

"Okay, hah-ah," concluded Marty, "if there're no more questions, you guys have the rest of the day off. Come back tomorrow morning at ten o'clock."

"Wow, the day off already!" exclaimed Nicky. "You're so nice, Marty!"

"Well, ah, I...ah..." he blushed.

"Yeah, this is awesome. Thanks!" appreciated Patricia.

The four employees gathered their purses and other belongings, heading for home. Marty chuckled and waved.

Cody watched them go with a wide-eyed stare. He then turned to Marty.

"Why'd you tell them to take the first day off?!" he asked.

"Heh, relax, Cody, heh. Come on, heh. You know? Eh? Ah? Ah heh heh?" Marty pointed to his nose.

"No...what do you mean?"

Marty put his hands together and rested his head on them in a sleeping gesture.

"Eh? Ah?" Marty arched his eyebrows up and down.

"Sleep? We don't need sleep!"

"Come on, Cody, heh heh, sleeping is what you, heh heh, need. You worked hard. You deserve it. Eh! Eh? Eh!"

"I...I guess. We did work for two nights straight," Cody concluded.

Marty patted him on the back and began writing on the dry erase board. He wrote the names of fifty clients, most of them seemingly from the restaurant or oil industry. Some were recognizable; most were not.

"Reliant? Wow. You got us Reliant?!" exclaimed Cody.

"Wah-uh, more like they got us," winked and nudged Marty.

"Wait, where's H-Mart on your board? Why isn't it on there?"

"Eh, they just called me. Remember when you went to the restroom earlier this morning?"

"Yeah?"

Marty made a throat-slashing gesture with his hand.

"They cut us?!" asked Cody.

Marty closed his eyes and nodded his head, sighing for a few seconds.

"It's okay, though," assured Marty. "We don't need them. I got us M.H. Productions!"

"That's great!...Wait, what the hell is M.H. Productions?"

"Ah ha-eh, you've never heard of them? Big production company. Quality work. I'm, heh-huh, frankly surprised. You should go out there more often, hoo-ah."

Guy walked back into the office wearing a tennis outfit. He bounced a tennis ball with one hand while fiddling with a racket on the other. Jack and Xia came in wearing similar attire.

"Wait, what's going on?" Cody asked.

"Relax, Cody...shh....heh-heh...you haven't slept," laughed Marty. "We need to take our minds out of the company. We're playing tennis. Wanna come?"

"Sounds fun," Cody contemplated. "But then again, I don't play tennis."

"Don't worry about it then. You should rest, you really should, hahuh." Once again, Marty patted Cody on the back. "We'll have plenty of days to get serious and celebrate. This is our first day, hmm-ah, heh heh, let's just treat it as a formality and nothing more."

"I guess. Yeah, you're right," agreed Cody. "We were too stressed from this morning to think properly."

"Mmm yeah, haha, see?" Marty gave him a thumbs-up.

By the second week, Sonia had gotten familiar with Lydia and Patricia. She had also convinced Cody to get her a fancier computer, a higher salary and the new title of Executive Secretary. It didn't take the vixen secretary long to realize that both bosses had underestimated her. Men, she grinned, so easy to understand; so easy to control. She evaluated everyone's current strengths and weaknesses and mentally made a list. It was true that she wasn't very knowledgeable about websites and design. It was also true that she had very little working experience. But she knew how to work things to her advantage, to accurately read people and charm others into doing the fighting for her. Ms. Pokerface, she labeled herself with a smile.

She and the two designer girls made a habit of having lunch at Hula Hoop Shakes, a new diner just across the street from the building where they worked. There, the designer girls delightfully ordered from the fun assortment of hot dogs, pancakes, Frito pies and other items typically found in diners. Sonia herself didn't care for fatty fast food, but the restaurant had something else she enjoyed: a handsome, blue-eyed, blond-haired waiter.

"So...the usual?" the waiter recollected. "A cheeseburger with extra onion, no ketchup. Chicago-style hot dogs and tater tots. And for you, Ms. Sonia, a chicken salad with ranch dressing."

"Lite ranch," Sonia winked, "and, of course, my daily dose of cappuccino."

"With cinnamon in the grounds," the waiter winked back, walking away.

She knew she could have him if she wanted to, but she decided to designate him as a reserve. There were already too many men she had taking care of her. Charm, she was taught by her mother at an early age, was beauty plus attitude. However, none of it mattered without the concealing of intelligence. Sonia knew it was best to delude men into thinking she was incapable of bold ideas and keen observations. Ego, after all, was men's kryptonite. Perhaps, she thought, it would be best to share this knowledge with her new coworkers.

"Oh my Gahhd," Sonia pointed at Lydia, "he's so cute like always. I think he likes you, Lydiaaaa!"

Lydia felt herself blushing beyond her control. She rarely heard herself being described as a thing of beauty. The tiny girl had accepted her fate of dating socially awkward geeks and weirdos. It was better this way, she decided—being average looking was a natural filter from superficial men. Whoever ended up loving her, she figured, would care about her for who she was on the inside. Now, however, Sonia had planted a forbidden fantasy into the girl's head—one that she secretly believed could come true.

"He'd...he'd never like me," Lydia said, brushing it off.

"Like yuuuh," Sonia countered, "white guys like Asian girls...it's the new 'thing.'"

"Ha ha ha! Guys are guys! They like pretty girls like you. It would be ridiculous if they passed you for me just because I'm Asian. Ha ha!"

"Totally not!" insisted Sonia. "I just have better game. I think for an Asian girl to get a white guy, all she has to do is stand still and say 'Hi. I'm Asian!'"

The three girls laughed. They were bonding.

"Nooo," Lydia smiled and sighed. "I'm all good. I...probably...wouldn't want a guy like that anyway. All these girls fighting for him if I was his girlfriend. They would always bug him about why he'd be with me. Ha ha. Better leave him to the beautiful ones like yourself, Sonia!"

"Oh, hon, it's all about how you carry yourself," advised Sonia. "Ever notice that whenever I needed something from him, I would slightly bend over and expose a bit of my chest?"

Lydia and Patricia giggled like schoolgirls. They admired Sonia's openness with sexuality and flirting—something their conservative backgrounds held them back from exploring. Their lunch conversations led them to ask questions they couldn't believe they were asking. Mostly, though, they respected Sonia because she knew how to control men—and that was tradable knowledge for their loyalty.

"The secret to getting men to do what you want," Sonia began, "is to make them feel like kings. This way they won't realize that the queen is always more powerful."

"Like chess," Patricia observed.

"Yuuuh," she nodded, "like getting them to think we work for them when, in fact, they work for us."

The two girls immediately picked up on Sonia's specific meaning.

"I don't think twelve vacation days in a year is enough," Lydia nodded.

"And nine o'clock in the morning for work?" Patricia said. "Ten-thirty is way better."

"Patricia, is getting to work a problem for you?" Sonia asked in a concerned voice.

"Yeah, I have to have my mom drive me. We live in Humble," she replied.

"Don't worry"," Sonia assured her. "Start coming in at ten-thirty then. Eleven if you must."

"Yeah, it's not like Cody comes in before two in the afternoon anyway," laughed Lydia.

"But what if Marty comes in and sees that we're not there?" asked Patricia.

"Seriously, are any of you really afraid of Marty?" smirked Sonia. "I noticed what a pushover he was during the night at The Oceanaire. His wife clearly wears the pants."

Sonia cleared her throat and began imitating Marty. "Um, ahhh, huh, ah huh ha, hahaha, I don't know what I'm doing. I just laugh. Ah ha ha. Ah huh huh. Ha huh ha!"

The girls burst out into a flurry of laughter. It wasn't a bad impression.

"Seriously," she continued, "I don't buy into all this bullshit about him being an experienced salesman. He's been training that Nicky girl for two weeks and they haven't gotten anything."

"Yeah," Lydia agreed. "I think they lied about H-Mart too."

"I bet he's trying to fuck her," said Sonia. "I can tell these things. It's also why they hired me. Like, oh my Gahhd, did you know that weird cousin of his...what's his name, Jack?...the one who's a drunk-ass loser...anyways, did y'all know what he asked me the other day?"

"No, what?" the two of them simultaneously wondered.

"He flat out asked me if I knew why I really got hired, and I said, 'yeah, for my tits'. And he laughed and said 'glad you know.' What a pig."

"I'd never date someone like that guy." Patricia shook her head. "He smells homeless."

"I heard from his brother Guy that he mooches off unsuspecting women and he's also an arsonist," Sonia added.

"Yeah. I can see that," Lydia agreed.

"They're all dumb," declared Sonia. "I can run a company better than any of them could. Nothing's organized. And speaking of dumb..."

Sonia's expression turned serious. She was about to get into the main point of their afternoon conversation.

"...I think Nicky is an absolute moron. There's air in between her ears. Tell you the truth, girls, I'm scared for the immediate future of Mosaic Design Studios if she's our hope for sales. I really am," said Sonia.

"Yeah, I've talked with her," said Lydia. "She's not very bright. She told me she used to be a Hooters girl."

"Not all Hooters girls are dumb," countered Patricia.

"Well, this one most certainly is," Sonia said, "and I got just the right person to replace her. I have a good friend who's smart, brilliant and charming. She would do a helluva better job than this bimbo."

"Here you go, girls!" interrupted their handsome waiter.

As he served their food, the girls were surprised that he was accompanied by a new waitress. Ever since they had started coming regularly, he was their favorite thing about Hula Hoop Shakes. The sign of an apprentice might mean what they had feared: an end to his services.

"So," Sonia observed, "who's this?"

The new waitress was a spunky-looking young woman of Korean descent. She had piercings on the most visible parts of her body, heavy makeup and spiked-up hair. The entire side of her left arm was covered with an interesting tattoo sleeve design.

"This is my replacement, Phoebe," introduced the handsome waiter. "She'll be here from now on. This will be my last week."

The girls' hearts sank; their instincts had been proven correct.

"Where are you going?" Sonia sweetly asked. "You know we'll miss you."

"I just got accepted to work for Halliburton," he explained. "Guess my days of waiting tables are over. I really liked talking with y'all. It was cool to see you girls almost every day."

"It doesn't have to end, you know." Sonia wrote her number on a napkin.

"I guess it doesn't," he laughed, taking the napkin.

Phoebe, the new waitress, refilled their drinks.

"I'll miss you," smiled Lydia.

"So," ignored the waiter, "anything else for you girls?"

"Yes," replied Sonia, "applications to Halliburton, please?"

"Hahaha, I'm sure they could use a hot girl for a secretary in there."

"Executive Secretary," she laughed and corrected him.

It was the scene that Marty loved the most. With only a small hacksaw and a tape recorder to set her free from the dilapidated bathroom, the chained blonde cheerleader realized her only two options. She was either to saw off her own foot or give oral sex to the corpse beside her. Marty salivated when she looked at the camera and gladly chose the latter. The corpse turned out to be alive; swanky guitar music started to play. The video had the three things Marty loved the most: a porno parody of his favorite movie *Saw*, blondes, and the activity the actress was about to perform.

"Uh-ho ho ha! Hooooo!" Marty breathed heavily. "Yeaaaah."

Keep your voice down, he reminded himself, he didn't want people to know he was in the back of his Oldsmobile, relieving himself on his laptop. The pants-less sales director would be embarrassed if anyone discovered this was how he spent his lunch hours. As the video got into its climax, his cell phone unexpectedly rang, causing him to spurt out a surprise both in expression and secretion.

"Huh-ah, h...hello?" he answered, quickly turning down the volume.

"Hey, Marty! It's me, Nicky, I don't see you here at Starbucks in the Town Square. Are you okay?"

"Wh-what? Um, hah. It's...it's only, heh, twelve-thirty," Marty said, glancing at his car's clock.

"Huh? It is? All the clocks in here must be broken then. They all say one o'clock on them," Nicky believed.

Marty silently cursed himself for forgetting about Guy's Jamba Juice accident earlier in the day. The drink had spilled onto the dashboard and damaged the car clock.

"Wuh-ha! Huh huh, mannn, can you believe that?" he laughed. "All the clocks in the Starbucks are wrong at the same time."

"I know!" giggled Nicky. "What are the chances of that happening? Oh, and guess what? Wow! My cell phone's clock is messed up too! So weird!"

"Well, shhh. Um, glad one of us has a working clock then!" Marty laughed.

"I guess I'm early!" she laughed.

"Don't you worry, I happen to be close by! Wait for me for fifteen minutes, okay?"

"Sure! Maybe I can occupy my time by telling everyone that their clocks are wrong," laughed Nicky.

"Er, ah, HA! No no no, don't do that. Shhh. Hush, heh. Heh-ha! They probably won't appreciate you correcting them. I'll be right down there, okay?"

Marty hung up and quickly put his pants back on. He was thankful that Nicky wasn't very bright; in fact, it made it better that she turned out to be a moron. A hot-looking moron, nevertheless. Still, he was a bit disappointed the video session ended prematurely, but then again, at least for once he was able to do something prematurely. The extensive watching of pornography had messed up his sexual appetite. Perhaps he should blame Xia for holding back intimacy during the past year. Didn't she know it tortured a man?

The phone rang again. It was from the office.

"Hey, bro," Guy's voice said, "you better get in here quick. Some crazy motherfucker is starting shit."

"Wuh-uh, what?" Marty couldn't believe it. "Where's Sonia? Why are you on her phone line?"

"You should just come quickly," Guy hinted before hanging up.

Marty contemplated whether he should meet with Nicky or attend to the office emergency. If he ignored either one, he realized, he'd be seen as the bad guy. It was a thought that greatly bothered him. Think, Marty, he pushed himself, think. After a few seconds, he dialed Nicky's number.

"Um, er, Nicky! Do you see me?" he lied. "No? Um, are you sure? I'm at the door...you, um, heh, sure you don't see me?...wait, what Starbucks are you in again?...no, noooo, hah-heh, I told you the one in the Pearland Town Square...see? You're so forgetful.....muh-heh, it's okay...... Well, you just stay there, I'll drive on over to the one in the Sugar Land Town Square..."

This was why he liked her. She wasn't smart enough to question things. Now he needed just an hour to handle whatever was happening at the office.

The scene that awaited him there was a frightening one. An angry, bald and physically imposing Hispanic man was in the middle of their office. He was yelling obscenities and pushing around loose office furniture from rage. Sonia was leaning toward a corner, paralyzed with fear. The two designer girls stayed at their desks, pretending to look at their screens. And for all his muscles and self-boasting bravado, Guy was hesitant to confront the enraged man. Marty recognized him. He was bad news.

"Now, now Jose," he called out, "ehhh, heh, this doesn't have to get violent."

"So you finally show yourself, eh?" Jose scowled. "Good. I was going to hurt your idiot staff and your whore secretary if you had not!"

Guy was offended by those words.

"Bro, I don't think you can hurtOOOF!" The quarterback dropped down after being kicked in his left calf. Jose proved himself a strong and formidable fighter.

Marty continued with the negotiations. "Ah, eh. Come...come on, Jose. Please? Heh. Eh? Ehhh!"

"Where is my website! Why isn't it ready! I paid you guys!" he yelled.

"Well, ah, uh...Lydia...why don't you show him that design you did. Heh-hah," Marty asked nervously.

"Yes, let me bring it up," she said softly.

"Oh no!" Jose stopped her. "I saw that one already! It sucks! Ugly design! Maybe because made from ugly girl!"

Lydia gave an offended expression.

"Ah, I'm...heh-ha-ha, hey, you want anything to drink?" asked Marty. "We have...what do we have, Patricia?"

Patricia cleared her throat. "Grape Capri Sun, Vita, Pepsi..."

"I don't fucking want a drink!" yelled Jose. "I want you to finish my site right now! I paid you two thousand already!"

"Now now, mm-mmm," Marty assured him, "why don't we go to my office and, heh, let me tell you a funny story!"

Behind closed doors, the staff heard Jose screaming at Marty. Even with Guy's assurance of his cousin's martial arts, all of them were certain it was only a matter of time before the giant man lost control and violently injured their boss. However, minutes later, the room fell quiet. He's dead, they thought, perhaps even witnesses to a murder. Then, unexpected laughter suddenly came from the room; it was Jose's voice. Ten minutes later, their boss' door opened; Jose exited in good spirits. He laughed and waved a friendly hello to everyone. Putting his giant arms around Marty's shoulder, they laughed together as he voluntarily left their office.

"I'm sorry, I'm sorry," he laughed and apologized.

"Ah huh-eh! Ha!" Marty said. "No problem, Jose. See? It was all just a little misunderstanding. Heh. Ha! Heh-ha."

With Jose's departure, Marty felt a rush of confidence; he wanted to do something bold, take whatever he wanted. Nicky, he suddenly remembered—she was still at the Starbucks.

It was now or never, he realized. He was going to drag her out, take her to his bedroom and make love to her.

The Starbucks was full of people by the time Marty arrived. Occupying the limited tables were mostly college kids and working professionals with their laptops and those new iPads he heard about. He searched for Nicky's blonde hair until finally, near the edge of the coffee shop, he recognized her unmistakable body. This was it, Marty told himself as he made his way closer to her, *Nicky, come sleep with me. Now.*

Unfortunately, at the expense of his heart, he saw a man next to her, holding her hand and kissing her. Marty's confidence was deflated. How did it never occur to him that she had a boyfriend? A black guy too. He shook his head. His drop back to earth was brutal. A slight buzz to his right thigh shook him out of his self-pity. It was his iPhone vibrating. Xia, he read from the caller ID.

"Mm-huh?" Marty answered.

"<Hey, don't forget to help my brother paint his house today while he's away from town. Also, be sure to walk our poodle around the FRONT of the house this time. Then call Wanda and tell her I'll be going to her girls' night out together this weekend. Did you remember to get the Japanese Blossom hand wash from Bath and Body Works? Oh, and hey, get me those tampons I wanted from the store next to your workplace.>" His wife hung up.

"<Uh-huh, uh-huh>," nodded Marty, talking to an already ended phone call. "<Yes, dear. Anything for you, babe. Mm-huh.>"

He let the phone slip out of his hands and watched it hit the floor. Nicky had a man. Nicky had to go.

His feelings didn't get any better later after midnight as he lay awake on his living room sofa. It didn't help that Guy's snoring could be heard from the first-floor guest room or that Jack was equally as loud wheezing in the recliner. A burst of light caught his eye; it was from Xia coming in from a night of clubbing. He could see her silhouette stagger, making its way awkwardly towards the stairs that led to their second-floor bedroom. Marty hated it when Wanda and her girls got his wife drunk.

"<Xia>," Marty called to her.

"<Oh, husband...my nice, nice husband...hicc...did you get my tampons for me?>" She laughed in a buzzed stupor.

"<Wah-oooh. Ooh, no.>" He walked up and consoled her. "<You're drunk.>"

"GET YOUR HAND OFF ME!" Xia yelled in accented English.

"<Mmuh, ah...>"

Xia laughed and copied him, "<Mmuh, ah! Mmuh, ah! Why do you always sound like you're retarded?>"

"<Sighhhh.>"

"<Don't follow me upstairs. You just...help me...if I command you...hicc...>" Xia stumbled her way into her bedroom.

"<Okay.>"

"<Oh...hicc...look>," giggled and pointed Xia. "<Your cousin Guy has fallen asleep with nothing on. But he...hicc...he still has more pants than you do. Hahahahaha!>"

He watched her as she found her way to the bedroom and locked its door. Today I almost cheated on you, Marty thought to himself. She had no idea how much his own family hadn't wanted him to marry her; his mother felt Shanghai girls were a materialistic and fickle bunch. He was told how they'd rather focus on outside appearances and didn't bother with the inside. Marty wouldn't listen at the time because he was in love with her. Or rather, he liked being married to a pretty woman. It gave him face; people patted him on his back. Xia gave him admiration but for a hefty price.

The gloominess of the topic persuaded Marty to distract himself with something else. He flipped his laptop open and went to his browser's favorites. There, in neatly organized links, he snooped at his employee's Facebook pages, blogs, and other personal pages. He had ways of overriding their privacy settings, courtesy of his I.T. friend. Sonia sure took a lot of risqué photos, he smiled, saving them onto his laptop. He also discovered she was a Maxim Hometown Hottie contestant. Nude? He searched deeper into the web. Yes, he excitedly realized. She had nude photos of herself. *Saved.*

As he was about to log off and enjoy the saved nude photos, he noticed Sonia's latest Facebook status from the corner of his eye. There, with Lydia and Patricia also responding, they were making fun of Nicky. *Dumb. Bimbo. Brainless. Marty lacks inability to choose good employees. I heard he tried to sleep with her. He hadn't the guts to ask.* Shocked that they were making fun of him, he immediately grabbed his iPhone and dialed Cody's number. Luckily for him, the device still worked after it was dropped earlier.

"Hey man, I was just about to call you!" greeted Cody. "We must have ESP!"

"Heh, ah, maybe," Marty agreed, "hey guess what? Jose came today and started shit. Heh. He was mad, but I calmed him down by talking to him."

"Yeah, I heard about that from Lydia," said Cody. "Good job."

"Huh? Heh-ha...Cody, they....they tell you things? They talk with you?" asked Marty.

"Sure. Why not?"

"I mean, ha...uh ha ha...no, no. It's...it's no big deal."

"Okay. Well, anyway, listen, Marty...I've been looking at our bank account and sales charts for the past month and we're not getting anywhere near the quota as we should. And with all the salary the girls eat up we'll—"

Marty needed to change the subject. "Oh, man! Guy and I played this game today. Guess...guess the name. City of Heroes. And then City of Villains. You get to make your own super hero or villain and run around this world. Wild, huh? You should play with us, Cody, you really should, heh. Ha! Heh-ha!"

"Hey, this is serious," Cody said, sticking to the original topic. "Why haven't you and Nicky been getting enough sales?

Aren't you guys going around meeting these fifty or so clients? And why hasn't M.H. Productions paid us yet? Lydia and Sonia emailed them the design for approval, but they haven't responded."

"Uh, ah, are you...you sure they, heh, didn't pay...no, no, shh, ffft...they paid. I'm certain of it!"

"No, Marty, I've looked everywhere. It's not there. Can you ask them again just to be sure?"

"Oh, of course. Wah-uh, eh."

"Dude, we're going to be out of money very soon. Haven't you checked the bank account?"

"Well...yer...hoo...ah, I mean, I thought that was your job...I...didn't know..."

"Marty, we used close to a hundred thousand dollars of my family's money in just under a few months. And so far you've only gotten us four thousand dollars in sales. Four thousand! What's happening here?"

"Well, sales take time, eh ah? Yeah?"

"But bills don't take time. We have to pay salary on time. You assured me you could do this."

"Sigh."

"Marty, we won't last past next month. I can't believe you haven't been checking on our bank account."

"Wer, ya...heh...I lost the password!"

"Then click on the button 'Forget Password.'"

"Nicky."

"Pardon me?"

"It's Nicky. She's...heh...she's the problem."

"Yeah, the other girls tell me she's kind of dumb."

"Er...ah...yes. Yes," Marty agreed. "She holds me back. She's not learning anything. Nothing. Sigh."

"I thought you said you liked her. You were telling me that your training was turning her into a killer salesman."

"I, ah, mmmeh, I made a mistake there. She's incapable of learning. Incapable. Heh...ha! So...let's...fire her, man."

"Okay," Cody slowly said.

"April Finley. Let's replace Nicky with her."

"I was going to suggest the same thing. April came across more capable in her interview than Nicky had."

"Woo-ha, okay," Marty nodded. "You, eh, I'll let you do the firing."

"I've never fired anyone before."

"Heh, uh, neither have I."

"Then let's fire Nicky together."

"Wa-ahh...no no. Um, I'll sit next to you while you do it."

"Fine. Okay. Not now though. Let's wait a few weeks later. Close to Thanksgiving."

"Meh...ah...I...okay. Uh, okay," Marty replied.

CHAPTER 20: DAREDEVIL

In the blink of an eye, autumn passed.

As business continued to slide, Cody found himself coping alone most nights at Hula Hoop Shakes. At first, he regularly ate there with Marty after work hours—they had to try it for themselves since the girls wouldn't stop raving about it—but after a couple of trips, its appeal had waned for Marty. Cody, however, made eating there a habit. He had found the Frito pie and chili dogs to die for, but mostly it was because he had fallen for the pretty Korean-American waitress.

He first met Phoebe during Halloween, when he had come along with Marty and Xia to the diner in full costume. Cody wore a giant light bulb over his head. It was held together by the wire of an old coat hanger, which was his idea of an "abstract costume." Xia and Marty came as a pair of Ranma characters: Akane Tendo and her panda Genma. The large doses of cotton and heavy eye shadow caused Marty to scratch himself constantly. Xia's dark purple wig wasn't nearly as troublesome. The heavily tattooed Phoebe, who wore bright hippie clothing and an assortment of body piercings, was at first mistaken to be in costume as well.

"Oh, I'm always like this," she shrugged, snapping around a piece of bubble gum in her mouth. "They let us wear anything tonight because it's Halloween."

Marty had once made fun of Cody for liking women who "seem like they'd knife ya" and perhaps he was right. He liked Phoebe's spunk, her naughty smile and heavy use of mascara. The attraction proved genuine; it passed several weeks' worth of time. He continued seeing her at Hula Hoop Shakes even after windy weather turned into rainy conditions. And then, to everyone's surprise, by December it became a white winter—for the first time in decades, there was an actual snowstorm in Houston, Texas.

As usual, Cody walked into the diner with Phoebe as the first priority on his mind. He shook the snow off his large black overcoat and dusted his gloves. There she was, he saw... his favorite waitress, busy with other tables at the far end of the diner.

"How many people?" asked another waitress.

"Just me," Cody replied.

To his disappointment, the other waitress led him to a booth near the doorway. He initially decided not to request a seat near Phoebe's section; he thought it might make him appear creepy. After fidgeting with the idea for a few minutes, however, he said to hell with it and waved over the nearest waiter.

"Hello, what would like to drink, sir?" he asked.

"You know what?" Cody replied. "I think I changed my mind about this table. Can I just say hello to Phoebe?"

"Oh, sure," replied the waiter.

Making his way toward his crush, Cody found her standing there, pausing for a moment to watch the television's weather forecast. He stopped a few feet from her, waiting for the segment to end. The news report switched to a story of a man found abducted inside of a Taiwanese cargo ship. Cody let out a heartfelt laugh when he saw a desolate Kirk Santiago being interviewed by the Taiwanese media.

Startled by his laughter, Phoebe let out a slight yelp.

"Oh!" she collected herself. "Hey!"

"Hey, hippie-hipster."

"What were you laughing about?" she giggled.

"The guy who got kidnapped to Taiwan." Cody pointed at the television. "That's hilarious. What a prank, eh?"

Phoebe frowned. "No, it's not. He probably had a family that was worried sick the whole time. Whoever did that to him must've been one self-serving bastard."

She was right, realized Cody. In his short-sightedness to get even with his former supervisor, he hadn't considered Kirk's mother worrying herself sick. She had probably cried hysterically for months, dreadfully awaiting word from investigators.

"W...Well," justified Cody, "maybe that Kirk Santiago guy was a jerk and he deserved it. I mean, why else would somebody do that to him?"

"Meh," Phoebe shrugged. "That's still a vengeance-filled thing to do. I hope they catch his kidnapper. Don't you?"

She looked at him with wandering eyes, waiting for his answer. Cody changed the subject before he could get lost in them.

"Anyway, I just...I just came in to say hi," he sheepishly confessed.

"Meh," Phoebe repeated.

"So, hey, you thought about coming to my Christmas party? There's going to be around seventy-five people there. I really want you to come."

"I'll, uh, I'll see. When is that on? Next Saturday, right?"

"Yeah," Cody answered, "I sent you an invite by email. You never wrote back."

Phoebe remembered the email. It was filled with cheesy flirting and numerous references to how beautiful she was. She didn't feel comfortable enough to say yes.

"I probably can't," she replied. "My boss says I've got to work that day."

"Come on, just tell him your grandma's in town."

"Haha! What? Cody, you are something else."

"Please. It's going to be huge. It would mean a lot for me if you came."

"You don't even know me," she smiled, sticking out her tongue in jest. Even her tongue had a piercing in it, he noticed.

"Well, if you change your mind, let me know," Cody laughed.

"Alright."

Cody mentally kicked himself as he turned to leave. He should've just been an assertive jerk and demanded her to come. Maybe his cousin Duke's seminars had a point; passivity doesn't work. As he stood outside lost in thought, the snow started covering the lenses of his glasses. Cody took them off and wiped them clean. It reminded him to keep moving and stay focused.

The Christmas party the following Saturday was an extravaganza. It was held at one of the fanciest hotels in town, financed by Cody's personal savings. As an ambitious attempt for a creative twist, both Marty and he bought out the staff and inserted their own. The volunteer waitstaff were dressed in Lone Ranger–type masks as a tribute to the Crazy 88 villains from one of Marty's favorite movies, *Kill Bill.* To accommodate their theme, "Home Cooking," the two also asked some of their guests to bring home-cooked meals. It was a direct violation of the hotel's rules due to safety reasons. Even with that in mind, they succeeded in fooling the hotel management by switching the hotel food with the home-cooked food behind large blue screen curtains. Marty was proud of himself for coming up with that idea.

True to Cody's prediction to Phoebe, there were seventy-five guests that arrived, most of them friends of Cody's and Marty's, although Mosaic Design Studios employees were invited too. Unfortunately, Phoebe wasn't among them; she had declined after all. Guests were treated to a beautiful setup, complete with a sea of wrapped gifts at the back and an open bar. They were also aware that there would be a game of Black Elephant, a twisted version of White Elephant where random guests would later be pitted against one another in various challenges. It was the first time many of Cody's friends were together in the same room.

"Hey!.......Hey!" screamed Herman, serving as the usher.

He quickly grabbed the guest who walked past him.

"What's your name?!!!" Herman continued yelling at her. "We have assigned seating here, you know!"

"Assigned seating?"

"Yeah! Bosses' orders. They have a seating chart."

"That's ridiculous. Why can't we just sit where we want?"

"Rules are rules. Tell me your name. Now!"

"Yuki," she said, "Yuki Yee. And I've read all about you, Herman Shu."

Cody's longtime Internet friend from New York had finally made a trip to see him. It was amazing how all the characters he blogged about were now in front of her in the flesh. There was Mindy Cheung and her husband, Wing Wei. His childhood friend Diana Li and her cousin Kiki, the dorky fresh-off-the-boat relative from Hong Kong. She recognized Zoey Vu and her gay best friend, Felix Lin. There were Lydia, Patricia, Sonia, Marty, Xia, Guy, Wanda...identifying all of them was like a game in and of itself.

"Sit here!" ordered Herman, pointing to her designated chair.

Like hell I'm gonna stay put, she thought. At least she was near the middle of the horseshoe-shaped arrangement of three long tables. It was easy to see everyone from there. As if on cue, her vision went out—someone had suddenly placed a pair of chubby hands over her eyes. Yuki immediately knew whom they belonged to.

"Guess whoooo?" sang a voice.

"I don't need to see you to know that it's you, Rain."

Rain uncovered Yuki's eyes and both women squealed in joy, hugging one another. They couldn't contain their thrill of meeting in person for the first time.

"You look...you look..."

"Chubbier in person?" laughed Rain.

"No," corrected Yuki, "you look even more hip!"

Yuki was telling the truth. Rain had an aura of confidence and a look to her that made it obvious she was bright and talented. Yuki also felt confident too, but it was in a much different way. She was comfortable with herself, even though she was a decade or two older than everyone else in the room. There was something to be said about elegance and class and wearing the proud mantle of a cougar.

"Hello to both of you, la!" interrupted a voice, "my name is Kiki. Are you friends of Cody? Ahehehehehe."

"We're Internet friends with him," Rain explained, shaking Kiki's hand. "We're meeting him for the first time."

"Internet?" Kiki had a confused expression on her face. "Wow! That's so dangerous!"

"Actually," Yuki realized, "you know what? I haven't actually met Cody in person yet. Where is he?"

"Oh, he's walking around somewhere," explained Rain. "I met his best friend, Marty. That's the guy fixing the stereo systems around the stage area. I think they're going to set up the Black Elephant games or something."

Yuki decided to stay and occupy herself with the other guests around her. Rain bounced around the ballroom, making small talk with anyone who was male.

Behind the blue screen "curtains," Cody was a nervous wreck. Nothing was going as planned. Many guests were coming late—on "Asian Time," he'd call it—and the volunteer Crazy 88 staff was slow and incompetent. Worse yet, the deejay had bailed out on them, but that didn't seem to matter anyway since Marty was still struggling to set up the sound system. He found himself orchestrating everything, keeping the party gears in motion, but it seemed to make things worse. He was worried the party would turn into a big disaster.

"Oh, fuck!" shouted Guy, who tripped and spilled someone's large container of soup all over the floor.

"What—what'd you do?!" alerted Cody. "Aw, hell! That was Diana's chicken gumbo soup! She spent the whole day on it."

Making sure no one was looking, he grabbed a stockpile of expensive hotel napkins and soaked up Diana's soup from the carpet. It was enough to make him curse up a storm. Perhaps he needed to push the volunteer staff harder.

"Go go go!" he shouted at them. "Put the food on the plates faster!"

"Hey, Cody, bro," asked Guy, "what do I do with the spilled gumbo soup? Do I just tell them there's no more?"

"No, don't do that! There's some vegetable soup that the hotel made us order," Cody explained, unveiling a hidden cache of it. "Use this. No one's going to know the difference."

Guy scratched his head. "I don't think so, dude. That doesn't look anything like gumbo."

"Then use the rice that Lydia brought and dump it in. There! Gumbo!"

"But that was for Lydia's Thai curry!"

"Well, now it's just curry soup, man! Market it as that!"

"'Curry soup'? What the hell?"

Cody stormed out from behind the blue screens in anger. It was worse than he thought—what was supposed to be a classy and organized evening had turned into a romping free-for-all. No one followed the assigned seating; they weren't even sitting. Worse, there was something about the guests. All the guests appeared more than tipsy—they were as loud as college kids at a frat party. The open bar, he suddenly realized. Jack Tsing had turned it into a constant stream of shots for everyone. Even the Crazy 88 staff were drinking.

"No, stop!" Cody screamed at Jack. "Don't get everyone drunk! You're skyrocketing the tab!"

"Stop?" laughed Jack. "Are you kidding me? This is the best damn Christmas party ever! You're the best!"

Jack ordered a straight shot of vodka and gave it to Cody.

"Drink, motherfucker!" Jack exclaimed.

"No!" refused Cody.

Suddenly a screech from the microphone could be heard from the stage. Marty finally got the stereo system working.

"Mm-hah. Testing, testing," Marty spoke into the microphone.

He stood in the center of the stage, grinning that he had finally gotten something to work. Cody ran up to him.

"Start the games!" Cody ordered off-mike. "Start the games now!"

"Wah-ah, okay we're going to do our Black Elephant event now," Marty announced on the microphone.

Scattered clapping followed. Marty looked at Cody for further instructions. Cody was irritated because he had gone through the Black Elephant details with him several times before. Now it was obvious that Marty's deer-in-the-headlight look meant that he hadn't understood or listened to Cody.

"Er...ah...heh...mah-wuh..." Marty didn't know what to say. From the corner of his eye, he noticed his wife Xia, giggling with one of Cody's male friends.

Cody couldn't wait for Marty to recover. He grabbed the mike and explained the game himself. "Okay, our first Black Elephant game is simple. We're going to draw the names of four guests from this box. If you get picked and you don't want to do it, you can pick a person to go in your place."

He pointed at the big pile of wrapped presents in the left corner of the stage.

"First prize gets to pick first, second picks second, and so forth," he continued.

"Wait, what's the game about?" shouted Zoey.

"Okay, good point," Cody nodded, "the objective of the first game is to do exactly what Herman does. He will perform various kung fu moves and we will have three judges. The highest overall grade wins."

The four who were selected for the game were Sonia, Mindy, Felix and Wanda. Cody handed the microphone back to Marty who announced, "Heh-ha, let the games begin!!!"

Dramatic music played. The lights were dimmed. A spotlight shined on Herman.

"Now I'm gonna start off with something easy!" Herman declared,"OoooooooooooooooOOOOOO!!!"

He unleashed a flurry of random spin kicks, roundhouses, punches and cartwheels.

"YOGA BOOM! JADED UPPERCUT! THE TIGER OF SAN PEDRO!" shouted Herman.

Marty added martial art sounds into the mike for effect. "Whaaa! Oooh! Raaaa! Hadouken!"

The room exploded with overwhelming laughter; some of the guests were so amused that they fell off their chairs. One of the Crazy 88 waiters cracked up so hard he spilled his food. Herman repeated what he did slowly for the contestants to understand.

"Okay, Sonia! Heh-ha!" Marty announced. "Ready? You're up!"

Sonia wore a mischievous smile. The beautiful executive secretary slowly walked up to the stage. Marty cued the dramatic music to play again.

"Haiiiii-YA!!!!" she hollered out, unleashing an athletic assortment of well-done martial arts moves. "Hai-ya! YA! YA! KAiiiIII!" It was better than anything Herman did. Sonia apparently had training.

"I just...I think I just got a boner," whispered Guy.

Jack nodded. "I had no idea our secretary was a black belt."

The judges immediately gave her all tens. Sonia ended up winning the first Black Elephant game, taking home a Sony Vaio laptop as her prize. As they went into the other games, Diana tugged Cody's arm and reminded him of the remaining time.

"We've got fifteen more minutes!" she warned. "And half the guests are only served soup!"

"Shit. Shit shit shit," Cody murmured.

The games were getting boring. Marty had spent too much time on each of them. Most of the guests had lost interest. Cody walked toward the stage and grabbed the mike from Marty.

"Sorry, everyone," Cody apologized. "We've only got fifteen minutes left."

A collective groan emerged from the tables.

"We're going to have to skip right to the Secret Santa and the gifts left over from the Black Elephant. So if you...hey...wait...stop...STOP!"

It was too late. The guests—mostly drunk—stampeded toward the gift tables, taking whatever gifts they could. Zoey proved to be the most vicious, throwing her little body into the middle of the melee while nabbing presents away from other people.

"Holy shit!" smiled a lucky guest, "a new Playstation 3!"

"Gimme that!" shoved Zoey. "I have a seven-year-old son!"

Jack leaned back at the bar, enjoying the mayhem while sipping his Crown Royal.

"That right there," he pointed at the pandemonium, "is a thing of beauty."

Finally, the party was over. By the time most of the guests had dissipated, the manager of the hotel entered the room aghast at finding the hotel room torn asunder. It was too late for Cody and Marty to completely remove evidence of their rule breaking.

"What is this?!" scolded the manager. "I heard you paid off our staff and used your own?! You...what did you...ooooahhhh! I charged you extra for this! No excuse!"

"I'm not the person in charge," replied Yuki.

The manager stared at her blankly. "Who then?"

She pointed at her friend Cody whom she still had yet to meet in person.

"Hey!" the manager approached Cody. "I heard what you guys did!"

Cody rolled his eyes, plopping his personal credit card into the manager's hands.

"Give your staff a nice gratuity tip," dismissed Cody.

Money solved everything.

To Cody's relief, he discovered the after-party was much better.

Held at the Happy KTV in Chinatown, the karaoke bar featured private rooms that were spacious and, just as important, soundproof. The remaining few from the Christmas party were mostly from Marty's family, but Cody also had his cousin's wife, Wanda, joining him as well his two Internet friends, Yuki and

Rain.

"Why're you feeling bad, man?" Jack asked, plopping a hand on Cody's shoulder.

Cody remained silent, looking at the floor in defeat.

"You want a cig?" offered Jack.

Cody shook his head. He didn't smoke.

"You really need to loosen up," Jack advised.

"The Christmas party was a complete failure," mumbled Cody.

"No, it wasn't, man. Shit, everyone loved the hell out of it."

"Really?"

"Fuck, yeah. I wouldn't lie to you about that. Here, let me get you something to drink. What's your poison?"

Cody finally surrendered. "A Crown and Coke."

"Good shit. Come on, get fucked up like the rest of us and enjoy the night."

Cody walked over and joined the rest of the group. Rain and Herman were having a karaoke showdown.

Herman grabbed the mike and blurted out of tune," jOSiE's On a VaCATion FAr aWaY, cOME iN mY hOuSE and TalK it oVeR. SO mANy tHIngS I LIke tO pLAy, yOU knOw I liKE thOSE gIRls tO bE oLDer..."

"Um, those aren't the exact lyrics," criticized Rain.

Cody approached Yuki and smiled. Finally, they had officially met face-to-face.

"Fancy meeting you here, Ms. Melody Bunny," he smiled.

"You look tired," Yuki observed and smiled. "Are you tired?"

Cody put an arm around her.

"I was tired," he smiled. "Not anymore."

The karaoke waitress entered the room with various drinks. Marty had a Heineken while his wife sipped a margarita. Wanda got herself a gin and tonic. Cody had his Crown and Coke. The rest of them had shots of Grey Goose.

"More! More!" Jack pushed.

It wasn't long before Cody lost count on how many drinks he had. He gave alcohol a rare invitation, allowing it to take over his body and eliminate the night's stress and imperfections. Once again, Jack pushed Herman to exceed his normal threshold. By the time Herman had consumed his twentieth shot, he was drunkenly screaming obscenities at his reflection in the mirrored walls.

"You wanna challenge me?! You wanna challenge me?!" he screamed at himself.

"I love white girls!" cried Guy. "I love them so much!"

The big guy was almost as wasted, unbuttoning his dress shirt and swinging it over his head.

"Woo-hoooooooo!" cheered Rain.

Cody grabbed the nearest female to him: his cousin's wife, Wanda.

"I love you, Wanda," muttered Cody, "you're...hic... my favorite cousin. Cousin-in-law. Hic. Whatever."

He leaned his head on her shoulder and placed his hand on her lap.

"Ew, Cody!" pushed Wanda, "get off me!"

Cody looked at her and continued in his drunken sincerity, "I...mean...I mean if...if it...wasn't...hicc...for your...wedding...Marty and I wouldn't have...met...hicc. And I love him. I love him like my brother. Like he was family."

"Aawwww," nodded Marty who overheard.

Jack wasn't going to let them stop.

"Drink some more! One more time! Come on, assholes!" he continued.

"No more. I drunk I also sleep," Xia replied in her usual broken English.

Herman stopped arguing with his reflection and took additional shots with the others.

"Wimps!" he mocked.

"Fuck you!" cursed Guy. "You were arguing with your own reflection!"

"I'm not...hicc...I'm not...fuck...I...whoa..." Herman muttered.

He crashed to the floor.

"Dude," noticed Yuki, "does he wax his eyebrows?"

In his drunken state, Cody cleared out a large spot on

the table. He stood at the top of it and placed a dollar bill over his eyes.

"I'M DAREDEVIL!!!!!!!" he screamed.

"Aha-eh aha-eh, ah, eh, wa-what?" laughed Marty.

Wanda walked up to Cody and pleaded for his car keys.

"You should let me drive," she insisted. "You're smashed."

"Come on, guys! More drinks!" pushed Jack.

"No!" waved off Wanda. "He's drunk. Cody, let me drive you okay?"

Five hours later, Cody woke up with a massive hangover. He was lying on a bench in the area near his office building in the Sugar Land Town Square. The rare winter snow was still there, but thankfully, the bench was in an area where there was shelter provided by some awning. He admired the beauty of the area; it was well-lit by traditional looking street lamps, intended to re-enact the old Texas towns of yesteryear mixed with a modern touch.

"Morning," came a voice next to him.

Still lying on his back and staring straight up into the dark sky, Cody rolled his eyes up and saw the semi-familiar face of the woman looking down at him. The hangover delayed his recognition, but he was used to seeing her from a low-resolution webcam anyway.

"Yuki," he finally recognized, "I'm sorry I only talked with you for a few minutes tonight."

He made himself sit straight up on the bench.

"What are we doing here?" asked Cody, still disorientated. "Sun hasn't come up yet."

"You don't remember at all, do you?"

"No," he replied, rubbing his eyes. "Who took us here?"

"Your cousin's wife, Wanda. She drove your car. Then she called her husband to pick her up."

"My car! Where is it?"

" *T'inquiète pas*," she replied. "Your car is safely in the parking garage."

"I'll be sure to thank her the next time I see her. God, my head hurts like crazy."

"I'll bet it does. That Jack guy made you guys drink shot after shot."

"And I just passed out?!"

"Um...not necessarily, Cody. Not immediately anyway."

"What do you mean by that?"

"We found out you were a happy drunk. Haha. You strutted around telling everyone that you were 'Daredevil: The Man Without Fear.' You held a dollar bill over your eyes and said that it was your 'mask.' Then you flirted with your cousin's wife."

Cody made a disgusted look with his face. "Who? Wanda?! Ewwww!"

"Yeah. But some of the others did worse. I'm not going to get into details with it, but trying to put Guy's clothes back on was like tackling a rhino. He's ridiculously strong. Hard enough to hold him down when it was mostly the women who were left sober."

"What happened to the guys?"

Yuki sighed, "You guys were such lightweights. All of you were knocked out, except—"

"I know, Jack."

"Actually, no. It was Marty."

"Haha. Marty? What? No way."

"Yes," Yuki replied and paused for a moment. "I noticed something weird about him. Each time you guys were picking up your shot glasses, he subtly poured his drink onto the floor with a flick of his wrist. He did it each time. He was deliberately drinking from an empty cup."

"He probably just wanted to stay sober to drive his wife home safely. What a great guy."

"Maybe. But I think it was something more."

Cody felt a little offended that she didn't trust his new best friend. What did she know? he thought. Cody was the one around him seven days a week. Who was she to come up with conspiracy theories? The nerve of this woman.

"Yeah?" Cody challenged defensively. "I'm sure you're reading too much into it."

"Your friend Mindy thought that way about him too."

"Aw, Mindy's just jealous! She used to be my bst friend, but then she had her twin girls and stopped talking with me. She's just pissed I didn't make her my business partner."

"Let's just say it wasn't only her and I who shared that opinion, okay?" Yuki shrugged. "I'm just looking out for you, Cody."

"Well, you should. You're like a big sister to me," laughed Cody.

Yuki frowned, but then pretended to laugh.

"It wasn't like that was all we talked about, of course," she continued. "I talked with Zoey the most. We're from the same neighborhood in New York. I knew her when she was a kid, you know."

"Wow, really? Small world."

"Yeah, we went to the same church. She was only a teenager back then. Was Duke there at the party? I didn't see anyone that fit his description."

"Nah," Cody replied, "I asked him to come but he gave a resounding no."

Yuki nudged him to get up.

"Come on," she said, "let's walk. I'm a big city girl. I'm tired of sitting down."

They strolled around the area, making a solid trail of footprints in the snowy ground. The scenery felt like a ghost town. Cody had never seen the Sugar Land Town Square so empty before. They headed towards the City Hall building, a pretty piece of architecture reminiscent of ancient Rome. Near the roof of it sat a giant clock with its hour hand pointing to four o'clock.

"So what do you think of Houston so far?" smiled Cody.

"Dull. Flat. Ugly," she replied. "Reminds me of Maryland."

Maryland was the state Yuki was frequently forced to visit because her cousin lived there.

"Everything reminds you of Maryland," Cody said, rolling his eyes.

"That's right," she shrugged. "If there isn't an adequate public transportation system, it's 'Maryland.'"

"But that limits you to only a few places in the world."

"I prefer to think of it as living in only the most ideal of places."

"What's so ideal about New York City?!!"

Yuki stopped and gave him an incredulous look.

"Convenience, interesting people, skyscraper malls and mass transportation! Hello?!" she threw her hands up in the air. "The fact that I never learned to drive suggests higher civilization."

"The fact that you've never learned to drive only suggests you're living in a big city bubble!" laughed Cody.

Yuki was noticeably irked.

"How can you defend Houston?" she asked. "Every city should be like Tokyo! The Japanese have it right. Futuristic thinking for maximum efficiency! When I went there, it was like...like...I didn't want to leave!"

"That's the place that has square watermelons for the price of a steak," dismissed Cody. "Nope, I love it here."

"Hah!"

"I'm serious."

"Why? Again, it's flat and it's boring."

"I grew up in this city, sweetie," Cody said in seriousness. "My home is where my friends and family are. As long as I'm with them, life's interesting. Besides, New York City has its own flaws. It's stinky and dirty. And a lot of people live paycheck to paycheck just to pay for its extravagant cost of living."

"Yeah, but I'm just saying it's more convenient there," Yuki continued. "Look at where we are now. I couldn't get some soda and fries if I wanted to."

"Well, actually there's an IHOP a block down. Don't let the Town Square scenery fool you. Anyway, I bet you were shocked to learn we have a big Asian population here."

Yuki chuckled. "Yeah. That and I kinda expected people to talk like hicks."

"You're joking."

"You think so?"

"Even the Asians?"

"Yeah."

They laughed and suddenly found themselves holding hands. Cody found something alluring about her. Yuki may have been in her forties, but there was a young woman inside. It was evident in the twinkle of her eye and the sincerity of her smile. She would have been a catch in her youth, he realized, perhaps an unfortunate victim of bad relationships. Now age had finally caught up with her. Whatever the reason, this much was certain: her fate as an unmarried person was not her own fault.

"I see us," she began, "and I see two people that get along. We're able to express ourselves, and laugh about it. Isn't that more than what most people have? We should give it a chance."

Her words took Cody to an unfamiliar place; he wasn't used to being pursued by women. The programming in his head wouldn't allow him to believe what he heard. Media and society had once too often drilled into his head that Asian men were unworthy and unwanted. But now that he was confronted with one who cared for him—an Asian-American woman, no less—he surprisingly felt fear. The bartender at the sushi bar all those months ago was right. What he felt as barriers were lies and he made them real by believing in them. But now that he knew it wasn't completely true, why was he scared? Perhaps men are like dogs that chased after things and when they caught them, they didn't necessarily know what to do next. Nonsense, thought Cody. Perhaps he was just scared of commitment. Perhaps—he couldn't really figure it out at the moment. All he could do was reply with what he felt in his heart, saying it in the way taught to him by Daphne Lee.

"Yuki, you're a great person," he began, "but I'm just not in the time of my life where I'm looking for a relationship. Let's just be friends. Friends are forever. We'll be like that TV show *Will and Grace*. You understand that reasoning, right?"

She looked at him in silence, reading his thoughts, knowing that it was a dishonest statement.

"There's always a reason, Cody," she sternly replied.

"But mine is justified."

"Everything can be justified. So...what do you think?"

"Yuki...I'm not sure. My family. They'd..."

She let go of his hands. It was only a few moments of vulnerability, but that was a lot for Yuki. She knew he would never tell her the real reason for not wanting a relationship. She could only guess. Was it really family? Was it distance? Was it her age? It was probably age, she guessed.

"I mean, we've just met," Cody stammered.

"No," Yuki countered, "we didn't 'just met.' We've been talking almost every night for four years. I know what you look like and you know what I look like. We know each other's life story. And now we're just going to pretend like we're strangers?"

"Yes. I mean...well...yes, because we don't know each other in person. Do you have a problem with unpunctual people? Because I have a lateness problem. Do you like sleeping with a blanket on top of your head? Because I fight for covers. We couldn't know these things unless we met face-to-face."

"And I'm willing to put up with all that. How do you know I wouldn't put up with that?!"

"You couldn't even stand getting out of New York for a few days!"

Cody and Yuki looked at each other angrily for a few moments.

"This isn't about that," Yuki said, "and you know it."

"I...I don't know what it's about. Besides...I thought you liked white guys."

Yuki laughed.

"What?" blurted Cody. "It's true, isn't it? Asian guys are nerdy, short, have small dicks and we beat our women. I've heard it all."

"I don't like white guys, Cody. I've always preferred Asian guys. You Asian guys just don't prefer Asian women unless they're supermodels."

"That's not true—"

"The real reason Asian men are single is because they're picky as hell!"

Yuki stared silently, challenging him for a rebuttal. When it became evident he had none, she smirked.

"I'm forty years old, Cody," Yuki continued. "I notice things. I was hoping you'd be different. But it's your choice. Take a while to decide what feels right for you. Just know that at this moment, I offered and you declined."

They paused, enduring the awkward silence.

"I'm sorry I opened up to you," she apologized, looking down.

"Don't be."

"I mean, I'm old enough to be your auntie."

"Come on, you're exaggerating. No, you're not. Your math sucks."

They both laughed. Yuki smiled and shed a lone tear, letting it flow down her right cheek before wiping it with the tips of her fingers.

"Well," she said, pointing toward the hotel, "I'm staying at the hotel over there."

"I should go get my car," Cody said. "Thanks for coming to Houston to see me."

"No problem. Sorry if I criticized your city."

"Yeah, well, I'm sorry that I said New York smells."

They both stayed a bit longer, staring at one another. Cody reached out and gave her a long hug. Lots of thoughts went inside his head. Could he justify walking away from such a good woman? Wasn't this what Daphne did to him? He wished he knew the right answers. Between the hug, he opened his eyes and looked at the restaurant in front of him. It told him part of the reason: Hula Hoop Shakes.

CHAPTER 21: IN THE RED

The start of the new year picked up where the drama had left off. Although Cody and Marty had given the staff two weeks of paid holiday vacation, Sonia ordered the designer girls not to express their gratitude. It was, she explained, their bosses' way of winning them over so that they could take advantage of them in the long run. The girls had unofficially started a union with Sonia as its leader. Now that it was January and her orchestration of Nicky's firing had been successful, it was time for phase two: getting her own friends into the company. Everything was going according to plan until one morning when a new woman approached the front desk.

"Hello," informed the new employee. "My name is April Finley and I'm here for my first day of work."

Bullshit, Sonia thought. So it appeared Cody and Marty had an ace up their sleeves. The imperious secretary loudly smacked her gum, silently looking up and down at April. April was young, beautiful, fashionable and very sure of herself. She was possibly very independent and intelligent as well. Sonia saw fit to initiate immediate removal of this potential competition; this woman might jeopardize her plans.

"Wait just one moment," Sonia commanded.

She stormed over to the conference room where Marty and Cody were meeting with local bank representatives. It didn't matter that she was given explicit instructions not to interrupt them; she entered with authority anyway.

"Wha-uh?" Marty turned around.

"HEY!" Sonia yelled. "WHO'S THE NEW GIRL, HUH? WHY DIDN'T YOU GIVE AN INTERVIEW TO THE FRIEND THAT I RECOMMENDED TO YOU?!"

"Ah ha ha, hush shhhh," Marty put a finger over his lips.

"Sonia," Cody calmly responded, "we're in the middle of an important meeting. We'll talk after we're done, okay?"

"You just discriminated from interviewing my friend who was a perfect candidate with the right experience and credentials! And I know justtttttt the reason!!!........ It's because she's not a pretty girl!"

The bank representatives slightly gasped.

"We will discuss this after our meeting, Sonia," Cody repeated in a firmer voice.

Marty chuckled and shrugged his shoulders at her in an I-don't-know gesture. Sonia remained infuriated. She continued to show her displeasure by staying in the room a few seconds longer before making her way out. When she arrived back to her desk, an unexpected sight further tested her fury; several more new hires were waiting there.

"Hi," one of them said, "we're here for our first day too."

"They're at a meeting!!!" growled Sonia. "Just sit there and wait!"

"But—"

"Hey!" Sonia snapped. "I'm the executive secretary around here! You'll learn to do as I say, got it?"

She ignored the rest of them, gesturing for Patricia and Lydia to put their headphones down and follow her. They immediately obeyed Sonia's orders, making haste as they walked over to the front desk.

"Girls, we're going to lunch," she commanded. "I've got a lot to say!"

"Who are they?" asked Patricia, pointing at the new employees.

"Overspending," Sonia replied.

———

"We got the monnnnney!" sang Cody.

Not long after the girls had gone for lunch, he and Marty were at the local tapioca tea house, toasting their transparent plastic cups like wine glasses. It wasn't an actual victory—they had merely suckered a desperate local bank into giving them a significant loan. It was, however, much needed money nonetheless. In a span of four months they had blown through Cody's retirement funds, Cody's grandfather's life savings, the big loan from Cody's uncle and even an additional fifty grand from Guy and Jack's father. They had only proved so far that they were good at borrowing money.

"Wooo...oh, man, sighhh. I thought Sonia almost ruined it when she interrupted the meeting," Marty admitted.

"Yeah," paused Cody, ".......yeah."

"Mu-hah, we gotta do something about her, you know? Eh? Huh-ha?"

"Damn straight. She's smart. She can calculate how much we spend on their salaries versus how many clients are coming through. She can conclude that we're not doing very well."

"Mm-hmm. Uh, hey, speaking of salaries, Cody. Mmm...eh...sigh, well, the wife's been yelling at me again. I might need to, heh-ha, take an additional paycheck this month."

"Is...everything okay between you and Xia?"

"Sigh, you know...heh....heh heh...no...I mean, I don't want to burden you with it."

"Come on, man, if something's bothering you..."

"Sigh," Marty looked at the floor while slowly shaking his head. "It's just hard on me. I've been sleeping on the couch every night. Last, heh heh, last night she gave me 'the talk'...again!"

"No offense, but your wife's a total bitch!" Cody exclaimed. "You should be firmer with her. Stop letting her run things, man!"

"Sighhhhhhh..." Marty said, looking sad.

"Look, Marty. We were fortunate to get this bank loan. We've recorded loss after loss each month with no signs of improvement. You might have to sacrifice taking paychecks like I've been doing."

Marty's eyes grew wide with fear.

"No...no no no. Wah-uh, no no," he replied. "Can't do that. That's a no. Heh heh. Cody, come on, I have a family to feed. Ah-eh?"

"You have a marriage without children. That's hardly what I would call a 'family.'"

"But we just got this bank loan!"

"Marty," Cody looked at him firmly, "you haven't been getting us a lot of clients. This loan preserves us."

"Huff...sigh..." Marty looked sad. "I'm trying my best."

"Then what's wrong?"

"It's, you know, heh, we take these people's money via contract, then we don't produce finished products. I can't keep giving us new clients when we, heh-ha, you know...you know? Wa-huh? When we don't finish the old projects."

"Well, that's why we've got more employees now. So we can increase production. And April just joined us."

"Yes, I know, I'll have to train her..."

"No. We can't have you spending time training a sales assistant again," Cody explained. "April will have to find her own methods. You go and get us some new clients."

"Come on, can't we take it easy? We just got a bank loan, heh!"

"It's a LOAN, Marty. We have to pay it back someday. Now luckily, I've put together a plan."

Cody opened up a binder and showed him some of the number crunching. They were to use the loan money aggressively, hiring more production people to match sales. Meanwhile, Cody set up new goals for Marty to match.

"Okay," finished Cody, "you said there's a market out there and you're just withholding potential clients from us because we weren't finishing our jobs. Well, now we have the capabilities. Can you meet your new quota?"

"Yes..heh...yeah, heh-ha, of course, yeah. But we...we've really got to get rid of our secretary."

Cody shook his head in disagreement. "Nah. Sonia's got a lot of heart and she does her job. She's just low on morale. We don't need to fire her."

Marty held his breath while looking at Cody. He wanted to tell Cody how much he disliked Sonia's explicit disrespect of him. She intentionally targeted him more than Cody. Perhaps she could change her attitude toward the company, but not toward Marty. He knew when people saw through him, which was what Sonia had done. In time, she would share her opinion on Marty with the new employees. Then they wouldn't respect him anymore. But how could he tell Cody this without losing face?

"Meh-heh," Marty agreed, "yeah, she does her job."

"Yeah, she'll turn around. Especially when she sees you kicking ass in sales!"

"Sure...yeah, wah-uh, I mean, I sure hope so. Mmm-uh, at least she would stop stealing stuff from the office."

"What?!" Cody did a double take. "What do you mean she's stealing stuff?"

"I mean, huh-heh, haven't you noticed we have less rulers and pushpins..."

Cody burst out laughing.

"So she took one or two rulers home," he dismissed. "My mom does the same shit with her factory work. I can't tell you how many staplers I have because of her."

"Wah-er-ahh...well, I mean, heh, that's not all Sonia took, you know? Remember that extra computer we had? Mm-ahhh, eh...no...shhhh...gone."

"Yeah? What about it? Didn't you tell me you took that computer home for your wife?"

"Wha-what?" Marty asked. "I...heh...there goes your memory again, heh."

"No, I'm sure that's what happened. I could ask Xia."

"Oooh! Uh-uh, shhh. Meh-ah, eh? Ahhhhhh...well, ahhhhh...sighhhhh. The truth is complicated, you see, about that computer. Wah-ha, I bought an exact duplicate of it because Xia wanted it, but, heh, I could never give her a company computer. Mmm mmm. No no. But she also doesn't like me using money, so I...heh...you know, heh, ha, I fibbed a little, and said it was the same one from the company."

Cody scratched his head. "So you're saying the extra computer we had since day one has been in our office somewhere the whole time. And the one your wife has is the same model, which you bought with your own money. You hid the original somewhere and somehow Sonia found it and stole it."

Marty smiled and tapped his right pointer finger at the side of his forehead. "Now you're thinking."

"Dude," Cody was skeptical, "are you really sure? Because we'd look like complete asses if we brought that accusation up to her and she's calling us liars."

"Come on, shhh, heh, she'll probably even deny it."

"Look, we're not firing her," Cody repeated. "She cares more about Mosaic Design Studios than our other employees. We just need to channel that intensity and turn it into productivity instead of rebellion. The designer girls listen to her anyway. If we make her happy, then she'll encourage them to be happy."

"Wah-er, arrr, ahh...Cody, heh, uh, come on...she might be too tainted already. Besides, she's a thief. Heh. HA! Enough reason for us to, woo-uh, heh? Ah? You know? Let her go?"

Marty was as nervous as much as he was frustrated. Why was Cody being so stubborn about something so replaceable? It wasn't like lascivious girls were difficult to find to offer a secretarial job to. His insecurities began taking over his thoughts. He wondered if Cody's refusal to let go of her was because she was his pick? Yes, Marty realized, that was the real reason. He wanted to show him up. Maybe she and Cody were secretly working together in an attempt to overthrow him. No...no, he calmed himself down, don't overthink it. He changed his mind; Cody wouldn't do that—Sonia hated him just as much. He quickly searched his thoughts for a way to have his partner agree on letting Sonia go. Something to pull Cody's heartstrings. Yes, Marty suddenly realized, he knew just what to say.

"Phoebe," he winkled. "Ah huh? Heh-eh?"

"What?"

"Er-ah, Phoebe. From Hula Hoop Shakes. The waitress that you're infatuated with."

"How did you know—"

"Mmm shhhh. Shh shh now," Marty smiled proudly. "I have spies all over Hula Hoop Shakes."

"You made the waiters of that restaurant spy on our employees for you?"

"Wah-huh, yeah. I mean, heh, not on any intimate level, of course."

"What else do you do to spy on them?"

"Now now, Cody, we can't have you saying the S-word now...ehhh...eh? EH? We could be in trouble for that..."

"Okay, but they better not find out that you do that, man," Cody insisted.

"Mm-hmm. So, uh-huh, they tell me Hula Hoop Shakes is going to close soon."

Cody's heart sank.

"Really?" Cody asked. "They seem to have good business."

Marty shrugged. "Wah-eh, just letting you know, because Phoebe might not be in your life anymore."

"Man," Cody sighed. "Maybe I can keep in touch with her by text and stuff."

"Ooh-heh, come now, heh-ha! You tried for the last two months. She didn't go to your Christmas party, did she? Heh heh. She never gave you her number and said you guys should hang out, eh? Eh? Ah-ehhhhh?"

"You're right," accepted Cody. "I guess it's over. She was the best part of my week. I'm going to miss her."

"Mm-huh. Too bad she'll be out of a job too."

"No job?" Cody's eyes suddenly widened. Marty had set the trap. "Hey! We could give her a job!"

"Hooooo! Woo-ah! Good thinking!"

"Yeah!" smiled Cody, "I mean, we were talking about that since we first met her, remember?"

"Heh! HA! But that was just you wishing like always."

"Oh, man! Marty, you have to ask her! It'd look too suspicious if I ask her. You do it. Come on!"

"Wah-uh, I don't know, we're already pretty full," Marty sighed. "If only we could, heh, let someone go, you know? Wah-huh-haha!"

"Yeah..." Cody had an epiphany. "We've got way too many new designers just hired. I'm going to let go of one of them and make Phoebe your sales assistant. I'll do the job interview myself! One on one...in a nice restaurant."

"Er, what about Soni—"

"I know just which of the new designers to let go too."

"Ah-heh, I'm sure Phoebe would use her voice well answering phones... "

"Let's do it, Marty! Ask her! Let's give Phoebe a new job as sales!"

Guy's final day came two weeks later; he had to return to school in Chicago for the new semester. He didn't want to leave, and the girls didn't want him to leave either. Besides being a useful guy with brute strength, he was also their informant about Cody and Marty. Sonia had secretly gotten to the big guy long ago, as early as their first week at work. With just a well-timed wink and a teasing view of her cleavage, she had made him loyal to her without him realizing it. It was sad that he had to go, but the girls understood and threw a small party for him in the kitchen room.

"We'll miss you, Guy," Sonia smiled sweetly.

She leaned toward him and gave him what he wanted: a tight body-to-body press with her breasts squashed against him. It made him turn into Jell-O.

"Will you come back and visit us?" asked Patricia.

"I want to, but I don't know, girls," Guy replied sheepishly. "Depends on my dad. He's pretty mad at Marty. He loaned Marty a lot of money because this company almost went broke."

"You don't say?" asked Sonia with a lot of intrigue. "And it's only been a few months."

"Yeah," Guy spilled, "and now all of that's gone and my cousin and Cody just borrowed more money from a bank."

"Oh reaaalllyy?" She paused and stopped Lydia from taking the best piece of cake. "Here, why don't you eat this part of the cake and tell us more about it."

She had him now. Sexual innuendos and food—it was all that took for Guy to pour out the details.

"Aw, this cake is so good," commended the quarterback, "...munch...mmm...I love pineapples. Okay, so yeah...Marty and Cody were stressed...munch...so Cody thinks production is the problem because Marty says he's got a lot of...munch...clients lined up if we...munch...finish the projects."

Checkmate. The smoking gun.

"See, y'all?" Sonia looked at the other girls. "We're probably not going to get paid on time this week. It'll take some time for that bank loan to go through. No wonder Cody switched our paychecks from biweekly to monthly. They're broke! They don't know how to run a company."

"Mmm...yeah, oh, and also," Guy continued, "...munch...my cousin has lingerie photos of you."

Sonia's eyes grew wide. The two designer girls snickered.

Guy flashed a smile. "I mean, wow, I didn't know you were in Maxim, Sonia! It's so awesome having a model in the company."

Sonia's face turned red. Of all the conniving, spying things that Marty was capable of doing, even she didn't expect he would stoop to that level.

"How did he...how did...that asshole...those weren't even published! How did he...?" Sonia was at a loss for words.

"Oh yeah, he also looks at your Facebook page, MySpace, Google Plus...all those things. One time he even typed your name in his Facebook status, mistaking it for the search bar. He had your name as his status for several hours until he noticed it and deleted it."

Guy left her with her thoughts as he felt his phone vibrating in his pocket. When he checked his text and learned that his ride was ready for him, he bid and hugged each of the girls good-bye. They playfully lined up and gave him a salute while he walked past them. He saluted them back. As he was leaving, Sonia had the stereo system play his favorite song: Taylor Swift's "You Belong with Me."

Once he left, Sonia called for a meeting between her and the two designer girls. They needed to discuss what they planned now that they'd received their newly processed information.

"Clearly we have a lawsuit, girls," she explained.

"Oh my God," muttered Patricia, "do you think he looks at our Facebook accounts too?"

"Of course he does. Don't be silly, hon," Sonia replied. "Perverts don't just stop with one woman. We're all in danger. Even the new employees eventually."

"Maybe we should tell Cody," Lydia offered.

"But aren't they friends?" reminded Patricia.

"Not necessarily," Sonia advised. "They're new friends. Did y'all know that Cody and Marty hadn't met until just half a year ago? Maybe we can turn Cody onto our side."

Marty had done Cody a major favor; at least on the surface, it seemed like a selfless act. He had set up a one-on-one dinner interview with Phoebe at a popular hot pot restaurant near his house. Cody relished his first chance at a date with the Hula Hoop Shakes waitress, getting past the job-related topics as quickly as possible before taking in casual conversation. He learned more about her during the first ten minutes than he had in two months from the diner. There were also so many more questions he had yet to ask, starting with why she had so much trouble with chopsticks. He knew she was whitewashed, but no Asian girl was so out-of-touch with her culture that she couldn't even use chopsticks.

"Aaah!" Phoebe screamed, dropping the food on her shirt.

"Here, let me help you with that," Cody said, wiping the food off her like she was a helpless baby. "Maybe we should ask them to give you a bib."

Phoebe laughed. "I had it. It was so close! It was inches away from my mouth!"

"Haha. Seriously, you're going to starve tonight if you keep trying with the chopsticks. Let's...get you a spoon, shall we?"

"No, it's okay," she insisted. "I got this. This is a learning process."

Her answer revealed this much: Behind the multiple piercings, tattoos and wild hair, Phoebe had a scholar's determination to learn. And, more so, there wasn't a hint of malice in her. She was a peacemaker, a neo-hippie with an egalitarian hope for the world. When the subject of her favorite city was brought up, the girl sat up with her heavy mascara eyes wide open.

"Portland," she beamed, "is where I want to eventually be. It's a wild place, man. The bands in the Aladdin Theater, the breweries on Distillery Road, the indie restaurants, pot..."

The subject of marijuana made him flinch. He should've expected it, though—her outer appearance did fit the stereotype. Then again, maybe it was a sign that she had gotten so comfortable, she had forgotten it was still a job interview. With that thought in mind, Cody reminded himself to look at her resume.

"Bowie," he read aloud, "your last name is Bowie?"

"Yeah. I know. Meh. I have a stupid name. Phoebe Bowie. I hardly say it in its entirety."

"No, no", laughed Cody. "I just didn't know that you were married."

"Married—? Oh no! No...ha ha. I'm adopted!" She twirled one of her chopsticks around. "That's why I don't know how to use these."

"Yeah, it all makes sense now actually."

He scooped some food from the boiling pot and offered it to her. Once he got around to looking closely at Phoebe from the table light, he realized she was probably just above legal age—much younger than he presumed. Perhaps just a kid who waited tables and went to school.

"People think it's great to be an orphan," she said with a distant stare in her eyes, "but you can never take away the fact that you were unwanted."

She took one of the chopsticks and twirled it around the hot pot sauce. They stayed silent for a few moments before she realized her comment might have depressed her new employer.

"But you know," Phoebe smiled and continued, "my adoptive parents have been wonderful. I didn't even come to the States until I was three."

"Really? Were you living in Korea?"

"No...haha. I was in Hong Kong. Didn't you say that's where you're from, Cody?"

"That's where my parents are from. I was made in the U.S.A.," he corrected proudly.

"Such a shame," Phoebe muttered, picking up a few raw pieces of beef and stuffing them into the boiling pot.

"W-why's that?"

"I always thought it'd be cooler to be born in an exotic land."

"Hong Kong's not an exotic land, Phoebe."

She shrugged. "Meh. More exotic than St. Louis, Missouri where I'm from. That's why I occasionally just tell people I'm from Hong Kong."

"Oh yeah?" laughed Cody, "how would anyone believe you if you couldn't mutter a word of Cantonese?"

"I can say something in Cantonese."

"Really?"

"Yeah," she smirked.

"Say something."

"<Hi, my name is Phoebe Bowie and if I'm ever lost, my parents live in 29 block C suite 5078 at Tsim Sha Tsui.>"

"Hahahahahahaha!"

"That's...all I can say in Cantonese. My parents taught me to say that when I was a kid," she grinned. "I've no idea what the individual words mean, but overall it tells them where my address was in Hong Kong."

"You're charming," Cody complimented her. "You'll do well in sales under Marty."

They took a pause in their conversation to order more shiitake mushrooms, raw chicken meat and napa cabbage. Giving the chopsticks one more try, Phoebe attempted to grab a piece of shrimp. Her clumsy attempt was noble, but ultimately futile—she ended up dropping her entire left chopstick into the pot.

"Dang it! I'll never get this right!" Phoebe shook her head.

"Patience. Practice," Cody advised, using one his chopsticks to fish out her dropped one. "That's the secret to mastering everything."

"You seem like a good teacher," she complimented, prematurely grabbing the hot chopstick too quickly. "Ow! Hot!"

"Well, you'll be under Marty anyway. I'm sure you'll pick up sales well."

Phoebe cooled her hand by grabbing her glass of ice water. "And what do you do?"

"Ah, you wouldn't want my job. It's boring. I stare at the computer all night long, sorting through code."

"You know, I've always wanted to program. I was good at it in school."

"I hate it. It's an introverted job."

"Meh, people-person jobs are so overrated. If it was up to me, I'd never want to put on a fake smile and serve people again. I dunno...I...I hate my waitressing job. It sucks. I've always dreamed of a desk job. You'd make my day if I ever got the chance. I'll work so hard for you guys. Really. I'm a fast learner. Can you teach me how to code instead?"

He couldn't imagine a beautiful girl like her sitting behind a desk all day sorting through lines of HTML. What a waste of her natural Korean beauty—she had a gorgeous slim, olive-skinned and toned body, he thought. It was shallow to think so, of course, and he realized maybe he had been seeing her wrong the whole time. Phoebe had an underrated intelligence to her and perhaps it was time someone took notice.

"Okay," Cody finally agreed, "but I gotta warn you, we don't pay much and you'll have to come every day for two weeks to learn from me."

"Anything," she smiled. "Does that mean I get to sit next to you and work?"

"Certainly," he replied, feeling butterflies in his stomach.

After their hot pot dinner, Phoebe let Cody give her a nightly tour around town. They drove through midtown, the medical center, City Centre, the museum district and, finally, the Sugar Land Town Square. She shuttered with anticipation as their elevator transported them up to the second floor where Mosaic Design Studios was. Her first office job, he realized, and he didn't even tell her she was hired. After Cody flipped on the switch, she squealed with delight as she skipped around the office like an excited child. Cody showed her the parts of the office.

"Here we have the kitchen," explained Cody, "and beyond that are the designers' desks. I do have someone coding with me right now, but she's about to go into labor at any time, so her desk will be free for you. Also—"

He looked back and saw Phoebe staring out the window. She was looking at the Hula Hoop Diner from across the street. Cody put a hand on her shoulder and looked at it with her. She leaned a little closer towards him.

"I used to look at you sometimes from out this window," he admitted, "...sorry if that came out creepy."

"Meh," Phoebe replied, "I'm just glad I won't be working there anymore."

It didn't take long for Sonia to implement her plan. She decided to unleash it on Valentine's Day, when the girls got flowers and her employers received a letter from her attorney. The courier came at noon, just after the workers had left for lunch. With the exception of April and Phoebe, the rest of them were loyal to Sonia now, joining her for daily lunches at the recently opened hibachi grill.

"Fuck," cursed Cody. "That bitch. Did you read the whole letter?"

Marty nodded while crunching his fried chicken and drinking his venti-sized frappuccino. He had a knack for eating foods that would greatly increase his risk of diabetes.

"Mmm, eh-ah, I told you," Marty agreed. "She's trouble, heh-ha."

Cody pounded his fists together.

"I can't wait until they get back. I'm going to have an immediate meeting and hold everyone accountable! Everyone!"

"Weh-ah, I can't make it. I have an appointment with April to meet our latest client. Guess what her last name is? Heh. Ha!...haha...it's Bigg Decks."

Cody wasn't amused. "Man, this isn't the time for sophomoric humor. We have a lawsuit on our hands. They weren't specific on the complaints though."

Marty looked at the letter again and grew a little worried. It occurred to him as to what Sonia might be referring to.

Cody continued ranting. "I mean, it says that they were working in a 'hostile and sexually inappropriate environment.' Geez, all you did was look at their Facebook accounts and found Sonia's Maxim photos. They're making a mountain out of a molehill."

Marty felt a lump in his throat.

"Wuh-ah, now now shhh heh, you might, eh, you might hear Sonia embellish some more things later on, Cody, but I assure you that when you hear them, she's making them up."

Cody gave his best friend and business partner a quizzical look.

"What...do you mean by that, Marty?"

"Shhh shhh, heh, ha!"

"Stop doing that stupid laugh, Marty. Is there something you aren't telling me?"

Before Marty could answer, April entered the office and urged Marty to head out. They were planning to carpool towards the Pearland area.

"Now now, wah-eh, remember not to believe anything they say, heh!" Marty reminded Cody once more before leaving.

He sat alone in the empty office, wondering what Marty cryptically meant. Forty-five minutes later, to his bewilderment, Sonia returned alone from her lunch break. Perhaps this was better, thought Cody, he could direct all his rage toward her instead of all the employees. He waited until she sat down at her desk before calling her. Knowing it was Cody, the rebellious secretary allowed the phone to ring until he gave up. They stared at one another through his office window. Cody slammed the phone down and made his way over to the front desk.

"Yes?" Sonia sarcastically asked.

"We've received your attorney's letter."

"Oh, good. It was planned that way. We told the courier the exact time."

Cody pulled over a chair and sat across from her. She looked like the boss and he, the lowly employee. How were things allowed to get this way?

"Sonia," he asked, "where's everyone? Why didn't they return from lunch?"

"Oh. I just gave them the day off," she shrugged, turning her attention toward Facebook.

"Haha...you what? You? You gave them the day off? Who the HELL do you think you are?!" shouted Cody, slamming his hand on her desk.

Sonia displayed a momentary expression of shock. She was not expecting him to stand his ground. Taking a moment to collect herself, she resumed her defiant attitude.

"I turned us into a union," she announced. "Not an official one, of course. But real enough that you'll have to follow our demands."

"Demands? What is this? Blackmail?" scoffed Cody.

"No!" she stood and looked angrily at him. "Protection. Protection against HIM."

That last statement confused Cody. "Who?"

"You know who!"

"Marty?"

"Yes!"

Cody was confused. He thought that between him and Marty in the good-cop-bad-cop roles, he was the bad cop. Now he realized the girls weren't mad at him. But what did Marty do?

"Come on, all he did was stalk your Facebook," concluded Cody. "And yeah, he found your Maxim submissions too. You'll have to forgive him. Sure, he was wrong, but he doesn't mean anything from it. I'll get him to apologize, okay? We don't need to get drastic and take this to court."

Sonia stared directly at him and let out a derisive laugh.

"Hah! Hahahahaha, " she laughed. "You think that's what this lawsuit's about?"

"Yeah. That and we didn't give your friend a chance to take over Nicky's vacancy. But I think April is doing a dandy job at sales, don't you?"

"Yeah," agreed Sonia. "You're right. April's good. Real good. She's cool...I admit I felt a bit threatened at first, but she's not exactly Marty's lapdog either. She's independent, but not a rival. I admire that."

She removed a tube of ChapStick between her breasts and moisturized her lips. Then she placed it back in between her breasts.

"What?" she asked, irritated that Cody was staring.

"I've kept you here because I stood up for you, Sonia. But this is crossing the line. You are so fired. Leave this office. Now."

Sonia remained sitting and smirked instead. Her beauty

no longer stunned Cody. It hadn't for awhile, but now she was at her utmost peak of unattractiveness. She was evil. No doubt she had planned this coup for a long time.

"Leave!!!" Cody repeated.

"No. I want Marty to come back and tell me to leave. Then I'll leave," she grinned. "But you know what? I bet he won't. He's afraid to hurt people's feelings. He thinks he's some kind of gentleman that cares about people's emotions. He loves to play victim. 'Oh poor Marty. Poor, poor Marty.' Hahahaha."

She stood up and walked over to Cody, pinching him on the left cheek.

"Look, Cody," she said, "the girls and I have nothing against you. In fact, I knew Marty wouldn't be here because I saw his schedule. But you've made a horrible mistake by choosing him as your business partner."

"You're out of line for saying that."

"I'm telling you something that you're too blind to see."

Cody paused and then asked, "What did he do?"

"Well, Cody darling, when you're not around," she continued, "he has made some...let's just say....advances at some of us. He had some disturbing requests for me and the other girls."

"You're lying," denied Cody. "He's in love with his wife. He wouldn't do that."

"Oh?" shrugged Sonia. "I've got a whole group of girls here who are more than willing to swear in court that he has. And you know Lydia wouldn't lie. Or Patricia. Or......Nicky."

"Nicky? Nicky was fired months ago."

"We've kept in touch," Sonia assured him. "He likes blondes a lot."

Sonia picked up her purse and pulled out a box with most of her belongings. It appeared she had been planning to leave Mosaic Design Studios for some time.

"I'll make it real clear," she concluded. "If you lose him as your partner, we'll stay and drop the lawsuit. If you keep him, not only will you lose most of your staff, but we'll be suing you guys too. After all, you guys just secured a large sum of money from the bank, I heard. This isn't about you. It's about him. Make the right choice."

Satisfied, Sonia picked up her stuff and left the office. Cody was alone again.

"Choose my company or choose my best friend," Cody repeated to himself.

Sexual harassment.

His head was telling him something that disagreed with his heart. Mosaic Design Studios making it big was stubbornly still in his hopes. They had every possible opportunity to succeed; why would Marty do something so careless to prevent that? Where was there to go back to? A dingy office job with a meager retirement fund? Sonia had to be lying, she had to. He paced around the empty office trying to convince himself of it. However, her body language and tone suggested she was too sure, too confident that what she claimed transpired actually happened. And what about Lydia and Patricia? They were saints and they claimed it happened too.

Those thoughts were still sticking with him three hours later when Marty came back, laughing and recalling funny incidents from his meeting. His humor charmed Cody enough that he ended up dismissing the incident with Sonia and keeping it a secret from Marty. This was his best friend, he realized, and friends give each other the benefit of the doubt. He decided to take on Sonia's lawsuit, choosing to defend Marty to the bitter end.

CHAPTER 22: THE EMO SAVIOR

After Cody's decision to stick with his best friend, a series of consequences occurred. Sonia followed through on her sexual harassment lawsuit, costing the company both a loss in staff and a chunk of their recent bank loan. The remaining finances for the company were only enough for the rest of the 2010 summer. With each monthly loss worse than the prior one, Marty had exhausted his excuses for the diminishing sales. Even his usual remedy of changing the subject and giving off a hearty chuckle didn't smooth things over with Cody.

Such as they were, there were still thanks to be given; at least, the company had one last chance to survive. The staff wasn't much, but the core components remained. April, now two months pregnant by her new boyfriend, assumed a less physically mobile role as the new secretary. Much to everyone's surprise, Lydia stayed, perhaps to ensure that she was the only one to see her designs to completion. And Phoebe, once the least skilled, had grown leaps and bounds as a web developer. Their loyalty should've been enough to make their final push over the summer worth it. At least, thought Cody, the girls were owed a debt of gratitude from him and Marty for their work ethic and faithfulness.

"Ah heh heh, ah heh ha, bye everyone!" Marty waved from his desk as the girls left the office.

Marty had made this statement on a mid-May afternoon, but it could've been any afternoon, which was what frustrated Cody about his business partner. His demeanor and attitude hadn't changed since day one, when he gave everyone the rest of the day off and left for tennis. A disturbing thought began swimming inside of Cody's head. Perhaps Marty wasn't either malicious or a mad genius—perhaps he was just not a very bright person. Oh sure, Cody realized, Marty may have consistently shown signs of cleverness when it came to manipulating people, but it was usually for shortsighted gains rather than for a bold, grand plan. It was the first time an opinion like that had crept inside of Cody's mind; it was the first time he had seriously doubted his best friend.

"So," Cody leaned forward in his chair after the wave-off. "What do we do now? Any large clients? Does your uncle have any more money to contribute to us? How about another loan from another bank? Maybe we could both put our houses up for sale."

His intention for that last statement was for sarcastic effect; instead, Marty took it seriously and agreed with it.

"Wuh-ah, you know," smiled Marty, "I was just thinking of that. My mom says she can sell her house and move in with Xia and me."

Leaning forward in his chair, Cody gave his best friend an expression of disbelief.

"Gee. I'd really appreciate the sacrifice your mother would make on our behalf, but I would hate it if it came down to that."

"Sigh," Marty expressed, "I know. But, ffft, we would do it. Even if Xia and my mother don't get along very well."

"No one gets along with that high-maintenance wife of yours very well."

"Huh, wah-er, I..."

As if on cue, Marty's phone rang: Xia, read the caller ID. Cody sat and stared at Marty while his wife gave him an earful over the phone.

"<Yes, huh>," he answered, "<oh...oooh, yeah, she, heh, she really shouldn't have called you that word at work...mmm-huh, mmm-huh...ah, wuh, eh, heh...well, I mean, we already have two poodles...uh, yes, sorry, I mean, heh, HA...of course we can have another little dog...sorry, ah-wuh, I...no, I didn't mean to...I didn't...no, we can have a third dog...mmm-ah, paycheck's coming soon...eh...wuh...no, no...please don't hang up...please...huh...heh...ah-meh, please no!>"

She ended the call. In a rare fit of displeasure, Marty displayed a natural reaction of anger.

"That...that BITCH!" Marty screamed.

"Damn, dude, you really shouldn't be calling your own wife a bitch. I mean, it's cool if others do it because she is one, but you shouldn't as her husband."

"Wuh...sighhhh..."

"What? You have to go?"

Marty nodded with a sad puppy face.

"Will she be at home when you get there?" asked Cody.

"No...she...I mean, sigh, there's this guy from her work she now spends time with. She, mm-heh, she wants me to feed our two poodles and have dinner ready for her when she gets, heh, home. Heh-ah."

Cody looked at him with intrigue. How could a man be so whipped? "Damn. That's kinda cold how she treats you."

"Sighhhh," expressed Marty, "I don't know. Gah-eh, huh ha ha, I don't think our marriage can survive if I go home for another month without a paycheck. Heh. Please, Cody, please. Loan me some more of your personal money."

This conversation again, realized Cody.

"Man, look, Marty, you're my friend and you don't have to pay back the money that I've given you, but I'm almost broke now. I've nothing more to give you, dude. I haven't even paid my own mortgage in months, you understand? You're going to have to save us through sales. It's the only way."

"But how?" Marty asked. "How am I going to get sales? Wuh-heh-heh?"

"How are you—?" Cody couldn't believe he heard Marty say that. "Listen, I don't know anything about sales. But you've got to try. This is your strength. It's what you assured me that you did well."

"Sigh..."

"There are no more saviors," Cody continued. "We've used up all of our lifelines. My uncle from Hong Kong...Guy and Jack's dad...the bank loan...all of it is almost gone. Mosaic Design Studios has three more months to get its act together. At some point, we have to save ourselves."

Marty reacted with more pouting noises. "I...I mean, heh, we don't finish our projects...we, mm-ah, we keep taking people's money first. It just stacks up the workload more and more."

"Yes, but we're going to need to keep getting new clients so that our own employees can get paid. Otherwise, we can't catch up."

"Yeah, I mean, heh...sighhhhh." Marty wanted to disagree and express his opinion, but he was afraid of hurting Cody's feelings or starting a fight. "You're right. You're right, man."

Cody gave him a quizzical look.

"Are you sure I'm right?" he countered Marty. "It's okay to speak your mind, you know."

"Wah-eh, well..."

"Okay, so you do have a conflicting opinion. Spill."

"Mah-uh. No no. Shhh. No no, heh. HA!" Marty was nervously shaking. "Don't pressure me, man. Mmm...ffft..."

Cody grew tired of his mind-reading games. "You think getting new clients will only increase our workload, right? You're worried that it'll be like Tetris and we'll stack and stack until we get in trouble. Is that it?"

"Hey, heh, you said it, not me!" laughed Marty. "You can't quote me on that. No no. Hush hush. Shhhhh."

"Well, I wish we had one more savior, but we don't. So..."

As he mentioned the word 'savior,' Marty had a sudden epiphany.

"Mm-wuhhh!" He raised a finger. "There, heh, there is someone! Heh...HA!"

Cody squinted his eyes and looked at Marty. "You're telling me that you know someone who would give us a shitload of money and save our company? Is...is that what you're telling me?

"You said it, not me!"

"What do you mean?" asked Cody. "You're the one who just said it, I heard you."

"Now now, Cody. Now now. Revisionist history, heh hah hehhh."

"Stop the bullshit! I just heard that you said you know someone who might invest in our company. Who is it?!"

"Really?!" Marty exclaimed. "Well, that's a good question, heh, mmm-ahhh. You're asking me if I may know someone. Good idea."

"The fuck—"

"It was your idea."

"Did I really?" Cody was confused. "Okay, maybe I brought it up first. I don't remember anymore. Anyway, do you know anyone that can help us or not?"

"Hmmmm, wa-uh, there IS someone, in fact."

"Who? God damn it, Marty...don't make me keep asking!"

Marty cleared his throat. "Wang's Restaurant."

The mere mention of the most successful Chinese restaurant in Houston's history made Cody spring up from his leather chair.

"What do you mean?" demanded Cody. "The Chinese restaurant where all the celebrities go to? The one that's internationally known from Houston? Those guys are loaded."

Marty smiled and nodded.

Cody laughed with joy. "You know Mr. Wang?! That guy's super rich!"

"Wah-ehhh, heh, well, ahhh, hmmm, heh. Heh. HA! Haha! Hoo. Ffttt."

"Is he a family friend of yours or something?"

Marty nodded.

"Dude, I...why didn't you mention it before?!" Cody realized. "Let's ask him for financial help! We'll give him partial ownership of the company. Tell him we've got over several hundred clients. Tell him we're doing well and that we need money to...to expand!...yes...that's a good reason. Whatever it is, ask him! He's insanely rich. Everyone in Chinatown knows Mr. Wang. I...I can't believe you know the guy."

Marty loosened his tie a bit; he needed to tell Cody the catch.

"Er, hmmm, heh, ahhh...well, it's...I mean, I'm not that close to Mr. Wang. I, heh, I'm actually just close with his son. We knew each other from a martial arts school when we were kids. Heh hah heh. Mr. Wang, eh, he's very disappointed in his son because, mm, his son doesn't, heh-eh, wanna follow in his footsteps!"

"That's even better!!!" exclaimed Cody. "We'll make his son the partner then!"

"Good idea!"

"What do you mean? It was your idea. How can it be my idea? I didn't even know this son of his existed."

"Huh? What were we talking about? Muh-eh?"

"We were talking about anointing Mr. Wang's son as a third partner if he financially supports us. We'll let this son dip his toes in responsibility and learn how to manage a company! I mean, he's a rich guy's kid, right? I figure he's our age, right? Probably spoiled as hell."

"That's a good idea! Remember, you thought of it!"

"I...what?...stop doing that psychological mindfuck!"

"Huh? Wah-uh? What are we talking about?"

"About making this rich man's son our business partner in exchange for financial help," explained Cody.

"Good idea!"

"Really?"

"Heh, yeah!"

"I know! I must've thought of it...I don't know how it got into my head...I..."

"Let's do it! Wah-huh, you're a genius, Cody!"

"I am!" He was too excited to care about who took credit.

A week later, unfortunately, Mr. Wang agreed to only the unwanted portion of their proposal. The infamous owner hastily accepted bringing his son in as a third partner; however, he refused to offer any financial help. Free labor, Mr. Wang insisted, was value in and of itself. Knowing that it wouldn't be enough incentive, the restaurant tycoon also dangled a grand financial reward—should Marty and Cody manage to do the impossible and prove that his son could responsibly run a company, he would offer to give them one million dollars in support.

Cody found out just how daunting their task was the day Wilbur Wang was brought in. Similar in age to both him and Marty, the overindulging adult child immediately showed his spoiled and high-maintenance side. Sharing wasn't something he knew—not in the partnership and not in the nature of the business. Rather than continue Mosaic Design Studios as a company that made websites, Wilbur demanded that it transform itself into a venture for promotional events.

Ever the neutral party, Marty muttered half-agreements and half-defenses. Cody, on the other hand, couldn't decide what he disliked more about Wilbur—the spoiled brat's obstinacy or his coddled prissiness and constant stuttering. Indeed, he had not met a more conscientious metrosexual. Considering Wilbur's well-maintained and deliberate bed-head hair, subtle use of eye shadow, perfectly moisturized skin, skinny jeans and carefully plucked hairless face, Cody didn't know whether to punch him or kiss him. He was irresistibly pretty, evidenced by the swooning reactions of the female employees. Meanwhile, his Filipina-American girlfriend, Rosie de Rosales—who also came to the meeting—was the epitome of masculinity. She was assertive, crass, vocal, bossy and openly competitive. In addition to the aforementioned traits, she was also physically well-toned, square-jawed and indifferent to fashion, and sported a short-cropped haircut that would fit better on Jack or Herman. Together, the paradoxical couple combined for an overbearing vexation of oppressiveness.

This, along with Cody's lack of an upper hand, resulted in his reluctance to try Wilbur's direction. Without further ado, everyone was mandated to show up for the meeting, including Herman and Jack.

"Alright, everyone," Cody began, handing out copies of the meeting's bullet points, "as you can see to my left, we've got a new member today. This is Wilbur Wang, our new...uh... director of marketing. We're changing the identity of our company to focus on promotions and catering. Marty suggested that we try building retainers as well. These are incomes that we can receive from restaurants and clubs on a monthly basis. Wilbur will be a vital part of our company by helping us establish this direction."

"What about websites?" Lydia asked.

"Yes. We—"

Rosie shoved herself into the forefront and interrupted, "You guys will only be doing design and websites for Wilbur's promotional events."

Cody could hardly contain his displeasure of being cut off in mid-conversation. Who did Wilbur's girlfriend think she was by interrupting? he wondered, she wasn't even a part of the company.

"No," countered Cody, "there are unfinished sites we still have to do. We're still going to be doing websites."

"L-L-Look," stuttered Wilbur, "y-y-you brought m-m-me in here to h-h-help you g-g-guys out. S-s-so we d-d-do this my way!"

"No," Cody repeated, "maybe you misunderstood. Again, we're still a web company but now we'll have a promotional.......side.......to it."

"T-t-this w-w-wasn't the d-d-deal, man!" Wilbur said with an accusing finger.

They both looked at Marty for his opinion on the matter.

"Wah-uh, ahhhhh...mmm...Wilbur has a point, heh," Marty nodded. "And Cody has a point too."

"The hell does that even mean?" Cody wondered out loud.

"God, you people are morons," Jack blurted, leaving the meeting room. "I'm heading out for a smoke."

Marty watched his cousin go without stopping him. "Heh-hmm, ah, heh, you know, heh heh, maybe we can share the staff."

"I wouldn't mind helping Wilbur," answered Lydia sweetly.

"Yeah," added April, "this party promotion thing sounds fun!"

The rest of the staff chimed in their favorable opinions about doing party promotions. Cody found it unbearable that his dream company was suddenly turning into Mosaic Wilbur Wang Party Promotions. He looked at Marty for help, but Marty was busy chuckling instead. Cody felt annoyed. Shouldn't Marty be on his side? Weren't they the best of friends? And why was he no longer surprised if the answer to both of those questions were "no"?

The transfer of power had already been completed by the time the meeting was over. It was manifested in the way the staff overwhelmingly welcomed and unquestionably obeyed any request from Wilbur and Rosie. It was further exhibited when the Mosaic Design Studios sign was taken down and a "Rawr Means I Love You in Dinosaur" sign was temporarily put up in its place.

"What the hell is happening?" commented Cody to Marty. "Didn't you just feel like our company got hijacked?"

"Heh heh, ahhhh, he's such a douche," agreed Marty.

"'Such a—,' dude, if that's how you felt the whole time, why didn't you stand up to him and She-Hulk?"

"Sighhhh. It's, heh, it's...I mean, what was I supposed to do, heh-ah?"

"I don't know! Maybe back me up when I'm defending our company? Show some spine?"

Marty nervously chuckled and shrugged. "I, heh ha ha, I'm doing my best, Cody! Maybe, meh-eh, he took the 'third partner' part a little too literally."

"That's what we said, didn't we? We told him 'third partner,' not 'sole dictator.' Man. I felt like we just exchanged Sonia for this guy! When is it our turn to be the bosses of our company?"

Regardless of Cody's fears, the company responded to the new direction with paramount enthusiasm. In less than a week, the now nameless company—temporarily referred to as Rawr Means I Love You in Dinosaur Promotions—had procured its first client: a jazz and sushi lounge called Purple Wasabi. The owner, an impassionate Cantonese entrepreneur named Roy, spared no expense in making the place a grand exhibition. He expected Purple Wasabi to achieve the triple crown of restaurant ownership: nightly packed parties, exemplified culinary delights and, above all, maximum profiteering. Unlike Mr. Wang, however, Roy was not wealthy, but he had so much confidence in his sushi lounge that it was worth gambling away his life savings.

Marty provided the man with every bit of empathy he could muster. It was almost a little too easy. By speaking to Roy in his native tongue and fitting the profile of someone he'd trust, Marty negotiated highly favorable opportunities for Wilbur to appear competent. Of course, the rewards were beneficial to his goals as well and it only made sense to go where his new bread was buttered. If the situation with Purple Wasabi made Wilbur look good, the million dollars his father offered was just three months away. And by then, who needed Cody?

He put all these thoughts aside while the three partners waited for Roy in his restaurant's private meeting room. The room was very well-decorated, luxuriated in the wealthy Hong Kong tradition: giant golden fu dogs, egg-shaped jadeite pieces, figurines of Cai Shen the God of Wealth, elaborately designed fish tanks filled with a thousand gold fish, and a beautiful scroll with four characters that read, in order, "Good Fortune," "Wealth," "Longevity, " and "Happiness." The owner entered with a small entourage—all from his hometown of Hong Kong, of course.

"<I am so glad to meet you guys>," Roy warmly greeted them. "<We Cantonese brothers need to stick together. Look around you. Look at all my employees. All Cantonese. Even the busboys. Hell, even these chairs and tables are made from Hong Kong!>"

Cody and Wilbur looked around their chairs, expecting to find a "Made in Hong Kong" label.

"<Muh-heh, of course, of course>," nodded Marty. "<Heh, if you can't trust your own people, who can you trust? Eh eh?>"

"<Yes>," Roy smiled, "<so happy that you feel what I feel. See what I see.>"

Marty smiled like a puppy dog. "<Wah-eh, you are my brother, Roy.>"

"<Cantonese brothers. For life.>" Roy shook his hand firmly. "<So, let us discuss what you have proposed in agreeable terms.>"

They reviewed giving Wilbur complete control of the event operations, with all external costs provided by Roy himself. The low monthly residual to their company, however, revealed an uncharacteristic stingy side of Roy. He was willing to spend thousands on deejays, photographers and go-go girls, but for the use of their company's services, he offered merely five hundred dollars. Cody immediately saw it as a red flag.

"How are we surviving with this guy?" he asked Marty the next afternoon in their office. "He's barely enough to pay for the printer toner."

"Meh-huh, ehhh." Marty thought about the situation as if contemplating it for the first time. "You're right, I didn't think of that. Heh. You know me. Heh heh heh! I suck at math!"

"What are you—your head in the clouds?" Cody expressed. "Get us some website jobs! We're bleeding all of our leftover money! I haven't paid my mortgage in months!"

"Sighhhhhh." Marty sadly looked at the floor. "I'm trying to, heh, make Wilbur happy. Wasn't that our goal? Meh-eh, wasn't that what you told me to do?"

Cody held back; Marty's point made sense. It was a million dollars or bust.

"Yeah," he nodded, "but what about our immediate survival? How do you know Roy's going to pan out? He gives a good spiel about being Cantonese brothers and all, but I wish he'd back it up with money!"

"Now now now, shh hush hmm-eh," Marty shushed as he checked to make sure their office door was closed. "I...I got us a plan, mm-heh."

"Oh, yeah?!" Cody chewed on the eraser of his pencil. "Tell me this plan, Marty. Does it involve us? Our original vision? Do you know that Wilbur is overriding all of my orders to the staff? They haven't been doing any of our work for days! They've been making his personal portfolio and website. They've been doing strictly Purple Wasabi stuff."

"Wooo, fffft, yeah, heh, that's bad," agreed Marty, "but isn't that what we wanted?"

"They're under the impression that Wilbur is the most important person in this company!!!" Cody said, overreacting. "And what if Mr. Wang sees our numbers and realizes Roy has ripped us off for half a grand a month? You think he's going to be impressed with Wilbur doing that? That's not leadership we're proving, that's foolish cheap labor!"

Marty paused and contemplated whether or not he should tell Cody something he didn't know. Cody knew him long enough to recognize that look.

"You know something more," he accused Marty. "What is it?"

"Er-ah...well...there's a big payoff coming from Roy."

Cody sat on the edge of his chair. It was starting to become a normal thing for him to do when talking with Marty. "What 'big payoff?'"

"Bluefin Tuna Night."

"...what's that?"

Marty took an unnecessary deep breath and then explained the concept of the Bluefin Tuna Night. Roy was planning to import a rare and expensive tuna straight from Japan. It would be gathered fresh from Asia, delivered to Houston in under twenty-four hours. This naturally made it exceptionally expensive, but also unique. Where else in Texas could anyone eat bluefin tuna?

"So you see, heh," Marty continued explaining. "Roy wants to make it a fancy suit and tie event."

"Charging several hundred dollars a person for V.I.P. and seventy-five for regular seats," said Cody, making the calculations on paper. "That's...that's a hell of a lot of money if he sold out."

Marty smiled and nodded.

"So how much did he say he'd give us in sales commission?" asked Cody.

"Well, er, ahhh, hmmm, it's, heh, it's not nice to bring up an exact negotiation amount when we were planning," Marty protested.

"You mean you didn't set a price and agreed to do it anyway?!!"

"Now now, Cody, shh shh, wah-eh, Roy doesn't work like that. He puts his trust in us and if we do well he'll, heh, he'll take care of us after the event is over. Besides, it doesn't matter as long as Wilbur looks good."

"No, this is business," countered Cody. "Enough of this brotherhood crap. We've got two months left or we die as a company. We need an exact amount to pay the employees, pay off rent and other expenses. I know the figure. It's fifteen thousand dollars. That's how much commission we get from Roy or else we take our talents elsewhere. He signs a contract or else."

With that said, Cody started dialing the number to Purple Wasabi. Marty immediately ran up to him and wrestled the phone away from his partner.

"What are you doing?" Cody struggled. "I'm telling Roy he has to sign a contract!"

"No...no...please...Cody...heh...ah-weh...ahh...don't...ehhh..."

Cody hung up.

"What else are you hiding from me?" he demanded from Marty. "Why were you so afraid I'd make that phone call?"

"Heh-ahhhh, nothing, no, I mean, he doesn't answer the restaurant line. Eh?" Marty smiled. "Look, I'll, heh, I'll just text his cell and tell him about it!"

Cody eyed his partner suspiciously—he had heard someone mention once that business partnerships were like a marriage. If that were so, they were on the edge of divorce because Cody didn't trust him. Ever since Sonia's warning, he had begun seeing Marty in a different light. As much as he didn't want to believe it, she was right about Marty's motives and nervous laughter seeming suspect. Now he was wondering if there was more going on than he was told. Perhaps adding

Wilbur as a partner had been planned all along. To ensure protection in their next meeting at Purple Wasabi, Cody surprised everyone by pulling out a contract in front of Roy.

"<What's this?>" the restaurant owner asked.

"Contract," Cody sternly explained in English. "Marty said he texted you about this."

An offended look fell upon Roy's face. It was obvious that he hadn't been told the contract was coming. Marty gulped.

"<Contract?>" Roy echoed in Cantonese.

"<Ah, heh, Roy, I didn't know...I...>" Marty stumbled to reply.

"Yeah," nodded Cody. "We'll agree to sellout the Bluefin Tuna Night event if you give us a commission of fifteen thousand dollars. That's about a thirty-three percent commission from the total profits. Pretty fair, if you ask me."

Roy looked Cody in the eye; the Asian-American traitor was betraying the gentleman's agreement. This wasn't how the Cantonese brotherhood does things, Roy believed. A contract symbolized a lack of trust, a lack of understanding and, above all, a lack of respect.

"<Okay>," Roy wryly smiled. "<You want to do this the American way. Okay. I thought we were Cantonese brothers. Dragon brothers. But you insult and challenge me with this contract. But okay.>"

He whipped out a pen and scrawled his signature on the contract.

"<Wah-uh>," Marty said, trying to smooth things out. "<You have to excuse my partner Cody here. He's—>"

Roy threw the contract back at Cody. "<Okay. Signed. You'll get your thirty-three percent if you sell out the tickets. All three hundred of them. Show me what you hot shots can do. Hunh!>"

The sushi restaurant owner got up and attended to his kitchen staff. The three partners were kindly escorted out by Roy's manager. They were left to argue amongst themselves in the parking lot.

"Y-y-you i-i-idiot! N-n-now he's m-m-mad!" stuttered Wilbur.

"Sigh, Cody." Marty shook his head. "You really shouldn't have done that."

"What? This is about principle, isn't it?" Cody defended. "I'm not going to risk using up my staff's time for a petty gentlemen's agreement!"

"Y-y-your s-s-staff?" Wilbur shook a finger at him. "I-i-it's my c-c-company n-n-now!!!"

Cody lost his temper. "WHY YOU SPOILED PIECE OF—"

Marty got between them and played peacemaker.

"Heh, come on guys, we're all on the same side now. Mm-hmm. Mmeh?" Marty looked at Cody. "Mm-hhhehhh...?"

"Yeah," Cody replied breathing hard.

Wilbur gave him a challenging stare.

Marty stammered a noise. "Mm-hhuhhhh."

"Yeah, I'm alright," Cody repeated. "I'm alright. Let's just fucking do this and get it over with."

Marty carpooled with Wilbur on their way to the office; Cody had noticed an obvious bonding between those two. Marty wasn't bright enough to set his Facebook exchanges with Wilbur to privacy, especially photos of their weekend hangouts. It was a clear message that Cody was a third wheel and that, out of everything that had happened, stung the hardest. Marty had merely pretended to sink with the ship, but he was probably abandoning it either way. With a million dollars he could start his own company; with a loss he would run away and scheme with someone else. Regardless of what happened, he had no more need for Cody and the rest of the staff. Now that they were down to nearly their final month, they were set on course for letting the success of the Bluefin Tuna Event determine their fate. All the eggs in one basket, Cody realized, with Marty the least of the victims should it fail.

Three weeks later, the Bluefin Tuna Night event failed.

Blame tumbled from one person to another like a setup of dominos falling. Cody was upset at Marty for not selling the tickets; Marty acted innocent and suggested Wilbur had taken care of it. Wilbur claimed all his time was spent preparing the party buses, dancing girls, band, photographers and a video crew. Meanwhile, Roy felt contempt toward Cody for promising a guaranteed sellout. The event had cost him tens of thousands—they ended up with enough uneaten bluefin tuna to feed the homeless.

In a fit of rage, the infuriated owner demanded that Cody be immediately sent to his office. The manager found him walking Phoebe to her car and delivered the indictment. After making his way through the restaurant, Cody found a hostile atmosphere awaiting him inside the familiar Purple Wasabi meeting room. The silence from everyone signified its seriousness. At the far end of the conference table sat a cigarette-smoking Roy, ready to explode. Beside him were Cody's two partners, seemingly blameless from the fiasco.

"Hey!" Roy barked in a thickly-accented English. "You stupid American boy! You know what you cost me tonight?!!!!!"

Cody stared back at him with equally challenging eyes.

"You say full house!" Roy continued. "I, Roy, I say okay. I believe, you see?! Then I order too much bluefin tuna! You see this? You see this tuna all around the table? All outside?! The bums are eating it!!!!!!!!"

Roy's face was as red as a lychee. One of his staff members urged him to calm down, but Roy pushed him out of the way.

"<That's all homeless food now>," Roy switched back to Cantonese. "<I gave you all so many chances. I even gave you guys an advertising budget! How come I didn't see any ads of my event anywhere, huh?>"

"What advertising budget?" scoffed Cody. "You didn't give us shit!"

"<Don't play dumb with me!>" yelled Roy. "<I'm already pissed!>"

Cody glared at Marty and then looked back at Roy.

"What advertising budget?!" Cody repeated.

Roy pointed at Cody with the cigarette between his fingers. "<Oh, you want to play this game, you bastard? I don't think you do. You've embarrassed me enough tonight. I gave you two thousand dollars—in cash because I trusted you guys—marketing budget...where did you use it?!>"

Cody's jaw dropped and he looked at Marty's eyes across the table. His partner shifted his gaze toward the floor. Marty must've taken the advertising money for himself, realized Cody.

"I see it so clearly now," Cody chastised Marty. "Asian brothers, eh?"

"Ah heh heh, Cody, please...heh...there's been a misunderstanding..."

Cody left the room before Marty could explain himself.

By instinct, he drove to the alleyway behind the CVS pharmacy near his house—the one where he, Marty, and Guy had made fun of Herman a year ago. The friendship back then had felt so real for him; he was naive enough to believe that life was more than people befriending one another just from necessity. He did not want to believe that what his cousin Duke had told him was right—that life was just looks, money and social status. But how else could he interpret this reality? How much smarter would it have been if he started his company without foolishly giving half of it to someone that he had just made friends with? To add insult to injury, his iPhone had been continuously vibrating with Marty's phone calls for the past half hour. It was a feeling of déjà vu; he had gotten used to face-saving apology calls.

"Yeah, man?" finally answered Cody.

"Wooah-ho, pshew, ffft," Marty said in his usual exaggerated tones, "emo boy was crying after we left Roy's place!"

"Who's emo boy?...Oh, you mean Wilbur."

"Yeah, shhh, heh! Yeah! Oh, man! He was stuttering even more than normal! Heh, he was devastated about it! Apparently he asked, like, a hundred friends to come and none of them showed up! Hah ha! That was why we didn't sell out!"

"That's still not the reason, Marty. We failed as a team. What'd you do, huh? What did you do this whole time we were organizing that event? At least Wilbur tried, as prima donna as he was."

"Huh," Marty struggled for words. "Er, ah, come on, heh heh, Cody. I was at the office taking care of production."

"Your title says 'CEO Sales Director'! That means you get sales!!!!" Cody lost his temper.

"But the workers needed me, they—"

"Yeah right. I saw you. You usually just sat there in the office, socializing with everyone! Not a damn time did you do anything, especially in the last month when we needed you the most! This is OUR company, man!!! And then you just sit there and crack jokes while Rome burned! I believed in you. I believed we had the opportunity of a lifetime to write our own path, create our own destiny, to escape this notion that people like us have to accept the role of a model minority!"

At this point, Cody wished Marty would respond with anger. A deep part of him hoped his best friend would care enough to defend a similar concern for their company. Marty didn't, of course. Instead, like always, he laughed it off.

"Well, ah, it's not, come on...it's not like that. Heh," was all Marty could reply with. "Oh man, heh, you should've seen Roy's expression when you left. Wuh-eh-ah!"

Cody expected to crush his iPhone with his bare hands as his grip tightened from displeasure.

"Listen, you asshole," he seethed at Marty. "We've inconvenienced a lot of people as a result of this company. We just lost Roy's bid and, by default, we've also lost Mr. Wang's confidence. I don't understand why you stole the advertising budget or how you could so casually laugh at what happened to us, but you are completely stupid for taking short-term rewards for long-term consequences!"

"Aarr-ah, now now Cody," Marty responded. "I mean, I believe in that too. Freedom, man. It's what it's all about. Breaking the bamboo ceiling! Heh! We can't give up what we built, muhhh, not without a fight we're not! I'm with you all the way, man! Heh, you know what really? Fuck Wilbur! We never should've catered to his party bus shit in the first place, huh?"

"Oh yeah? You really believe that? You seem to have gotten pretty chummy with 'emo boy.'"

"Ffft, come on, heh. Chummy. Me? Him? I was always on your side, man."

"You're on everybody's side, Marty. That means you're on nobody's side."

"Heh-ha! Yer-ah, you don't understand. I really am on your side."

"Really...prove it. I want you to tell Wilbur that he's no longer welcome in our company tomorrow. Tell all the girls that the event was a disaster and that we're broke. You're going to let April, Lydia and Phoebe go. You're going to be the bad cop this time. Then we're going to run the company together, just you and me."

"Er, ahhh, yeah, I got it, man! No problem! Psssh! Fuck emo boy. We're going to save this company, heh, you and me together! Like real Cantonese brothers, man! Not that fake brother stuff that Roy was spouting! Heh! Like Double Dragon, man!"

CHAPTER 23: DISAPPEARING ACT

With his stomach in knots, Marty was dreading to tell the girls it was all over; yes-men like him always did. But with four kamikaze shots already, he really couldn't continue with a fifth one. As for the news Cody asked him to deliver, he had been trying to do so, but the timing was never right for Marty. They usually ended up talking about something else, watching a movie or, like the present moment, celebrating his birthday with drinking games. There was no choice, Marty convinced himself, he just couldn't think of a nice way to tell them they were laid off. So he never told them.

As a result, he had a good birthday, the best one he ever had. Rosie bought him a Batman-themed cake, Wilbur bought him free shots, the girls sang "Happy Birthday" together and that was enough for him to believe it was better to remain the good guy.

"T-t-to my b-b-best friend, M-M-Marty Ho! A b-b-brother to me," Wilbur toasted.

"Maw-uh, ah! Heh!" Marty gushed. "HA!"

"D-d-drink!" Wilbur insisted. "Drink drink d-d-drink!"

Rosie and the girls joined the chant. "DRINK! DRINK! DRINK!"

Succumbing to their persistency, Marty unwisely gulped down the fifth shot. It was all that his lightweight threshold could withstand. His defenses had raised a white flag. In those rare times that he had gotten drunk, Marty found alcohol to be a truth serum—dangerous to someone who was used to filling every sentence with half-truths and tactical cognizance. Worse, it made him into even more of a yes-man. In a state of embarrassment, he began muttering incoherently and stumbled his way upon a rotating world.

"Wha-uhhhh...ahhhhhhh....hehhhh...haaaaaa."

As April waved her hand in front of his face, the trail of motion from the movement seemingly created ten hands.

"Areee youuuuuu oookkkaaaayyy?" Her words came across to him in slow motion.

"Merrrrr-ahhhhh....woooo..." Marty found his own words taking their time to come out as well. As he looked down and focused on her dazzling cleavage, the drunken Marty felt drool descending from his mouth.

"Ohhh myyyy Godddd." Who was it? Marty figured it was Rosie who said that.

His current dizziness notwithstanding, the birthday boy was ignored for a moment when Wilbur loudly declared that he had an announcement. The staff and Wilbur's girlfriend gathered around him as well as some curious nearby bar patrons.

"M-M-Marty a-a-and I are gonna s-s-s-s-s-s-sssss...ssssss—"

"'Start', hic," helped Marty.

"—s-s-start our o-o-o-o-o-o-o-o—"

His stuttering only heightened the anticipation of whatever news he was trying to spew. After a few more 'o's, the group lost patience and began guessing his next word out loud. Fortunately, Wilbur blurted out the word he wanted to say.

"—o-o-OWN company! Y-y-yeah t-t-that's r-r-right! A c-c-company! This t-t-time we're gonna d-d-do it r-r-right."

Even in his less than perceptive state, Marty wished Wilbur wouldn't have announced their new business so soon. After all, he hadn't even told Cody he was leaving his current one yet. And how confused would the girls be as they still believed they were on Mosaic Design Studios' payroll? Ah well, dismissed Marty, that was his former best friend's problem, not his.

"Cool," remarked Rosie. "What'll it be called?"

Wilbur gave a proud smile and replied, "'Y-Y-You're t-t-the C-C-Celebrity'!"

"Wait, what about the current company?" questioned April.

Wilbur gave a smug shrugging of his shoulders. Several days ago, he had demanded that Marty leave Mosaic Design

Studios and join him. Marty, as always, agreed, but he balked at informing Cody like he promised.

"A-A-And I'm g-g-gonna g-g-give L-L-Lydia the honor t-t-to m-m-make my l-l-logo!" beamed Wilbur.

"Awesome!" The lilliputian designer held her smile, forgetting for a moment to conceal her crush on him.

"Wow, a company designed to make people feel special," April replied.

"Y-y-yeah!" proudly proclaimed Wilbur. "B-b-because we believe that p-p-people should be t-t-treated right! Unlike how C-C-Cody runs his business! F-f-fuck Cody, man!!!"

"Heh, ha!" agreed the drunken Marty, toasting an empty shot glass to Wilbur's empty shot glass. "Yeah, fuck him, heh! Woo-HA! Wah-uh, he doesn't have your vision, Wilbur! He doesn't know how to, wa-eh, treat people right like you do!"

"F-F-FUCK MOSAIC DESIGN STUDIOS! FUCK THAT SHITHEAD C-C-CODY QUAN!" Wilbur toasted with a sixth round of kamikaze shots.

Marty chuckled, "Wah-heh-ha, er ah-hah!"

The interns and employees hesitated for a moment and weakly toasted back.

"I...I have to go," Phoebe excused herself as she left the bar.

The former waitress had been quiet for most of Marty's little birthday bash. She was as queasy as much as she was confused. Unlike Lydia and April, she had seen a lot of Cody's good side. But then again, she was often inclined to see everyone's positive side, including Wilbur's and Marty's. It was disheartening for her to witness a splitting of the company; worse yet, her immediate future was in question. Reverting to her usual habit, she treated herself to a cigarette and, after it was down to its last inch, discarded it for another one. The events that had transpired frustrated her. Cody had promised her a better future if she gave him her best. She was peeved that her new job had likely ended prematurely because of childish bickering. The thought of it was so distracting that she barely made out the footsteps from behind her.

"Hey!" called out Lydia.

Phoebe fumbled to put her cigarette out, dropping and stepping on it on the sidewalk. Although everyone knew she was a chain smoker, she was still ashamed of being seen with a Marlboro in hand.

"Oh, uh, hi," Phoebe stammered. "I thought...I thought you were still with them, Lydia. Are they done?"

It was rare for them to have a conversation together; Phoebe suspected it was because Lydia figuratively looked down on her. Of course, there wasn't any actual evidence to support that feeling of insecurity. Her coworker seemed nice enough, but she was always distant—much more so than with the others. It was also natural for girls who were polar opposites to misjudge and make assumptions. Phoebe knew that Lydia had come from a good family and had a great education; Lydia had never mentioned taking a blue collar job before and with her talent she might never have to. It was only natural if Lydia considered Phoebe beneath her, even if she failed to see Phoebe's positives. After all, she thought, Lydia wouldn't be the first one or the last.

"No, they're still drinking," Lydia answered with a reserved tone. "I felt a little unnerved. I can't drink, you know. Christian upbringing and all. So...what are you doing out here? Smoke break?"

Phoebe gave off a look of shame. "I was hoping you wouldn't catch that. But yeah. I was...I needed a cig."

The two young women stood silently on the sidewalk, watching a few people pass by as they struggled to come up with conversation.

"You can smoke inside the bar, you know," Lydia finally said, suggesting the obvious.

Phoebe rolled her eyes but remained composed on being nice. She knew her diminutive coworker didn't mean to sound as condescending as she did. "I...um...well, I just didn't want them to see me. None of you guys smoke, so I just didn't want you all to think that I'm a bad person. I know it's silly. But I don't like it when...yeah..."

"It's okay," Lydia eased. "I just wanted a proper chance to say it's been nice working with you. Maybe you didn't recognize me back then, but you were our waitress back in Hula

Hoop Shakes. We've never talked much and I'm sorry. You probably thought I was a snob."

"Meh," Phoebe shrugged, trying to change the subject. "You're very talented. I wish I had your talent. Cody always assured me that I could one day be as talented as you, but I think that's just pep talk from him."

Lydia waved off her compliment. "Talent's overrated. I guess I just got lucky."

Phoebe appreciated Lydia's olive branch for friendship, but she also knew the timing of it signified the end of Mosaic Design Studios. If she could figure it out, certainly her brainy coworker could as well. Only the most important question remained.

"So...are you gonna join Wilbur and Marty?" Phoebe asked.

To her surprise, Lydia shook her head. "I think Wilbur's cute but I don't trust Marty."

Phoebe didn't know if it was appropriate to pry about Sonia's sexual harassment accusations, but she secretly wanted to know. It had always seemed a little out of character for Marty, who appeared to be a friendly and caring person. She wanted to believe he was simply misunderstood, but something about the way Lydia spat out his name indicated he wasn't the pleasant person he appeared to be.

Sensing Phoebe's hesitation, Lydia offered an interpretive answer. "He did some...questionable...things before you joined the company. Maybe they weren't that bad. It depends on perspective. To us who were there, I suppose, it was pretty out of line. Maybe you wouldn't have thought so. Maybe we overreacted."

The former waitress appreciated her coworker's attempt for fairness, but both of them knew Lydia felt otherwise.

Older men like Patrick Hui knew better than to be frustrated; opportunities for romance did not come often at his age. For over a year, he had remained behaved with Cody's Aunt Hannah, always placing himself within striking distance yet savoring her like a precious bottle of 1982 Chateau Lafleur Pomerol. He made himself believe it was because he wanted her to feel comfortable, but in his own honesty he knew the situation was a tangled web. The problem with romance was that it hinged so much on anticipation. It was why married couples got bored and why Patrick was convinced cheating saved marriages. Loyalty was such an unnecessary ruse; certainly back in the day of concubines, society understood and accepted this necessity to continue a happy marriage. He wondered if it was so wrong to pursue a woman that was happy with him while he was married. Was it so wrong to desire someone who cared when his own wife didn't? These weren't the obstacles, of course. The real problem was because no one else would approve of his pursuit. Hannah's family was a constant thorn. Between her teenage daughter's animosity and her own sister's meddlesomeness, it was enough to consider the romance unachievable. Yet, he had gained her trust and she loved his company. Why else would she frequently invite him to her house—the same house that he sold to her—to fix things? A middle-aged man like himself, he admitted, just desired to be wanted.

"<This door to my daughter's old room>," Hannah complained during a usual afternoon visit, "<it never did completely close. See? You have to force it to close correctly. The home association warned us that a lot of these houses were built from cheap labor. The construction companies contracted illegal Mexicans. Isn't that horrible? I knew you wouldn't have any idea about this and it wasn't your fault.>"

Patrick kept his lips sealed; he had had the house inspected and had known of its flaws and construction shortcuts. Yet, as long as Hannah wasn't aware of his involvement, it was far more convenient to blame phantom illegal Mexicans.

"<You know, this isn't difficult to fix>," observed Patrick.

"<Really?>"

He smiled, assuring her of his confidence. "<Yes, certainly. You just measure the length of the door to the angle and readjust the hinges. The calculations shouldn't be difficult at all. Let me go get the toolbox.>"

As promised, the gray-haired realtor turned handyman came back and re-screwed the hinges on Megan's bedroom door and reapplied them at their appropriate angles. Throughout this process he could feel Hannah's eyes undressing him—a disposition suitable for their first official rendezvous. With an electric screwdriver in hand, he began unbuttoning his shirt only to turn around and discover a teacup inches away from his nose. Hannah insisted that he drink.

"<Hot?>" she inquired. "<Let me turn on the A/C.>"

He reluctantly took the teacup and sipped it as his consolation prize. Funny how the Chinese culture quenches thirst with warm drinks, he mused. A slight moment of doubt arose within Patrick, but he knew his instinct wasn't entirely incorrect. She just needed to be taken slowly, he realized, that's all.

"<I can't thank you enough for helping me once again>," Hannah smiled with a schoolgirl's twinkle in her eye. "<I'm always ashamed that I couldn't repay the favor. It's just that you're so brilliant and I'm such a dummy.>"

Patrick laughed it off with a modest wave. "<It's...it's just a door, Hannah. You give me too much credit. Just a piece of wood held together by screws and hinges. Not like it's a car or rocket.>"

Hannah opened her mouth to say something, but she hesitated for a moment, trying to fight off her better judgment. As if he could read her intentions, Patrick placed his cup on a nearby table stand and happily leaned over to her with a smile. They both giggled like schoolchildren before he initiated some action.

"<Yes?>" Patrick smiled. "< Don't be shy, what's on your mind?>"

"<Well, I...I do have a second favor to ask you this afternoon.>" She bit her lip and continued. "<Remember around last year, while Megan was still in high school...and...and you were showing us this house? And you gave me that quick massage?>"

Patrick replied in agreement with a slow blink of his eyes and a calm nod.

"<I...ahem...I liked it>," Hannah admitted. "<Can you give me another one? My daughter's not here this time around.>"

"<No interruptions>," added Patrick.

She smiled. "<No interruptions.>"

By instinct, he took her by the hand and whisked her downstairs to the living room. The silver-haired realtor hadn't felt so alive in a long time. He couldn't even remember the last time he had made love to his own wife. A decade at least, he calculated. Then, in the same thought, he dismissed it because he didn't care. This afternoon was the moment. He would be lucky and he would be participating in a moment to remember. He vacillated between starting with the main course and soothing her first with his homemade brand of reflexology. Why rush, he ultimately decided.

"<There>," Patrick made her comfortable on her living room sofa. "<Just relax and enjoy the magic.>"

He started rubbing the soles of her feet, soothing pressure points that were specifically designed for sexual arousal. Patrick knew he could make her orgasm with merely a foot massage, a perfect way to start their first encounter of intimacy.

"<OOOOOH>," moaned Cody's aunt.

Mid-fifty-year-olds shouldn't be having THIS much fun, she thought. Meanwhile, Patrick smiled, knowing that an older gentleman uses every tool at his disposal. Within a minute he had worked every sensual nerve in her body by timely-placed pressure points to her left foot. For fifteen minutes they continued this variation of reflexology sex until Hannah could stand it no more—married or not, she demanded Patrick perform intercourse the standard way. With no words needed, the lustful realtor climbed atop Cody's aunt and unbuttoned the rest of his shirt.

"<I am the South China Tiger!!!>" he declared. "<Feel my conquest!>"

In a moment of shock, however, they were unpleasantly interrupted by loud knocking on the front door. At first, they dismissed it as a mere trick of the mind, but the knocking persisted.

"<My sister!>" Hannah gasped. "<She probably brought me some food from Chinatown.>"

"<Oh>," replied Patrick in an icy tone. "<You don't have to answer it, you know.>"

As Hannah wondered whether or not she should heed Patrick's advice, the knocking continued.

"<Damn it, doesn't that woman quit?>" he growled.

Hannah scrambled to the front door and peered through the peephole. She had been correct—Cody's mother was standing outside with plastic grocery bags in hand.

"<Just ignore her>," hissed Patrick.

"<Hey!>" Cody's mother shouted. "<I know you're in there, sister! Your car's outside.>"

Patrick's eyes widened like saucers; he knew he had carelessly parked his car next to hers as well. Hannah looked at him to signify she had a similar realization.

"<Mui's car is here too. Why is he in there with you?>" demanded her sister.

Patrick quickly put on his shirt and signaled for Hannah to open the door.

"<Finally!>" Cody's mother exclaimed, seeing her face-to-face. "<So what's going on?>"

She craned her neck past her nervous sister and caught a glimpse of Patrick in the living room.

"<Well>," Hannah scratched her head. "<Um, Patrick was upstairs fixing my daughter's door. You know how it never closed properly—>"

Cody's mother pushed her aside and wagged a finger at him from the entrance. "<You bastard! What are you doing with my sister? Go back to your wife!>"

"<What?>" the realtor barked back. "< I came to help a friend. I can't help a friend?>"

"<Yes>," Hannah agreed. "<We're just friends. That's all. Just friends.">

Cody's mother let out a mocking laugh."<Hunh! Use your brain, sister! He's a man! Men always want something more!>"

With a lesser restraint on his temper, Patrick walked closer to the two of them in a bid to defend himself. "<Oh, you vile woman! Don't be so jealous! Just because you don't have any friends, let alone male ones, you're thinking the worst intentions! Your sister is every bit more the woman than you are!>"

"<Oh? Is that right?>" scoffed Cody's mother, who never backed down from a challenge. "<Maybe it's better to be friendless than to shame myself in tempting other people to cheat!>"

In a fit of rage, Patrick grabbed and put on his shoes, storming past the two sisters. Hannah served as a human barricade between her secret lover and her enraged sister. Halfway towards his car, however, he turned around and clinched his fist at Cody's mother.

"<Someday you'll know better than to interfere with other people's happiness>," he threatened, "<and I won't promise to be as civil next time.>"

It came as no surprise to Cody when he got involved in his first car accident during September; after all, short of death, every other bad thing had happened to him in the year 2010. He didn't believe in curses, though it was probably as good a time as any to explain the worst year of his life. This time he couldn't even blame Jesus; the pursuit of money did this to him. Or rather, as he stood near the wrecked mess that used to be his Integra, he did this to himself. A brief but frightening truth emerged from that realization—maybe anything bad that had ever happened to him he had done to himself; though as much he tried, he wasn't courageous enough to accept that. There was no use contemplating it during this moment, he thought, it was a bigger priority to find a ride home. By instinct, he reached out to Marty, perhaps because he had gotten used to speed-dialing his number or perhaps a part of Cody still considered him his best friend.

"Hey," he barked. "I just got into an accident. Come pick me up."

"Wah-huh, okay," Marty responded.

The ride back to Cody's house started with trivial chatter—no mention of the Bluefin Tuna Event collapse or Wilbur's continual presence at the office. It offended Cody that Marty tried to skirt the issue, as though they could sit the whole way through without talking about what was important. The growing insult nagged at Cody until he changed his mind and ordered Marty to eat with him somewhere in Chinatown. Always eager to play the role of the harmless nice guy, Marty complied, though he steered their decision to an udon restaurant whose staff were familiar with him—and could protect him should Cody snap and get out of line.

They arrived at the restaurant late afternoon, finding it packed with Mainland Chinese patrons. Cody always felt a bit uncomfortable with these types of hole-in-the-wall eating places because they were openly disdainful toward Asian-Americans. Marty, of course, found it easier to camouflage himself as one of them since he was fluent enough in Mandarin Chinese to blend in. Unbeknownst to Cody, Marty gave a signal to the waiter and hinted for a table near the middle of the packed restaurant. He hoped being surrounded would discourage his partner from displaying open fits of anger, but Cody ended up snapping anyway.

"What have you been doing with your time?!" Cody barked after they ordered food. "I've been seeing you and Wilbur hanging out together. I thought I told you I didn't want him around the company anymore! And don't get me started on the staff still being there."

"Sigh..." Marty protested. "I did, I guess they didn't understand. It's been one big misunderstanding, Cody."

Cody had an expression of disbelief. "What's there not to understand?! Wilbur is worse than ever. He acts like he owns the place!"

"Hah, er...woo-ha! Oh that!" chuckled Marty. "Let me tell you a funny story—"

"I DON'T WANT ANY FUNNY STORIES!" screamed Cody, catching the attention of nearby customers. "You never told him he wasn't welcomed anymore, did you?"

Marty started wiping beads of sweat from his forehead with a napkin. "I...no, I, I did! No, I swear, I did! It's just...woo-hah...he's always asking to see me, that's all. You know? I told him 'Now now, Wilbur, you can't keep hanging around the company anymore.' Heh. Mm-huh. But he keeps persisting. I...I have to hang out with him. I don't want to, but he makes me."

"So what the fuck?! Tell him no! What you're doing is disrespectful and insulting! By the end of this month, we'll be owing our employees thousands of fucking dollars, man! Where are we going to get the money to pay them? Holy shit, I thought having zero was bad, but being in the negative! Fuck, man!"

"Muuuh, then why don't you fire the staff yourself already?"

Cody knew it was the smart thing for him to do, but he had been blinded with pride, rather keeping the girls until Marty fired them. He was sick of always being the one who delivered bad news.

"Because I asked you to do it. Because you owe me this. Because you're just going to wait until I do it and then take them out to drinking with you and Wilbur."

Marty adjusted the collar of his shirt. He couldn't believe Cody already knew about his new company.

Cody smirked. "Oh, don't think I don't know."

"Now now, shhh shhh!" Marty replied. "It's all just a big misunderstanding. You're still my best friend. And Wilbur? Shhh. I don't have anything to do with emo boy."

"I wish you did a better job hiding that. Bringing him in and out of the office everyday doesn't help. Laughing and eating with him and posting Facebook photos of yourselves hanging out doesn't help. DO YOU THINK I'M AN UTTER MORON, MARTY?"

"Shhh...shhh...ah heh heh, ah wah uh! Calm down, Cody. You, heh, you sound like a jilted lover."

Cody stood up in anger. "You 'shhh,' you motherfucking strange talking weirdo! How are we paying the staff now? You claimed you have clients. Who have you gotten in the past few weeks?"

"Sighhhh...you don't...sighhh..."

"WHAT?!"

"My mother has cancer!" shouted Marty in uncharacteristic seriousness. "There, heh, I said it, okay? Huh? Huh? It's put so much stress on me! That's what's been happening. Nah nah er, ah!"

Marty had expected Cody to exhibit sympathy. To his surprise, this news somehow made Cody angrier.

"You mean to tell me that you knew your mom had cancer all this time? That you wouldn't be able to get any sales?! That you decided not to tell me?!"

"Wah-huh, please, shush shh! Heh! It's personal! That's why I didn't have time to do anything! I...heh...eh? You just misunderstood!"

"FUCKING ASS MOTHERFUCKER!!!" Cody screamed standing. He had his pointer finger inches from Marty's nose. "We're business partners! You need to tell me this shit! I could've just let all the employees go!!! Now we owe them money we don't have!!!"

"Please, heh, please Cody, my mother..."

"I don't fucking care about your mother! For her sake I hope you're lying like you always do! You didn't have a sale all this time!!! Why the hell didn't you just say so? Are you a fucking idiot?!"

"Ah-wah...er...mahhhh." Marty was at a loss for words. "The doctors said she has a tumor growing behind her left eye. Heh-ha! We couldn't detect it until it was too late!"

Cody dropped his chopsticks and looked at him in disbelief. Marty was giving the best puppy dog expression that he could muster. Cody wondered if it was possible for even Marty to lie about his own mother.

"Have you ever heard of the boy who cried 'wolf,' Marty?" Cody asked.

"Ffft, fine!" Marty rolled his eyes. "It's true. Heh-haw! But you don't believe me."

"You've always lied with every chance you've gotten."

"Hah-waaaaa?!!!!!!! Me?! I...I don't lie!"

"Yeah, you! You're a damn compulsive liar!!!!"

"Mahhh, er, ah, I've never ever told a lie in my life!"

"Fuck you, man!"

"What? What are we talking about? Fuck me about, heh, what?"

"About your shitfaced lying!!!"

"You're a liar? When? Cody, what did you lie about? Heh-wa?"

"Oh no! You're not doing that psychological game with me! Not this time!"

"Mmm heh, wah? You're a liar? Please, shh, shhh! Hush now! Meh-gah, maybe you shouldn't lie so much, ffff."

"I'm not lying! You're the one who's lying! Oh my God! I let you steal from me and my friends! My family! All of it! MY FAMILY TRUSTED YOU! And all you can do is make up some story about your mother having cancer."

"Now now, Cody. If your mom has cancer, you really need to think things through."

"No! What are you talking about? You said YOUR mom has cancer! You said that! How dare you even lie about it? Now you're...wait...ahhh..."

"Cody." Marty put a hand on his shoulder. "It's okay to let it out. Heh, humm. If your mom is going through treatments, maybe you should take it easy."

"My mom," Cody assured, "is a hundred percent okay!!! Don't jinx her! Don't bring her into this game!"

"What game? Why are we in this restaurant? Who are you? I'm me, you're you, you're you but you're not you. Mah-heh. Your name is Cody Quan, your mother just got cancer and I saved you from a car crash."

Whatever mind trick Marty was pulling was finding its way into Cody's head. "Shut up! Shut up! Shut up!"

"Meh-ah, I've never met you, hi, my name is Marty." Marty gave him the friendliest of chuckles. "Don't you remember? You look familiar. Heh, we have the...ah hah!...I know! You were in my Chinese class. Remember? Wuh-hah! What are we talking about? Why are we in this restaurant? Don't you remember me? You're going through a nervous breakdown, Cody. Let me help you, meh-heh. You're going through a nervous breakdown, Cody. Let me help you. Hey, you look familiar, wait, meh-heh, you're in my Chinese class. Hi, I'm Marty. You're going through a nervous breakdown, Cody. Mah-hah, mah-heh—"

"SHUT UP SHUT UP SHUT UP! I'M SANE!"

Cody couldn't take it anymore. Marty was doing something to him and it was working. Whatever control Cody had left demanded him to do one thing: stop Marty from penetrating his mind at all costs. Deep resentment had already bubbled onto the surface of Cody's temper. He found his decision to unleash a good hard right to Marty's jaw a straightforward and effortless one. *POW!* Despite Marty's many claims of mastering martial arts, he was a surprisingly easy opponent. Cody's best friend immediately fell down on the floor.

"<Hey!>" the manager shouted at Cody in Mandarin Chinese. "<I saw what you just did! Get out of this restaurant!>"

Cody could not understand him, but it was universal that fighting in any restaurant was not encouraged. A waitress quickly rushed up to the fallen Marty.

"<Are you alright?>" she asked. "<Oh, you poor soul. You were just talking to him and he hit you.>"

"<Ah-weh, mahhh. It hurts, sigh. It hurts.>" Marty shook his head, managing to extract a tear or two from his eye.

"Aiya!" The manager shook his head. "<How can this be? A Chinese hitting another Chinese!>"

The confrontation drew a crowd; the two of them were smothered with accusing patrons. Cody found himself shaking from the adrenaline of hitting his best friend—perhaps it was now more appropriate to label Marty as his former best friend. From the floor, Marty continued to wail. Come on, thought Cody, it wasn't that good of a punch. Regardless of what he thought of Marty's acting, the mob of customers were quite sold on it, pointing incriminating fingers in Cody's direction.

"STOP IT!" Cody angrily demanded. "STOP SHOUTING AT ME! I HAVEN'T DONE ANYTHING WRONG!!!!!"

"<He doesn't understand Mandarin Chinese!>" observed a patron.

"<Figures>," tsk-tsked another, "<with that temper that guy's obviously corrupted with American influences.>"

"<Ohhh, my jaw, hhhuhhhh.>" Marty continued moaning as he rolled over in pain. "<I need help.>"

"<And this one>," one of the customers pointed at Marty. "<He speaks such fluent Chinese! And well too! He's one of us!>"

One after another the faces of the crowd directed their angry glares in Cody direction.

"<What happened, sir?>" a nearby patron asked Marty.

"<Huh, I...I don't know...>" Marty explained. "<I was just asking how his mother was doing. Then he hit me. She must not be doing well. But still. Heh. Ha...why punch me? You know? Huh-ha? Temper temper.>"

The hostile atmosphere encouraged Cody to back away until he was able to reach the exit. He doubted anyone from the mob of customers would actually attack him, but he ran anyway. He weaved himself between alleyway after alleyway until he was certain he was alone, finally seeking refuge behind a dumpster near the edge of Chinatown. Whatever illusions he had about preserving his friendship with Marty were now completely gone. More importantly, there wasn't time for self-pity or anger; he was facing massive debts and something had to be done quickly. There were salaries to be paid, rent to be covered, not to mention all the massive credit card payments that had piled up. He had no qualms about suing Marty. That was the obvious thing to try and do. But something needed to be done soon and he feared Marty could weasel his way around the loopholes of the legal system. Cody collected himself and accepted that immediate action was needed.

"You want how much again, Bobbie?!" asked Cody's longtime friend Mindy.

Cody stammered for the right words as night-time mosquitoes feasted on his neck outside of her home. She was the first person he could think of when it came to borrowing money. It was frightening how hanging out with Marty had made him accustomed to being a beggar.

"Fifteen thousand dollars," he answered, "I'll...I'll even give you partnership of the company. Half of it. Three-thirds of it. All of it. I don't care."

Mindy silently stared at him with concern as he stood there, occasionally slapping a mosquito or two. She didn't like seeing her friend like this, not when he used to be so confident and financially well-off.

"Bobbie," Mindy replied affectionately, "what is happening to you? You were once so bright. So smart. It hurt me to see you in this way."

"I was a fool, Mindy," Cody humbly responded. "I opened up this company for all the wrong reasons. And now this snake of a partner abandoned me."

"That's right," she tsk-tsked. "He was never your best friend like I was! I told you he was taking advantage of you since that Oceanaire dinner! Now did you regret not choosing me instead?"

"Okay, okay. You were right," Cody paused, "can I, you know, come in or something? These mosquitoes are biting the hell out of me."

Mindy paused for a moment and then finally gave in. "Okay, but please take off your shoes."

Her new house was a decent two-story dwelling, littered with children's toys and old Taiwanese newspapers. Cody figured there must have been several televisions turned on at once because he could hear a dissonance of various TV programs in English and Taiwanese. Somewhere in the back was one of Mindy's twin girls crying, probably because of bath time given the time of night and what appeared to sound like water splashing. Mindy asked him to excuse the mess as they found a resemblance of privacy in the kids' playroom. Cody pulled out two miniature children's chairs while she closed the bifold doors in an attempt to reduce the outer noise. The ridiculousness of two adults squatting on tiny plastic chairs countered the seriousness of Cody's request.

"I cannot give you that much," Mindy began."I save everything and put it into a certificate of deposit account for the girls."

Cody looked at her in disappointment. She was his best hope.

"Well, how much can you loan me?" he asked.

Mindy twitched her eyebrows and gave him a familiar, frustrated look. Like old times, she gave him a loud and hard slap on his shoulder.

"Ow!" yelped out Cody.

"You only talk to me now when you need to borrow money, huh?"

Cody rubbed the spot on his shoulder where Mindy had slapped him. For a thin woman she had an unusual amount of strength. "Could you be a little more understanding? All my time was spent on running a company. You encouraged me to blaze trails."

"Yeah, but I never told you to be stupid and foolish! Okay, okay. I can let you borrow some money. Two hundred dollars."

"That's it?!" Cody tried to remain calm. "Mindy, you

know I wouldn't be asking for help if I wasn't in such dire circumstances."

"Bobbie, you should just sue him!"

"These things are harder to prove then you think!"

"Sue him, Bobbie!" Mindy repeated. "Why do you need your friends' money, eh?"

"What about the employees? I can't just delay their paychecks!"

"Yes, you can!"

"Well, I won't do it," Cody dismissed. "That would be something Marty would do."

"Don't be stupid! Protect yourself! Tell them 'Too bad, no paycheck. sorry! This is America. Ha ha!' Just like that."

Cody's glare showed disapproval of her absurd suggestion. "I can't do that. Come on. They'll get pissed! How can you even suggest that, Mindy?"

"Well, you cannot also ask anyone to just loan you fifteen thousand dollars, Bobbie!"

Cody eventually left her house with a check for two hundred dollars. For awhile he cursed Mindy's stinginess but then considered himself lucky she loaned him anything at all. His mind quickly brainstormed on who else could help him—it didn't take long for him to remember Yuki. They hadn't talked since the previous holiday season when he rejected her advances and considered their friendship on hold. Fortunately, he found her to be as goodhearted as usual, despite his sudden awkward return into her life.

"Please," he typed to MyMelodyBunny, "I wouldn't ask this unless I needed it."

"I don't know," she replied. "I haven't heard from you since you rejected me during last Christmas holiday. And now that I finally do, it's for money."

"I didn't reject you!" corrected Cody as Quanster7.

"Call it what you'd like."

RainYSkIEs589 entered their chat room.

"Hey, guys!" she interrupted. "Long time no see! What're you guys talking about? Wanna see my new artwork?"

"Nothing, Rain," they both typed.

"I'll email you about this later," MyMelodyBunny answered.

Yuki ended up contributing a substantially bigger loan than Mindy, though it was still far from the fifteen thousand dollars he needed. After receiving loans from a few sympathetic distant cousins and old high school friends, he had half the amount he needed but time was running out. Frustrated, Cody considered drastic solutions like robbing Marty or kidnapping Wilbur—but he probably wouldn't get much money doing either. It wasn't like Marty had a lot of money or that Wilbur's father would seriously consider saving his kidnapped son. Through his desperation, however, he had sunk low enough to consider a previously forbidden source for money: the reserve account for his grandfather's funeral.

Would he dare?

Granted, his grandfather was in wonderful health, but beyond the principle of taking such sacred money, senior citizens of that age were at risk to pass away at a moment's notice. If his grandfather passed away and his family found out the account was empty, there would be hell for Cody to pay. Ultimately, he decided to risk his luck and empty the money from the funeral reserve anyway.

But first, he decided to pray about it.

CHAPTER 24: LOSS

The familiarity of the scene hit Cody all at once. The beautiful pews, the choir warming up, the exquisite height from floor to ceiling that gave the church just the right amount of echo. As a show of humility, Cody did the one thing that he had rarely done: show up anywhere an hour early. With all the problems that had arisen, he needed Jesus' help and forgiveness. He felt sorry for flushing the crucifix down the toilet and he was sorry for denying Christ—even if the prior relationship had been severely abusive and catastrophic. None of it mattered anymore; he was out of options.

He had selected this particular church, knowing it provided a notably beautiful setting. Indeed, the soothing ambiance briefly erased any reason he had for breaking his spiritual relationship off. It brought back pleasurable memories of his baptism and the sensation of peace. That was when his faith was intact. Cody looked around, observing the scattered early birds who also sought solace amongst God. He had always felt a little envious of these happy Christians. Why didn't Jesus bully them? Then again, Cody realized, who's to say they had never been tested. Perhaps their sense of peace was the aftermath of Jesus' wrath—a challenge that came across to Cody as abuse. Wasn't that the lesson of Job? God purposely allowed the devil to torture this wonderful man beyond the confines of cruelty just to reward him again. It was funny logic without the humor, certainly similar to child abuse.

With those negative questions in mind, Cody decided to pray anyway. It was a good time to speak with Jesus, especially since the church was still barely filled. He found a relatively quiet area near the back where several rows of pews were left unoccupied. There, he slipped into the farthest pew and got on his knees to pray. It was strange what a foreign feeling it was, having never done so for more than half a decade. Slowly, he closed his eyes and spoke from the desires of his heart. Cody prayed for guidance, he prayed for money; mostly, he prayed for an audience with Jesus Christ.

"Dear Jesus," he began, "I..."

Thump. His thoughts were interrupted by an external sound. Yet, what was even more noticeable was the lack of other sounds. The choir had suddenly stopped; the loose chatter had vanished. A chill crept down his spine; something had happened. Cody reluctantly opened his eyes to find a dark, empty church. The walls were a bit distorted as though part of another world; indeed, he realized, it was another world altogether. Cody looked at his watch to confirm what he had suspected—time had frozen. It didn't take long for him to realize it was a mistake to summon Jesus. A very bad one.

"Hello?" Cody inquired out loud. "Anybody here?"

The echoes of the dark, empty church greeted him back. He felt a strong wave of fear seeping into his soul. The floor slowly began rumbling underneath him. Suddenly, there came a crash followed by a succession of crashes. To his horror, Cody caught sight of the empty pews toppling one after another. From the stage, the pulpit fell down. Chandeliers dropped from various parts of the ceiling. The rumbling turned into a violent shaking as though the dark world church was in the middle of a small earthquake. Of all the objects vying for Cody's immediate attention, however, were the locked entrance doors that had him fixated. He saw the attempts of someone—or something—trying to break through; it was only a matter of time before the locked doors gave way. Cody was proved right. No sooner had he convinced himself of this, the doors burst open to a very strong power. Entering through them was an angry Jesus Christ.

"No!" pleaded Cody. "Stay back! Don't hurt me!"

His appeals for mercy seemed denied by Jesus, who wore dark gray garments. The Messiah stared intensely at Cody with a lone eye that shone through his dark and wet long hair. The intimidating Deity calmly walked towards Cody, inching slowly toward him until the distance between them was a mere few feet. For a moment, Jesus stopped, offering nothing but a disapproving frown. Cody was certain punishment would soon come.

"Hahahaha!" Jesus laughed in a gesture that surprised Cody. "AHAHAHAHAHAA!!!!!!"

With uncanny speed, the dark Messiah grabbed Cody and began sprouting a large pair of black wings.

Cody pleaded, though he knew it wouldn't help. "No! Nooooo!!!!"

Without a second's hesitation, Jesus flew upward into the black sky at an astronomical speed. Their flight caused them to crash through the glass rooftop and Cody immediately found himself covered in blood. They soared so high above the clouds that Cody could see Houston as a collection of bright dots. The city, too, seemed frozen in time.

"P...please," begged a semiconscious Cody, "why are you doing this? Why do you...torture...me..."

"Because I can," replied Jesus, tightly holding on to him.

"But all people do for you is love and worship. Why do you hurt them? Why...do...you...hurt...me..." Cody felt himself fainting.

"Because. I. Can. And. I. Don't. Love. You."

"Is that...why you...made us?...to...torture and...and play with..."

"This is going to hurt, Cody. I'm going to drop you and you're going to be in a lot of pain." Jesus let out a malicious laugh. "But please, I insist, keep praying for me. Maybe I'll feel nice someday and follow through. HAHAHAHAHAHAHA!"

"You're...nothing...nothing but a sadist..."

Jesus wouldn't let Cody finish his sentence. Instead, the dark Messiah let go of him, watching him drop quickly down through the Earth's stratosphere. As Cody descended, he made sure to give Jesus a glaring, hateful stare. If God created man simply to make him suffer, then never was there a God so unworthy of praise. He decided he would never give Jesus another chance, even if it meant living in eternal hell. That was all Cody had in mind while his body quickly plunged into the world and promptly into an envelope of darkness.

"Cody! Hey Cody!"

It was the next morning, a late October Monday. Cody opened his eyes and found himself staring at Phoebe. He was lying on top of the conference room table.

"Where...where am I?" He sat up, making his way off.

"You're in the office, boss," Phoebe explained.

"Please don't call me that. What happened?"

"I'm not sure. You had me worried," she replied. "I was the first one in.......geez, what happened? You got cuts all over you. Did you crash through a glass window?"

It took Cody a little longer than usual to remember how Phoebe could enter the office. Then he recalled giving her an extra set of keys because the employees had been managing themselves. They were saints for coming to work on time without supervision. It was little wonder that Marty didn't have the heart to let them go; of all the wrong that had happened, they were lucky to have some of the most honest employees a company could ask for. Pity they had to be let go.

"Boss?" Phoebe said, trying to snap him out of his thoughts. "Hey?"

"I don't know what happened," Cody finally replied. "I was in that church..."

"Church? Meh. You were lying here unconscious when I found you."

She sat him down and told him to stay there while fetching him a cup of water. Cody was amazed at how thirsty he was the moment he drank it. A quick look at his reflection on the table glass showed cuts over his visible body, but they were also healing with an astonishing quickness.

"What time is it?" he asked when Phoebe returned with more water.

"Eight-thirty."

"Eight-thirty?!" Cody did a double take at the office clock.

"Yeah, you told us last Friday to come here at nine because you had a special meeting."

The meeting, he realized. After his fight with Marty and his scramble to collect fifteen thousand dollars, he had mandated a meeting for the final Friday of October. Today was the day Cody would deliver the bad news: Mosaic Design Studios was no more. However, because there were still plenty of projects left to be done, he was going to keep one of them for an extra month.

"So you're telling us it's officially over," April summarized once the meeting started and the rest of the girls arrived.

"Yes. In so many words," Cody replied, looking tired and defeated.

Lydia raised her hand. Feeling like a schoolteacher, Cody pointed at her. "Lydia?"

"What happened to Marty?" she asked.

"Marty has...well..." Cody collected his thoughts carefully. He decided to be cautiously candid about it. "We haven't seen him get a sale in the past four months. In the past month, he hadn't even made an effort."

"Did you guys fight?" prodded Lydia.

"That's...not important," he tactically explained. "He's gone. And he won't be with us anymore."

"You know he was working on his own company behind your back," continued Lydia. "I just thought you should know because it was wrong for him to do so."

Cody nodded, confirming that he already knew.

"Yeah," April agreed. "Remember M.H. Productions?"

The three girls paused, letting Cody put the rest together.

"Marty...Ho...Productions," realized Cody. He let out a groan of regret. "Oh, how could I have been so blind and stupid?"

"Hey, it's okay," April offered her condolences. "He's had his own company set up long before Wilbur."

"Well, Sonia should get a lot of credit," replied Lydia modestly. "She discovered his secrets while she was going through the projects. Also, his cousin Guy told her a lot of things as well."

"So he never did get us any clients before opening day," Cody concluded. "That scumbag."

The four of them let out a collective sigh.

"You might want to ask some of the clients what they actually paid too," April insisted. "Some of them have been saying they paid an amount different than what I saw in the contracts. They said they wrote a second check to—"

"Marty Ho Productions," finished Cody.

"Yeah," nodded April, "but there's a line in the contract that says Mosaic would refund the whole amount if either we or Marty didn't fulfill obligations."

"Holy shit," he sighed.

"Is the company broke?" interjected Phoebe.

Cody paused. He didn't think delivering the bad news would be this difficult.

"Yes," he replied after a long silence. "I'm sorry, girls. None of you deserved this. You were all so professional and tried your best. I was lucky to have you all as my employees. After your last paycheck you're free to find work with another company."

Phoebe held back tears.

"However, Lydia, I'd like for you to stay. Just to wrap up loose projects," Cody requested.

"Cody, I..." Lydia paused, "I think you should give the job to Phoebe."

He tried to bring Lydia to her senses, "I'd love to, but—"

"No, I...I figure it's best if I moved on, Cody," she insisted. "I think it's time for me to seek new challenges in my career."

Phoebe smiled, silently thanking Lydia with a slight nod.

"Okay," Cody faced the former Hula Hoop Shakes waitress. "Phoebe, can you stay?"

Excited to know that there was still some resemblance of an office career left, Phoebe joyfully reacted in her own unique way. "Meh. Sure."

When Patrick Mui's cell phone buzzed earlier in the afternoon, he leapt up from his recliner and felt a strong tinge of excitement. It was either a rare call from an interested homebuyer or, better yet, Hannah; secretly, he was hoping it was the latter. To his delight, the caller ID on his phone showed him just that: "Hannah Wong, Calling." He had worried that their last encounter—a passionate rendezvous thwarted by Cody's mother—scared her for good, that it might have been his only chance at making love not only to her but with any woman in general. At his age and modest income, intimate opportunities were miracles.

"<I was hoping I could bother you for a well-needed massage>," Hannah hinted. "<If you don't mind, of course.>"

"<Of course I don't mind>," he grinned.

Neither heaven nor hell would stop him this time around. There was, of course, that accursed sister of hers, he reminded himself. The mere thought of Cody's mother put a frown on his face. *If that woman dare interrupt us again...* He decided to stop thinking about it and resumed his concentration on the upcoming lovemaking instead. Fortunately for Patrick, the distance between his house and Hannah's was a mere fifteen-minute drive. He didn't let the three school zones he breezed through serve as obstacles. Besides, he opined, children in urban cities learned early on to dodge traffic; it was high time suburban kids did as well.

Absorbed in his determination, he paid no attention to a familiar car exiting the post office. Earlier on, Cody's mother had purchased yet another round of groceries for her sister. She knew Hannah gave her the stink eye for being pushy, but Hannah wasn't exactly the most responsible person, in her opinion. Even when they were children, Hannah needed to be taken care of and Cody's mother found it difficult to stop doing so. As she waited patiently at the first red traffic light, she immediately recognized the car in front of hers: Patrick Mui's.

She could only take a guess as to what he planned on doing in her sister's neighborhood.

Meanwhile, Patrick glanced at his rear view mirror and noticed Cody's mother. In his frantic state of mind, he could only reason with one explanation why her car was behind his: the intrusive woman was out to stop him. She must've planned it all along.

"<No—"> Patrick damned in revulsion. "<No! NO! How did she realize...>"

Fumes came out of his head. That woman is always cock-blocking me! he cursed to himself. When he arrived in front of Hannah's house, he stormed out of his little gray Kia Optima, ready to confront Cody's mother. With Chinese groceries in hand, she got out of her car too, ready for the confrontation.

"<You BITCH! YOU TOTAL BITCH!>" he yelled.

"<What are you doing here? Stop screaming at me!>"

"<YOU FOLLOWED ME! YOU KNEW ABOUT THIS! WHY DON'T YOU MIND YOUR OWN BUSINESS?!>"

"<What are you talking about? I'm just here to give groceries to my sister! I live in this neighborhood as well!>"

Hannah heard the two familiar voices and shuddered at the worst-case scenario happening in her front yard. She quickly concealed her lingerie with a bathrobe and rushed out of her house to calm the situation.

"<Little Sister!>" scolded Cody's mother when she saw Hannah. "<Why's this married man coming to your house again? And why are you wearing a bathrobe? You never do that!>"

"<It's just a little misunderstanding!>" Hannah insisted. "<He's here to offer some reflexology treatments. He—>"

"<'Reflexology treatments'?! Ha!>" mocked her sister. "<Oh, you always did fall for the wrong men...>"

"<HEY!>" Patrick snapped in her direction. "<What we do is NONE of your business! You better scram! I told you I won't be as civil the next time you stopped us!>"

His threat came across as an empty one as Cody's mother stood her ground.

"<Oh yeah?!>" she exclaimed.

Her defiance inflamed him. Patrick couldn't stand it any longer. "<DON'T THINK FOR ONE MOMENT I WOULDN'T PUSH YOU!>"

He had little reason to be intimidated by her. The woman was tiny, no taller than a prepubescent child and no heavier than a sack of rice. She was foolish to hold her ground; even at his advanced age, Patrick could put her in a world of pain.

"<PUSH ME?!>" challenged Cody's mother. "<I DARE YOU.>"

Her words were an invitation to attack her; with a brutal shove, the silver-haired realtor sent Cody's mother face first into the concrete driveway. She lay still on the ground, absorbing both the physical and psychological damage she immediately suffered. Patrick resumed standing before her, dreaming up of further things he could do. He could kick her in the stomach, he mused to himself, yes, that would show her he meant business. Before he could act on his impulse, however, Hannah came between them and pleaded to him to cool off inside her house. With a tinge of guilt, Patrick obliged but not before he heard Cody's mother surprising them with another bout of determined words.

"<How dare you?>" she shouted at Hannah as she lay there on the driveway. "<Choosing a man, over your own sister!>"

Hannah hung her head in shame as she closed her front door, leaving Cody's mother to recover alone outside. The hurt woman eventually pulled herself up, wiping away the dirt and blood that poured out from the new cuts. It took some effort to get herself into her car. Once she had, she took a long look at herself in the mirror and saw a mess. Mostly scrapes and bruises, she dismissed; maybe back when she was young she cared about her looks, but now she prided herself in her fortitude. She drove herself a block north where her home was and made an immediate phone call to her husband at work. Mr. Quan took awhile to answer.

"<It's me>," Cody's mother replied. "<I was just visiting Little Sister to give her some groceries. Mui was there and he shoved me to the ground.>"

The incident was further explained in detail. Not surprisingly, Cody's father didn't feel the need for action.

"<That doesn't sound good>," he casually answered. "<I hope you're okay.>"

"<Well?>" Cody's mother insisted. "<Aren't you going to do something?">

"<What do you mean?>"

"<That disgusting man just pushed me! Come over here!>"

"<Oh. Okay, I'm coming>," he declared.

Cody's father cancelled his game of Angry Birds and took a detour to the men's room. After reading a funny article about sea monkeys, he headed to Hannah's house while relaying to Cody on the phone the details of the incident.

"What?" Cody asked in disbelief.

"<What do you mean 'what'?>" his father chuckled. "<I'm sure it was nothing. You know how your mother overreacts.>"

Cody didn't feel the same sense of casualness; the news of someone harming his mother was enough to send him into a rage.

"No," he declared, "I'm coming over there."

"<Hey now, hold on—>"

Cody slammed his desk phone down, hurrying to the parking garage where his rental car was. On his way over to his aunt's house—a good half-hour long drive—he continually slammed his fists into the rental car's steering wheel, imagining it was Patrick Mui's face. That slimebag! he cursed to himself, and that floozy aunt of his deserved some yelling too! How could anyone hurt his dear sweet mother? He put the pedal to the metal, ignoring school zones and making the crossing guards earn their pay. It was high time suburban kids learned to cross the street on their own anyway, he thought.

"PATRICK MUI! COME OUT!" Cody screamed once he arrived in front of his Aunt Hannah's house.

He banged continuously on the door until it drove his aunt insane. When she couldn't take it anymore, he heard footsteps rushing downstairs.

"<Please, Cody>," she pleaded from the garden window. "<Be an obedient boy and don't worry about it.>"

This angered him and sent him pounding his fists into the door harder.

"<Go away, boy!>" he heard a man's voice say. Patrick had shown his face next to Hannah's in the garden window. "<Your mother deserved it! She had it coming!>"

"<FUCK HOLE ASS I KICK YOURS!>" screamed Cody in broken Cantonese.

"<Oh yeah?>" mocked Patrick. "<You can't do anything to me!>"

Cody kicked the door until dents started appearing in it. Neighbors were coming out to watch the incident.

"<PLEASE!>" pleaded his Aunt Hannah from the window. "<Cody, this is an adult situation. Be an obedient boy. Please.>"

"<Obedient?!>" scoffed Cody's mother, who was making her way back to Hannah's front yard. "<Why don't you tell your dog of a boyfriend to obey my son's order to come out?!>"

"Mom!" Cody's face lit up. "Are you okay?"

His mother pushed him aside and joined the door banging. "<Come out, you cowards!!! I'm ready for round two!>"

"<Give up!>" advised Patrick. "<This isn't your business! You're not coming through that door!>"

"<Oh yeah?>" defied Cody's mother. "<And how will you get back home to your wife?>"

Her words stung Patrick; the realization hadn't dawned on him that he had trapped himself. The Quans could easily stake outside forever. Besides, there was also Hannah's daughter Megan too. She would eventually be returning home from school.

Hannah attempted to soothe the situation. "<Come on, Big Sister. This is just a minor thing. No need to get worked up about it.>"

"<Oh, I definitely need to get worked up about it>," Cody's mother replied.

As Cody contemplated throwing a brick through the garden window, he heard the screeching tires of his father's car pulling into the driveway. At last, Cody smiled, his father could join him in what surely would be a father and son team-up ass-kicking fest. That dirtball was going to get it now.

"Come on, dad!" Cody encouraged. "I'll throw a brick through the window and we'll rush him out together!"

"<No, no, son>," calmed Mr. Quan. "< Let's just go home and pretend this never happened.>"

Cody paused in surprise, "...what?"

With an apologetic smile he walked toward the garden window where Patrick was and bowed. "<I'm sorry my wife and son has caused this unnecessary disturbance, Mr. Mui.>"

"<You better be!>" Patrick grunted. "<And next time you tell your bitch of a wife that she won't be so lucky! And I'll kick you and your shithead son too!>"

Mr. Quan repeatedly bowed. "<It won't happen again. We don't need to have confrontation. We've embarrassed us all.>"

"What are you doing, dad?!" screamed Cody. "This guy pushed Mom! He pushed your wife!"

Mr. Quan took Cody's arm and pulled him away from the front door.

"<Please, son",> he offered in hush tones. "<This is embarrassing. A bunch of Chinese people yelling at one another. What will the neighbors think? Save face...save face...let's go.>"

Cody refused to leave, picking up a brick instead.

"<No!>" his father stopped him. "<You're going to regret doing that!>"

His father's words carried through; he was right, Cody realized. It would've been an invitation to foolishness to directly attack that treacherous man. They weren't street thugs and who knows what would happen if they actually fought? Patrick Mui wasn't exactly the kind of man who hesitated on suing for preposterous reasons.

Still, something inside nagged him; he couldn't just let Patrick get away with it. Some justice had to be done. Picking up his iPhone, he texted Rain, hoping his long-distance friend was free enough at the moment to respond. She did.

"What's up, Bubbleman?" RainYSkIEs589 responded.

"Hi, Rain," texted Cody, "sorry to bother you but I need an emergency favor..."

Moments later, Cody walked back to face Patrick and Hannah at the garden window.

"Patrick! I just had my friend look up and call the local police number. We filed charges against you! The cops are going to haul your ass to the police station. My friend also looked up your home number and called your wife too! Feel free to explain everything to her when she bails you out of jail!"

As promised, two squad cars arrived ten minutes later. Patrick willingly came out with his hands up. The police interrogated him and eventually hauled him to the station. While it wasn't the action-packed beating that Patrick probably deserved, a part of Cody was nonetheless proud things were resolved in an uncharacteristically refined way.

"You should have been the one doing something," Cody glared at his father.

Mr. Quan replied with a lengthy sigh, staring regretfully at the grassy ground. Cody's father didn't like the way they lost face in front of their neighbors. What transpired was not worthy of the victory his son so proudly cherished. The incident was enough for him to consider looking for another neighborhood, one where no one knew anything embarrassing about the Quans.

Cody didn't have too long to dwell on the afternoon incident with Patrick. There was some unfinished business between him and Marty later on in the night in the lobby area of the Sugar Land Town Center Marriott. Neither was prompt as usual—one of the many things they shared in common. However, looking back, Cody realized that their differences, while few and far between, were vast in philosophy and morality. Perhaps those two things were what mattered the most.

As per usual on an uneventful weeknight, the lobby area was quiet and devoid of workers. Even the desk clerk was nowhere to be found. The two former friends sat opposite each other, focusing on the papers scattered across the glass coffee table between them. The document in the center was the most important one, indicating a legal breakup on Marty's behalf of the company. As Cody predicted, his business partner hurriedly agreed to give the entire ownership of the company to Cody now that it was in heavy debt and ruined beyond repair. This was okay, decided Cody, also realizing beforehand that suing Marty would be futile. Like always, Marty put a lot of effort into such an unrewarding hustle, leaving him with intangible triumphs that meant so little to most people. All he had won was an absolved responsibility he could never pay back and the love of Wilbur and Rosie. None of it mattered. Marty was destined to run the same deceit with someone else again and come out happy with only the public acceptance he so pathetically cherished.

"Wah-uh, I'm glad things worked out alright in the end," Marty chuckled.

His laughter sounded so phony to Cody now. Everything about him became so predictable. Once he started out with a lame attempt at humor, Marty would slide in what he really needed to say.

"Er, ah, heh-heh, I made a slight change, ah heh heh," Marty insisted.

Cody gave out a mocking snort, knowing his partner would try something sleazy.

"What change? I told you not to change anything," Cody replied, looking at the first page of the contract.

"Meh-ah," Marty adjusted his collar. "No no. It's nothing bad. See? I just added my middle name. Ah heh."

Cody rolled his eyes and read out loud Marty's full name, "Marty Lai Ying Ho."

"Ha! Yeah. Lai as in 'good intentions.' Ying as in 'brave.'"

"That's ironic. Your full name in English sounds like 'Marty Lying Ho,'" Cody observed.

"Hah! Heh! Good one, Cody!"

"Not funny, because it's true."

Cody thoroughly looked over the rest of the contract papers. Once he was certain nothing seemed awry, he signed his name on the appropriate line. Now it was official: their partnership had ended and, Cody hoped, as was Marty's future presence in his life. Marty seemed more than glad that he was free from responsibility.

"Mm-huh, if it means anything, I'm really sorry that the company fell apart," said Marty. "I mean, heh, if it wasn't for Sonia and emo boy, wah-uh, we'd definitely turn things around together. You know! Eh? Haha, eh?"

Cody silently stared, unmoved by his former friend's spurious comforting.

"Oh, hey!" Marty suddenly announced. "I brought you something."

Cody looked at him suspiciously as he pulled out a wrapped gift from a shopping bag.

"Heh! Thought of you, man!" Marty smiled.

"Why are you giving me this? It's not even Christmas or my birthday."

A reply wasn't need; Cody already knew what it was—a bribe. A bribe for good feelings. A bribe to suggest Marty wasn't the deceitful opportunist that he had proved himself to be. Cody needn't open it; he decided it would be better thrown away unopened.

"Wah-eh, why aren't you opening it?" asked Marty.

"I'll, um, I'll do that... later," Cody replied.

With business taken care of, they both got up from their chairs. Marty offered a handshake, one that Cody ultimately decided to refuse. With his back turned, Cody walked away from his former friend, disgusted at himself for ever trusting someone so noticeably deceitful. He also found a nearby trash can to dump the present in.

"Wuh...uh...hey, wait!" Marty called out to him, his voice echoing across the empty lobby. "I'm not the bad guy, you know! I, heh, I'm not!...Cody?...Cody?...heh heh? Eh?...Cody? Codyyyy!"

Soon he discovered he was talking to only himself.

"Hey, do you need help with that box?" smiled Phoebe the next morning.

It was the second to last day of Mosaic Design Studios. Cody had found Duke, of all people, willing to help out with tomorrow's moving. Until then, only Cody and Phoebe were left to haul the smaller boxes to the front of their building. They both found the temperature outside to be fantastic; the late autumn weather was just cool enough to quell the usual Texas heat.

"Sure," replied Cody, "if you think you can lift it."

Phoebe gave out a teasing laugh. "Hey! I used to lift trays of food heavier than this!"

She helped carry the box and place it with the others sitting on the curb. As she was stacking the rest, Cody couldn't help but notice how spectacularly beautiful she was in her plaid-patterned red shirt and dark blue Wranglers; if only she didn't smell like a ten-gallon ashtray, he thought to himself.

"There," she huffed, "I think that's all of the supplies."

They rested by leaning on the large stack of boxes, facing the second floor window they both once shared. Despite its failure, at least Mosaic Design Studios brought Phoebe into his life, if only temporarily. Cody never stopped appreciating the moment; it was a gift to spend the final moment of his dream company with the waitress he once fawned over. A moving truck pulled up and stopped at the corner of the building. It was from a private charter company that was moving into Cody's office space.

"Prestigious Air Flights," Phoebe read the sign that was being moved upstairs. "What a totally different business than ours."

After Phoebe and Cody watched the movers for the new company make a few trips upstairs with office furniture, their stomachs began to growl.

"You know," Cody suggested, "I've always wanted to try that five-star steak place around here."

"Let's go," Phoebe replied, smiling slyly.

"This late in the morning? It's eleven o'clock!"

"Meh, why not?"

"Because it's still kinda morning...and because... " Cody began feeling his pockets. Something was missing. "Shit."

"What?"

Cody lowered his head in embarrassment. "Phoebe, I think I...I think I lost my wallet."

"Haha. Ah, don't worry, boss," she smiled, holding her paycheck. "My treat."

"You sure? We can just eat at Taco Bell."

"You can't afford Taco Bell," laughed Phoebe. "You're broke. I'm paying, so I get to decide. A steak dinner it is."

"You mean an early steak lunch."

"Meh. Steak's a steak."

Cody sighed. "Alright. But only because I want to end this company on a happy note."

He retrieved his rental car and drove it toward the front of the building. Together with Phoebe's help, they filled it with all the boxes that would later go into public storage. The Mosaic Design Studios office supplies would soon join the Mosaic Decor counterfeit decorations. After parking the car and heading towards the steakhouse, Cody hesitated walking too quickly away from their building. Staring sadly back at their former office, he stopped Phoebe. He knew he would probably never be anyone's boss again. It was back to cubicle jobs and facing that old familiar bamboo ceiling—the life of the model minority.

"I'll miss this place," Cody mumbled. "This will go down as the worst defeat of my life."

"Hey." Phoebe patted his back, trying to cheer him up. "Don't say that. You'll bounce back. Some way. Somehow."

He shook his head. "No, this was a once-in-a-lifetime opportunity and I blew it. I let someone else dictate my fate. I shouldn't have had a partner. I should've been the captain of my own destiny. And now that it's over, I'll never be rich. I'll never amount to anything. And I'm broke. I'm even going to lose my house and live with my parents.

Phoebe leaned in and, to his surprise, planted a soft kiss on his cheek.

"You'll be okay from this," she promised. "You know why?"

"Why?" he asked.

"Because you're Cody Quan."

END OF ACT II

ACKNOWLEDGEMENTS

I've always told my father that I'm supposed to achieve more than him and my mother. Without their help and hard work, I wouldn't have had the opportunities to exceed them. That's the sign of progression and the ultimate way of rewarding a previous generation's lifetime of dedication and sacrifice. I will never forget that they were the ones who brought me here and they were the ones who stuck with me during a struggling time in my life. The existence of this book shall long outlive us and future generations of the Leung family. By showing my parents proper recognition here, their loving and unselfishness will hopefully be immortalized. I know it's not enough to repay them as wonderful parents, but it's a start. I would also like to thank a very good friend in Nori Choy who encouraged and pushed me to start and finish this book. Her constant feedback and early grammar fixing made writing this book very enjoyable. To my editor, Ron Lewis, I thank him for his professionalism and hard work; like all great editors, he's made me look smarter than I really am. Finally, I'd like to give a special appreciation to all the ones who helped in the marketing of the second act of Cody Quan.

PLEASE LIKE US ON FACEBOOK:

www.facebook.com/louisleungauthor

PLEASE FOLLOW US ON TWITTER:

@louisleungautho

WEBSITE:
http://www.louisleungauthor.com

Please write your honest thoughts on Amazon.com.

Simply log on Amazon.com, search "Cody Quan Act II: Mosaic Design Studios" and click on the Write a Customer Review button.